SIGHT UNSEEN

Susan Mac Nicol

with Nicholas Downs

ALSO BY SUSAN MAC NICOL

THE MEN OF LONDON SERIES
Love You Senseless
Sight & Sinners
Suit Yourself
Feat of Clay
Cross to Bare
Flying Solo
Damaged Goods
Hard Climate

THE STARLIGHT SERIES
Cassandra by Starlight
Together in Starlight

OTHER TITLES
Stripped Bare
Saving Alexander
Worth Keeping
Double Alchemy
Double Alchemy: Climax
Love and Punishment

Boroughs
Publishing Group

www.BOROUGHSPUBLISHINGGROUP.com

SIGHT UNSEEN

Copyright © 2017 Susan Elaine Mac Nicol

ISBN 978-1-542536-33-2

This book is for all those people out there who get through the day with a smile despite their lack of one of their five senses. It's for those who take this in their stride and don't let it become WHO they are, but only a small part of them. It's to those people who are able to do anything their spirit wants them to do, and who don't let this lack deter them. I salute each and every one of you—your tenacity is a breath of fresh air in an often jaded world.

ACKNOWLEDGMENTS

A friend called Lynsey helped me a lot with this book, giving me her witty insight into what it's like to be one of those visually impaired individuals, yet who still manages to become a talented pole dancer and win awards for her performance. Just goes to show you can achieve anything you want with determination and guts.

Of course, without Nicholas Downs, this book wouldn't have been written. His original screenplay fanned the elements of this story to turn into a full-blown fire. Thanks for your faith in me, Nicholas, to write this story, and may we go on to take this idea even further.

Thanks also to John from the Headway organization in Cambridgeshire for his time in helping me with some questions and sending me some material to make my research easier. You can see the work this organization does here: www.**headway**.org.uk.

SIGHT UNSEEN

Chapter 1

Nate

Beep. Beep. Beep. Whirr. Hiss. Laughter and low voices. For a split second on waking, I imagined myself in some alternate universe, like a scene from a Wile E. Coyote cartoon where the sound effects were magnified for dramatic effect.

The clamor was unnerving and unfamiliar. I tried to sit up, got halfway then fell back against stiff, starched pillows, definitely not luxurious and soft with the scent of sex and male vanity: Jon's Paco Rabanne or my Artisan.

My hip and left side ached, and something unfamiliar tugged at my wrist, causing a spike of pain. The room was black, no light or shadows anywhere.

"What the hell?" My question stuck and slurred from a bad case of Sahara dry mouth. I reached around with my good hand to find something familiar. My alarm clock at the side of our bed or the metal table lamp would go a long way to reassure me, and take away this feeling of being a stranger in a strange land. Groping, I managed to knock something off the cold surface of what was probably a bedside unit. Whatever it was fell to the floor with a resounding clatter.

My breathing sped up, the fear in my chest swelled like a sponge dropped in water. The beeping got louder, more strident.

Over the turmoil in my head, there was the soft shuffle of footsteps coming nearer. A strong hand tried to push me back onto the pillows as a female voice spoke soothingly. "Please relax, Mr. Powell. You're safe, you're in the hospital." Her hands stroked my arms and I flailed wildly while trying to make sense of it all.

"Hospital? How can I be in the hospital? I don't remember anything happening to me. Where am I, who are you? Where's Jon?

Cody? Let me get up—" Surely my boyfriend or best friend would tell me what the fuck was going on.

"Mr. Powell." This tone was brisk, sharper and male. "Nurse Sandra is trying to help you. You've been out of it for a while. Lie back and try to calm down and I'll explain it to you. But I need you to calm down, we don't need any more damage being done." There was a muted conversation I couldn't make out as I pushed their hands away, trying to get these people from encroaching on my space.

"Fuck off, will you. Leave me alone, let me get up and see what's going on. Why can't I see anything? What do you mean damage? What have you done to me?"

My heart hammered against my chest, my breathing became even more erratic and when something warm flooded into my veins, a sense of peace and darkness overtook me and I spiraled down back into whatever hell I'd come from.

I was happy to leave. Where I was going had to be better than the world I faced while conscious.

***

"Nate, can you hear me? It's Jon. I'm here. Are you awake? Can you see me?" Warm hands caressed my face as I dragged myself up from sleep tainted with fuzzy thoughts. My head was muggy, pounding and it was still dark.

I groaned and reached out to the voice beside me. "Jon?" I needed my lover's comforting and familiar touch.

"Yeah, Nate, it's me. The doctor says you went a bit ballistic earlier so they gave you something to calm you down. It will make you feel a bit drowsy, maybe a bit sick. If you feel like vomiting, tell me and I'll call the nurse."

His hands were on mine, soft and soothing.

I sighed. "Okay. Why is there a doctor involved? What happened to me?"

His silence made my skin prickle.

"Jon, you still there?" Stupid question. I could still feel his hand in mine but I couldn't see anything.

Finally, he said, "I'm here. You don't remember anything about the accident or coming to the hospital two days ago? Can you see me?"

I shook my head slowly and tried to wave my right hand toward his voice, but a stinging sensation zinged through my veins. A strong grip stayed my arm.

"Nate, you have a drip in your hand. Don't pull it loose like last time or the nurse will have to plug you back in. Just keep still and I'll try to explain."

"Why can't I see?" Panic spiralled down my spine. "What day is it? What do you mean, two days ago?"

"It's Sunday, June twelfth, Nate. Do you remember being at the Gravity Awards ceremony Friday night?"

I nodded and wished I hadn't as my brain exploded. "I remember—some of it." Vague memories swam around my brain of being up on stage accepting an award then the open-to-the-public after-party. I had a hazy recollection of drinking alcohol, gyrating on a dance floor and having a vicious argument with Jon's ex-boyfriend who'd appeared to be on a mission to win Jon back.

"We argued about Caleb touching you all the time," I croaked through my ever-present parched throat. "I remember that asshole's face being in mine and wanting to punch it." Someone huffed loudly and I looked across the room in that direction.

"Was my head damaged? Have I got bandages over my eyes? Is that why I can't see anything?"

There was a hesitation then Jon spoke again

"Yes, you suffered a blow to the back of your head."

I heaved a sigh of relief. "Thank God. I thought I'd gone blind." Vaguely I remembered white light, flashes of pain and murmured words of comfort. I shivered.

Jon breath hitched and his hand tightened in mine. He whispered something I thought sounded like, "Oh God, this is the worst thing ever" to whoever else was in the room, and I squinted in that direction.

"Did someone hit me? Was I mugged?"

Jon cleared his throat. There was more low whispering between him and the mystery person, but it was gone before I could comment on it. "No, you weren't mugged. Do you remember going for a run after the taxi dropped us off at home?"

I frowned. "I think so. I remember changing and going out on the road." The memory I had was the smell of sweat, hearing a night bird call out above me in the trees, the sensation of light behind me, and then nothing.

"I went for a run after that stupid argument we had when we got home," I said faintly. "That's about it. Nothing else."

A chair scraped closer, the sound of it making me wince. Jon's aftershave wafted into my nostrils as he leaned in. "You were hit by a car. It veered off the road, clipped your left side and sent you rolling down into the ravine. You rolled quite a way before you stopped."

That explained the stabbing ache in my side and back. "So what about my head? Did I knock myself out?"

"Yeah. Your head bashed into a rock. You were out cold when the nine-one-one call came in. The driver had the decency to call and report the accident but didn't leave any details. She did it from the phone booth about five miles down the road. The police have no idea who she was."

I digested the information then asked, "So I damaged my hip and my head and the bandages are doing what? Protecting my eyes, covering up a wound?"

Ignoring the gasps from Jon and the unknown someone in the room, I reached up with my left hand and felt for the bandage. A chair scraped back and I heard Jon mutter, his voice sounding tight, like he couldn't speak. "I can't do this. I can't. Call the doctor, he'll need to tell him."

Confusion swirled in my already muddled brain. "Um, is this some special bandage, because all I feel is skin and hair and eyelids. I don't feel any bandage over my eyes. What the hell?" Panic rose again.

Will someone tell me what the fuck is going on?

"I'm sorry, Nate, I can't. The doctor's here now, he's going to explain it all. I'm going to get some air. Come with me, please." Jon's strained voice echoed away from me and back into the room. At first I thought he was talking to me, but when I tried to get up, a strong arm restrained me.

"Your partner has left with his friend. I think he needs some time alone. I'm Doctor Malik. I'll explain, and answer your questions. Please try to stay calm. I don't want to have to sedate you again."

I nodded. I would have agreed to almost anything at this stage to hear what the hell was happening. I drew in heaving, awkward gasps, thinking dimly my heart might burst with from fear. "As long as you tell me straight," I managed to get out. "No bullshit. I need to know."

Ten minutes later I regretted that request. My world had fallen apart. Life as I knew it was over and I had no idea how I was supposed to make it through. Patient yet deadly phrases transformed the world as I'd known it to one of despair and desolation.

Damage to occipital lobe. Trauma to the back of the head. Potential permanent blindness. More tests. I'm so sorry. We'd hoped it wouldn't be that serious, that we'd have better news for you...

After what seemed like an eternity of breath-stealing disbelief while my heart pounded like an angry drum, I shut the doctor's voice out and sank back, waiting for the drowsy to turn into sleep.

I welcomed the darkness of slumber to act as a balm as much as the thought of my new enduring darkness terrified me to death.

Perhaps when I woke, it would all have been a dream and I could see the world again. When I woke up, Jon or Cody would no doubt tell me it had all been a nightmare and we'd laugh about it.

Until then, I'd sleep.

Chapter 2

Cody

I shouldn't wish I was lying curled there beside Nate, smoothing away the frown lines from his forehead, perhaps giving him some measure of comfort.

Unfortunately, as the man who was crazy in love with his best friend, my thoughts tended to stray to places they shouldn't. It was the sad story of my life. Well, at least from when I'd been fifteen and realized Nate did things for me no one else ever had.

I tucked a curl of stray dark lock of hair behind Nate's ear, and shifted irritably on the plastic chair beside the hospital bed in the private room. At six-three, a few inches taller than Nate, I found the chair not particularly comfortable. I'd flown in from Rome earlier this morning, cutting short my attendance at the art show I'd set up.

Getting back to Nate had been my priority the minute I'd heard of his accident a day ago. I was thankful Jon had chosen to tell me the news, albeit a little late, and begrudgingly since I knew how he felt about me.

I'd been filled in on the basics of Nate's condition and was devastated at the thought he might lose his sight permanently. Not my Nate, my irascible, moody, generous and passionate best friend. The Nate whose hands sculpted magnificent works of art enjoyed the world over.

Apparently, there was still some hope it might be temporary, but reading between the lines, that hope was bleak.

"I sold all your pieces," I murmured, hoping he could hear me. I owned an art gallery in L.A. called Artisana, and Nate's pieces were always in demand. "They're desperate for more, so when you're up and about, bud, I need you to get busy." I nudged him softly. "Hey, maybe you can wake up now and we'll talk about it."

The doctor had told me Nate was resting well. It had been half a day since they'd delivered the life-changing news, and Nate had decided to sleep most of that time away. I understood. It must have broken him. At least in sleep he didn't have to deal with all the ramifications of knowing what his future held.

I tried to smooth away the creases on his forehead. His eyes moved restlessly in his sleep and I shushed him softly. "You've got a long road ahead of you. And I promise I'll be there every step of the way."

We'd been inseparable since we'd met at a school swim event when we were eight. Nate had knocked me into the pool in his rush to get to the podium for his race. He'd immediately dived in to save me, even though I was probably the better swimmer. Seeing that determined, water-flecked face with eyes the color of warm chestnuts, and the unruly lock of dark hair falling over his broad forehead, I'd been lost. To this day, Nate drew people into his orbit with his smile, warmth and determination.

It was also the reason why, at seventeen, during one long weekend we'd planned on fishing in the Florida Keys, our friendship had turned into something else. Something heated, intimate and real. Memories of that time warmed my body, bringing back that which we'd both agreed never to talk about. Moans, groans, flesh against flesh and the slow slide of one cock against another.

I sighed. Neither of us talked about that time. Ever. It was like Voldemort, something about which we could never speak.

To Nate, that weekend had only been about sex and as soon as it had ended, so had my hopes of anything deeper. We hadn't exchanged undying vows of love or anything; we hadn't progressed that far, and to his credit, he'd been honest with me. We were both young, off to college, and he'd wanted to be able to pursue his sexuality freely. But it was more than us being too young to commit. After that weekend, Nate had withdrawn, distancing himself, and I'd had to deal with losing hope, and I forced myself to get on with my life.

After college, we reunited as best friends. As if time hadn't passed, and as if that amazing weekend had never happened.

The old familiar ache of longing started in my chest and I pushed it away. Thinking there'd ever be anything more between us was emotional suicide.

"No time for that sort of thinking, is there, Clayman?" I muttered.

Clayman had been Nate's boyhood nickname, coined when he'd begun to fashion small animals out of the clay-like mud in the river winding through the fields down the road from where we'd lived.

Beneath my palm Nate's hands moved on the white coverlet, forever in motion like the man himself when he sculpted. His long fingers twitched and I could still see traces of the dark materials he sculpted with under his nails. No matter what he did, he could never seem to get rid of the evidence of his genius and his passion.

Art had always been one of the things cementing us. I had a love of art and the business acumen to recognize what would sell, but I had no discernible talent for creating it. I had a BA in Fine Art from CalArts in Valencia and had scraped through. Nate had aced his studies, graduating top of his class at the California College of the Arts in Oakland. Those four years apart had been tough, and while we'd gotten together from time to time, I'd wished it could have been more, but Nate kept his distance. To this day, I didn't know why.

I gazed at a face I adored, and knew better than my own. Nate's freckles stood out against his pale cheeks, long eyelashes resting against the skin. His mouth was slightly parted, as if he was on the verge of saying something. Soft exhalations of air echoed in the quiet room.

Under the covers, Nate's lean body twisted, and he muttered something I couldn't make out. As I leaned over to hear what he was saying, there was a noise behind me; I turned and saw Jon and Caleb staring at me. They looked in sync in a way Nate and Jon had never been.

Caleb, dark, olive-skinned and broad-shouldered, was a stunning contrast to Jon's blond, tanned, boy-next-door look.

I sighed. I might not like Caleb but I could see his appeal.

The challenging look on his face was to be expected as he stood close to Jon, who moved over to Nate and placed a hand on his chest. Not protective, more possessive.

"When did you get here? I thought you were abroad." Jon fussed around Nate's covers, tucking them around his body. "I didn't think you'd make it here that quickly."

"I flew in a few hours ago from Rome, came straight here. A friend at the airline owed me a favor."

Caleb raised one eyebrow. "Really, you were in Rome and got on a plane dressed like that?" He motioned in my direction.

Even in these circumstances, I grinned. Caleb was such a clothes snob, as was Jon. I guess that's what happened when you were both fashion models.

"Yep. Why, what's wrong with faded blue jeans and a chambray shirt? And these flip-flops are comfortable."

Caleb shuddered. "God, Cody, you're such a flower child. You should have lived in the sixties. Even your hair and face stubble suit the period."

"*The period*? Bro, you sound like someone out of a cheesy historical novel. And what's wrong with my hair?" Instinctively I raised a hand to the short ponytail at my nape.

"I hate to tell you but bleached-blond ponytails went out a long time ago." Caleb sneered.

Jon stepped forward and touched Caleb's arm. "Stop being such a bitch, Caleb. This isn't the time to debate what Cody looks like. There's more important things to think about." He directed his gaze at Nate.

While I appreciated Jon's sentiments, I wasn't sure if it was a compliment. To be fair, he looked tired and stressed, and he *was* Nate's significant other, so I gave him the benefit of the doubt. And my bleached-blond hair was natural, colored so by sun and sea. Damn, he could check my pubes if he wanted confirmation. I'd whip them out right now.

"You had an art show, didn't you? Is Rachel picking up the slack?" Jon moved over to Nate's side and stroked his arm softly.

I drew my eyes away from the intimate gesture and nodded. "Yeah, Rachel is holding the fort. She understands I needed to be here." Rachel Norman was the floor manager at my gallery, and more than capable of acting in my stead.

Jon sighed. "Thanks for coming. He'd be pleased to know you were here." It was said begrudgingly but it *was* said. That was something.

"He's my best friend. Where else would I be?"

Caleb made a small groaning sound and I ignored it.

"So have his folks been told? Or are they pretending he never existed like they usually do?" I glanced at Jon. That job had been left to him to do because there was no way on God's green earth I wanted to speak to any of the toxic people who were Nate's blood relatives. Especially his father. I despised him.

That family—*and I use that word loosely*—were traditional old money from the South and devoutly religious. Nate's coming out at seventeen, coupled with the fact he'd never been the son his father wanted, had led to an ugliness no child should feel from his parents. When they disowned him, he'd lived with my family for three months before we went off to different colleges.

Now Nate's parents lived in Christchurch, New Zealand, where they'd emigrated to when Nate was nineteen.

Jon shook his head, his eyes stormy. "I talked to Duncan briefly yesterday. I thought no matter what bad blood there was between them, he deserved to know his son had been badly injured. I wish I hadn't bothered. His exact words were, 'Well, Nate made his choice to be a sodomite and this is God's punishment.'"

I winced. Duncan. A bastard if ever there was one. I'd expected nothing less but it still stung to hear that said by a father about his only son.

Jon drew a breath. "His mother Monica said the same thing. Neither of them wanted to know anything about him or his health." Jon scowled. "Duncan was quick to snidely point out that he's sure Nate has enough money to tide him over, what with his so-called sculpting job and the money Duncan's brother left him."

It had always rankled Nate's father that at nineteen Nate's uncle had chosen to leave a large sum of money to his only nephew.

Jon sighed. "It was basically a 'fuck off, we don't really care' from them. We didn't expect anything else, though. They're too busy running their hotel empire, and wrote Nate off long ago."

He sounded a little wistful at the thought of their thriving family business.

I frowned. "Yeah, well that empire is built on the blood, sweat and tears of honest men and women who are nothing like their employers. Duncan Powell takes anything he wants and destroys anyone who stands in his way. He's a nasty piece of work. Nate hated that business and despised the way his father treated his employees."

Jon's eyes widened and Caleb threw a sneer in my direction.

Scowling at the pair of mannequins, I said, "They'd never really liked each other *before* Nate came out. He wasn't their idea of the perfect son. He was too independent and decent." I gestured to the man in the bed. "And they kicked him out because they wouldn't condone his 'gay lifestyle,' being the good *Christian* people they are." I stood and began to pace the room. "Gay lifestyle, really? A lifestyle was what my parents chose when they decided to become hippies and raise me as a free spirit. Being gay *so* isn't that," I huffed.

Throughout the years, I'd thought there was something even worse than Nate's parents disapproving of his sexuality, something Nate had never shared. He'd told me once it belonged in the past and there was no need to dwell on it.

Jon murmured, "I didn't realize it was quite that bad. Nate never says much about his family other than they're estranged."

Petty, but satisfaction surged that I knew more about Nate's past than Jon. Of course, I had been there, but I felt it had more to do with Jon not caring enough to ask the questions.

Jon said, "I would have thought they might like to reconcile given what's happened. It seems things are worse than I expected." He shook his head.

I fisted my hands, wishing Nate's father bore the brunt of them right now. "God, if it were me in that hospital bed, my folks, brothers and sisters would be rallying the entire Topanga Canyon community to come out here and shake their hippie sticks in support." True and comforting. "There'd be nakedness, ukuleles and a whole lot of free hugs. As it is, they're already planning a family pilgrimage to the hospital to see Nate. They're on their way down now."

"Yes, well," Caleb sneered. "I've no doubt that would be quite a spectacle. I mean what do you expect from people like that?"

My temper flared. I was easy-going but Caleb got up my nose like a bad smell. "What do you mean, people like that? That's my family you're talking about, asshole. And me."

Caleb's comment reminded me of what Nate's father had sneered about my family. The words "no-good pot-smoking hillbillies" and "white trash" had infuriated me. Especially when said parental hillbillies had taken in the man's son and given him a home after Nate had been kicked out of the one he should have had.

True, I'd seen more naked bodies in my lifetime than a porn film director. I'd also smoked pot from the age of ten and learned to drive in a beat-up old Ford Thunderbird when I was twelve. But my family were genuine, non-judgmental and loving people, and both Nate and I adored them.

Through the open door, a harassed-looking nurse wearing a deep frown scurried down the hallway toward us. I gestured to her. "I think we're about to get kicked out. Visiting hours were over about ten minutes ago."

Jon leaned forward and placed a soft kiss on Nate's lips, murmuring something. I contented myself with running a hand down Nate's naked arm, and closing my eyes for a split second as I promised him I'd be back.

"Sleep tight," I said as I stepped away. "Wake up soon. I'll be back later to see how you're doing. We're all rooting for you, buddy."

Well, maybe not Caleb. The only reason he was here was for Jon. No doubt this whole tragic event was going to be the catalyst to enable Jon's dependency so Caleb could strike while the iron was hot. The calculating look in his eyes as he gazed over at Jon kissing Nate reinforced my supposition.

I smiled at the nurse as she entered the room and, surprisingly, she gave one back. "See you next time, gentlemen," she said and drew the curtains around Nate's bed, effectively shutting him from our sight. Clearly, our cue to leave.

As I pulled the coated elastic from my hair, which was more of a pigtail than a ponytail, Caleb made a sound like a teenage girl. I re-did it, tucking a wayward strand of hair away behind my ear. It wouldn't stay there. Experience had proven that. My hair was thick and a little wavy: a product of wayward Scandinavian genes from many ancestors ago.

Jon looked at Caleb. "I'll come back later tonight and see if he's any better," he said.

Caleb shrugged. "The hospital will call you if he wakes up. There's not much you can do for him while he's sleeping."

Callous bastard. He needed a good head butt. For openers.

Jon shook his head. "No, I'll come back later. On my own. If he wakes up, I'd like to be here for him."

Silently I saluted Jon, who was proving to be quite the caring boyfriend, and deep down, while impressed, feelings of envy and resentment weren't far away. "I'll pop back tomorrow."

I hated not being at Nate's side. If Jon were a different type of man, he'd welcome having Nate's best friend there. But Jon's emotional context didn't run that deep. "If anything changes though, in the meantime, you promise to let me know?"

Jon nodded. "I'll call you, don't worry." His look of relief at my leaving spoke volumes. We got on okay because of Nate, but I knew Jon wasn't fond of me.

"Cool. Right, I'll be off. Caleb." I acknowledged him curtly and brushed past, leaving them staring after me. I felt the tug of an invisible thread as I walked away, that thin precious binding tethering Nate and me together. I cherished that thread and never wanted it to break.

As I got out into the waning sunlight, my cell rang. "Light my Fire" by The Doors heralded a call from one of my parents.

"Hi, Mom. I'm leaving the hospital now."

My mother sounded exasperated. "We're on our way to your place because I guessed visiting hours are over. I thought you were going to call me earlier. How's Nate?"

"He's still asleep. The doctor says it's stress and trauma and he'll wake up and join us when he's ready. I wanted to take the tambourine in and shake it at him, but I thought the nurses would frown at the racket."

My mother chuckled. "Probably. How was your flight back from Europe?"

I reached my car, an old-model blue Chevrolet Cruz, and opened the doors. "As you'd expect. Tight spaces, cramped leg room and unpalatable food." I slid into the car and shut the door. "I'm on my way home now. We'll all go back tomorrow. I didn't want to encroach on Jon's time with Nate today."

"Oh, Shaggy," my mother huffed.

I shuddered. She was using my nickname from when I was a kid, which was a sure sign she was ramping up to one of her homespun hippie homilies. I liked to think I didn't resemble the beatnik in Scooby Doo that much. Yeah, I had stubble, a carefully trimmed beard and a short pigtail, but I thought I was better looking. Sexier. At least that's what Nate had told me.

"What, Mom? And you do know I'm all grown up now, right? Like twenty-nine years old? That nickname really doesn't apply anymore."

Except when it's Nate gasping it as I push my cock inside him.

My stomach tightened. Yet another memory that needed to be consigned to the scrap heap of my undercover memory spank bank.

"Child, I'm your mother, and I can call you what I like. And you know what they say— 'love is a friendship set to music.' I'm just sayin'."

For a moment, as I started the car, her words didn't register. When they did, I sat there, stunned, my mouth agape and pushing pieces of hair back from my now sweating forehead. The car had baked in the California sun.

"What the hell do you mean by that?"

"You know exactly what I'm saying, son. You think your dad and I don't know you carry a Statue of Liberty-size torch for that boy? And now he's going to need you even more, so I'm saying— love takes off masks that we fear we cannot live without and know we cannot live within. Time to take off *your* mask, honey."

Crap, the homilies were even more probing than anticipated.

Worse. My mouth opened and closed like a goldfish, thunderstruck my parents knew how I felt about Nate.

And I thought I'd kept it so well hidden.

"You still there, son?"

"You're wrong," I finally managed to sputter, knowing she'd see through the bluster, but giving it a try anyway. "Nate is my best friend."

My mother cackled. Bernadette Fisher aka Moondust Petal made a sound like a dying hen. "Yeah, and hippies don't shit in the woods. You've loved that boy since you were a teen, and some days I thought he felt the same 'bout you. I never understood why you didn't end up a couple. It's one of the great mysteries of the universe, along with how to tie-dye a damn shirt, 'cause you know I never managed to get that right."

My mom's efforts at creating funky clothing had backfired spectacularly more than once, and she'd ended up blasting several people anywhere in the vicinity of her experiments with neon splashes of dye. Dad had banned her from doing it ever again after his mustache had turned bright pink.

"He has Jon," I muttered as I thrummed my fingers on the steering wheel. "And like I said, we're only friends."

"You go on telling everyone that. Some of us know the truth. Some of us can smell it." I knew she'd be tapping a finger alongside her nose as she said that. "The thing is, Jon boy isn't going to cope with Nate if he's going to be truly blind, mark my words. Jon is an attention whore. He likes to be looked at and appreciated, and who's going to do the looking now? That Caleb fella is who. Not our Nate."

"You make their relationship sound so shallow, Mom. I'm sure it's not like that." My gut roiled as I saw the wisdom of my mother's words. Jon was narcissistic and needy, but in his own way, surely he loved Nate. I couldn't believe he'd be so superficial that he'd give up Nate because he couldn't see his lover, pay him a compliment or enjoy the visual world with him. Even Jon couldn't be that callous.

"Cody, my child, I say it like I see it. Maybe I'm wrong. Time will tell." Her voice grew fierce. "Did that no-good family of Nate's say anything about his accident? I'm guessing not. Those people were always poison. I'm surprised someone as good as Nate came from them."

"Jon called them but they didn't care. Anyway, you know we're his family, and have been for years."

My mother sighed. "I'll never understand how parents can throw away a child. It's got to be the biggest sin in my book." Her tone grew brisk. "Anyway, I can hear that engine of yours running, polluting the atmosphere and sending all those nasty gases into the ether. I'll let you get home to ponder my words. All I'm saying is maybe it's time to tell Nate how you really feel and let him decide who he spends his time with."

I nodded even though I knew she couldn't see me. "Love you, Mom. Say hi to dad for me and try not to kill each other on the drive down."

My car ate up the miles toward my home in Long Beach as I thought about what my mom had said. Her words fizzled in my gut and caused a welcome warmth to flood my body with hope.

My biggest fear was telling Nate how I felt about him and risk losing his friendship. It was why I'd never done it before, especially after what went down in the Keys.

Sometimes, your feelings were worth keeping to yourself.

Chapter 3

Nate

Flashes of luminescence and gray, followed by darkness, with occasional random shapes that flitted in and out of sight but I knew were nothing tangible. This was what remained of my vision.

I'd once spent Christmas in Norway during the *mørketiden*—the dark time—and I'd loved every minute. The quaintness of the Norwegian winter had been exciting. The novelty of spending time without bright sunlight, watching the twinkling of the Christmas lights as they shone against the black depths of the town had delighted me. As a born-and-bred Southern Californian used to the endless summer of Los Angeles, the contrast had been startling.

This darkness, I hated.

And now, sitting in my hospital room waiting for Jon to take me to the home we'd shared for the past year, I stared fixedly at where I knew the hospital room door was and saw only the dark light. I'd never see the Norwegian twinkling fairy lights again; I'd never see the face of my lover as he came. Never see the sun rise over the mountains.

How in hell's name do I do this? How do I just go home and accept what's happened to me?

The lead butterflies in my stomach battered my insides, flying to the beat of the erratic pounding in my chest.

I'd had a panic attack a few days ago, scaring the shit out of Jon, who called out to the nurses' desk for help. The fear I'd heard in his voice as he'd held my shoulders down, trying to comfort me, was almost as scary as the meltdown. When the nurses ran in, they shooed him away as they tried to get me under control. He'd given up by the time they were administering a sedative. To one of the nurses, he'd said, "I'll be outside. Let me know when he calms down."

The last time Cody had visited, I'd had another attack. Except Cody hadn't called for help, he hadn't moved away, he hadn't given up. He'd wrapped me in his strong arms and murmured words of comfort as I struggled to push him away. He'd cursed at me, insisted that I let him help, vowing that he wasn't going anywhere and that I had to shut up and accept it. Finally, I'd settled, and he'd sat with me on the bed until I'd fallen into an exhausted sleep.

And he'd been there when I had woken up.

His ferocity reminded me of that passion-filled weekend we'd spent in the Keys so many years ago. Even though our sex had been all youthful lust, and heat, his loyalty and intensity were apparent even then. And yet we were doomed before we'd even begun. My father made sure the consequences would have been catastrophic for Cody and his family.

I didn't fight him then, or later. And that decision to allow my father to cow me followed me into adulthood and shaped the man I was today.

Now something so far out of my control that no amount of fight could change would shape my life, and I wondered if I had the strength to find my way through.

These last two weeks, waking up to the endless barrage of tests, murmured platitudes, compassionate voices and visits from psychiatrists, psychologists and social workers, had been hell. I'd been scanned, re-scanned, soothed, counseled and comforted. The bottom line: I was blind and I had to face the rest of my life in darkness.

There was no hope, no miracle cure.

My life is fucked.

Although I knew it could be worse, I could be dead—the time spent in hospital had brought that home and given me time to reflect on the fact that I'd been given a second chance, even with my sight loss—still, I couldn't wrap my mind around how I would go on.

Grateful my life had been spared, my mind wandered down the "what if" path and I asked myself some tough questions. Questions I wasn't ready to answer.

A noise at the door made me turn. A warm hand clasped my shoulder as Jon's scent wrapped around my remaining senses.

Shit and balls, I thought as my pulse pounded in my temple. Is this what I have to look forward to? Able to tell who people are because of the smell, like a dog?

"Hi, honey," Jon murmured in my ear. "Are you ready to go? All packed?"

"I don't know. Why don't *you* tell me?" Instantly ashamed for lashing out like a petulant child, I murmured, "Sorry. I'm being a bastard. Ignore me. I shouldn't have said that."

Jon planted a soft kiss on the top of my head. "Don't worry, I get it. This is tough. For both of us." His voice was hesitant, an undercurrent of something in it I couldn't identify. But I couldn't find fault in whatever and everything he was feeling.

I reached out, searching for his arm. "Has anyone from my family called?"

No matter what they'd done to me in the past, I still clung to the desperate hope that one day they'd come to their senses and accept me for who and what I was, especially after an accident that could have killed me. I was the gay man who'd chosen not to follow in his father's footsteps. A son who'd disappointed his family with his choices.

Jon cleared his throat. "No," he said softly. "After I called to tell them about the accident they haven't called back. My folks called though. They sent flowers." Jon's parents doted on him, and had always thought he deserved better than me. Sending flowers had been more for Jon than me; I'd met them only twice, such was their disregard.

"Oh." The desolation in my tone must have been obvious because Jon squeezed my arm.

What did you expect? That the people who'd tossed you aside would get into a plane and fly across an ocean to see you because you'd had an accident? Yeah. Stupid idea. I need to come to grips with the fact I am never *seeing them again.*

"Forget your idiot family. Come on, let's get you ready to leave this place."

I nodded, heart heavy as Jon moved away. I already resented the pity in his voice.

Who was I now? A sculptor without his art, which would surely make me a miserable bastard. No doubt. The ache of loss at probably no longer being able to live my passion flooded my chest as I tried to hold back the lump that rose in my throat.

Jon moved away, probably to pick up my bags. I stood, feeling a swell of panic as I did. I'd fallen down a lot in therapy, where they tried to teach me how to get my bearings. I'd learned to hate the words "orientation" and "mobility" and being told to use my remaining senses to get about. The fact I'd need an orientation and mobility specialist as part of aftercare treatment when I got home to help me overcome day-to-day living pissed me off and scared the shit out of me.

My rehab therapist at the hospital, Marty, was a no-nonsense guy who'd helped many returning soldiers face their impairments. Marty took no prisoners, and, in fact, had been my rock. I'd miss everything about him, most importantly, how he didn't pity me. He'd told me time and again how he couldn't wait to see my new works.

"Hey, man." Speak of the devil. I smiled at hearing Marty's voice. "A little bird told me you were going home today. I thought I'd swing by, say good-bye and good luck."

He enfolded me in strong arms that smelled of sweat and cigarette smoke, familiar scents that grounded me. "Hey, Marty. Yeah, Jon's here to take me home so I can start my journey into the land of the blind."

A fist punched my arm and I yowled.

"Stop being such a damn douche, man," Marty growled. "What did I tell you?"

"Yeah, yeah. 'The only thing worse than being blind is having sight but no vision.' I remember the quote."

Helen Keller had a lot to answer for. That had been Marty's mantra each time I'd broken down or decided to get pissed with him.

"Too right, my man. You keep that in mind when you're out there in the wide world and remember Big Marty has eyes on you. I'll know when you get that look that says you're giving up and I'll be there to kick your ass." Marty squeezed my shoulder.

All I could do was smile and nod.

"We're ready to go, Nate." Jon moved up and placed a hand on my arm. "Hang on to me and I'll guide you out to the car. It's not far from the exit." The strain in his voice was my undoing.

Shit, this is so damn embarrassing.

"Jon, I'm sorry that you have to do this. It's not fair to put you in this situation," I choked out, and to my horror tears pricked my useless eyes.

At least my tears ducts still work.

Marty's deep voice sounded in my ear. "Nate, nothing about this is fair to either of you. It wasn't your fault, bud. I'm sure Jon knows that." The slight edge in his tone surprised me as I held on to his firm bicep. Beside me Jon sighed heavily and muttered something I couldn't catch.

Marty's warm hand covered mine with comfort and reassurance. "Once you're home among familiar surroundings, even if you can't see them, things will be better. You'll adapt because you have no choice but to adapt. You're strong. You'll get there. It will take time, that's all. You need to be patient." He slapped my back. "And remember, I've given you all the contacts and links for that blind artists' network. I want to see you sculpting again, and if anyone can help you get there, they will. I've seen your stuff, and you're talented. It would be a shame to let that go to waste."

"He can't see, Marty." Jon's tone was frosty. "How is he supposed to sculpt? You shouldn't be giving him hope like that. It's cruel."

I drew in a breath, about to say Marty was trying to help when Marty spoke again, his voice fierce.

"Don't you be saying shit like that. Nate can do whatever the hell he wants to do, and this organization has blind artists and sculptors who've found a way to keep working on what they love. It is possible so don't be filling Nate's head with that crap. His friends think he can make it, so you should too."

I put a placatory hand on Jon's arm. The muscles beneath were taut as he stood rigidly next to me.

"Yeah, his friends? You mean Cody?" Jon said sharply, derision skating just beneath the surface. Not for the first time I wished the two men in my life got along. "Well, you guys aren't the ones who'll be there with him. You get to say good-bye now, 'cause your job's done. I'm the one who's going to have watch him struggle and get frustrated, and support him."

Jon gripped my hand on his arm. "Forgive me if I need to be the realist here. Come on, Nate, let's go. Traffic right now is a bitch."

I raised a hand and rubbed my temple.

Christ, another headache. All I want to do is get home and crawl into bed and put my number one coping mechanism into play: sleep.

Come to think of it, where was Cody? I was hurt he hadn't come to be with me when I left the hospital like he'd promised. He'd visited often, more than Jon in fact, but now when I truly needed him, no Cody.

Did I do something wrong? Is he giving up on me?

I was enveloped in another bear hug, and my despair lessened with that affectionate gesture. "Nate, listen to me," Marty whispered. "You can do it. You have my number if you need to talk. Anytime."

The warmth of his solid body left mine and I felt bereft. I could have spent all day in those reassuring strong arms, but it was time to man up and get on the road.

"Thanks, I appreciate that." I cleared my throat. "Okay, Jon, lead the way. I'm ready to go home. See you around, Marty." I managed a weak smile at a phrase that now became a joke.

Jon moved closer. "Take my right arm, Nate. Here, the elbow." He took my left hand, putting it into the crook of his arm. I grasped it firmly, thinking I was grateful he'd paid attention during those short conversations he'd had with Marty about guiding the blind. I followed Jon out of the room, trying to keep in step with him, holding on like a limpet on a submarine.

Just don't leave me alone. I'm not ready for that.

My skin prickled as I walked along what I imagined was the hospital corridor. Jon's usual fast pace slowed for my more hesitant one. Now and again, I heard him give a huff or a sigh.

He stopped and I stumbled, and clutched onto his arm even tighter.

"Ouch," Jon muttered. "Not so hard, Nate. You know how easily I bruise."

Well, I'm sorry, bitch. Maybe you forgot I can't fucking see?

Sorry," I murmured. "Why have you stopped?"

"The nurses are waving for us to go to the nurses' station. I think they want to say good-bye. Come on, let's go over."

Again, I followed. *As if I had a choice.* As we neared the clamor, the scent of female perfume and disinfectant along with the other smells I'd learned to associate with the hospital grew stronger. I wrinkled my nose.

Starched linen, hair shampoo, sweat and urine. Lovely.

Perhaps there was something to the "now that you can't see, your other senses kick in" thing everyone had told me about.

"Nate, were you leaving us without saying good-bye? How dare you?" Nurse Caroline. She wrapped long arms around me. Caroline had been one of my favorites. Always ready with a smile in her voice, patient to a fault and a font of gossip about the goings-on in the seedy underbelly of the hospital.

"I wouldn't dare," I managed to get out in between being pressed against a soft bosom. "You know my boyfriend." I waved in the general direction of Jon, noting he was silent.

"Oh yes, your gorgeous man. He's a sight for sore eyes indeed. All the ladies think he's handsome. You too of course," she said quickly with a laugh. "You make a striking couple."

She couldn't have known her kindness was a stab to my chest, cutting deep into the flesh and muscle and leaving nothing but a painful mess.

I'll never see Jon again. Never see him dressed up in his tux, or watch his cute move of sticking his tongue out when we play Scrabble. I'll never see the artwork scattered around our home, pieces I made or favorite object d'art we bought together.

I'd miss seeing Cody's expressions, like when he does that exasperated eye roll when I get insecure about a piece of sculpture I'm working on. I'd miss watching him dance with abandon or his perfect form when he surfed.

All things I'd taken for granted, gone—lost in one roll down a roadside embankment.

Surely everyone could hear my heart pounding and see the panic on my face. The hospital smells now seemed overpowering, the surrounding noise deafening and I needed to leave before I lost it completely. My fragile psyche was unravelling with every kind word, reinforcing every thought of what I would be missing.

Clamping down a scream of frustration, I pulled away from Caroline, my hands dropping to my sides. "Thanks, everyone, for everything you did for me, for taking such good care of me." I touched my fingers to my mouth and blew them a kiss. "Now we need to get going, the traffic will be horrible." I swallowed past the growing tightness in my throat. "Jon, can you help me outside to the car please?"

Christ, is this my future? Dependent on another person for every little thing? Jon turned on his charm and smoothly voiced our farewells. Then he placed my hand on his arm again and guided me away.

My senses seemed to go into overdrive as I walked. The swish of people's clothing as they passed, the clink of some piece of hospital equipment and the muted voices and occasional moans all assaulted my ears. Nausea built in my gut and I tried to clamp it down.

Jon must have seen my agitation. "You okay?"

"No. I'm not okay." I groaned, feeling desperate. "I want to get home and go to bed."

There was a pregnant pause. "Nate, it's eleven in the morning. It's not night time." His tone was sympathetic and I hated it. Hated that he sounded that way for me. Hated that I couldn't tell anymore when night began and day ended.

I grasped his arm tighter, ignoring his hiss of discomfort. "I don't care. Just take me home."

***

The drive home was fraught with tension, which escalated when Jon pulled over to answer a phone call. It had to be Caleb. After a few muttered words, Jon hung up and took me home.

Home should have been a refuge. Instead it had become a minefield. I'd have to learn to negotiate my own house in a new way. Cupboards would need to be rearranged so I could find plates, glasses and food without breaking everything or killing myself trying. Walkways needed to be cleared, and everything had to be put in the same place every day so I could navigate—again without killing myself.

Walking into my house, supported by Jon, was both a blessing and a curse. I needed the support, but hated the reason why.

New smells assailed me. The overpowering scent of lilies and sweetness exploded in my brain. The fresh flowers Jon had told me about; bouquets delivered from friends who wished me a speedy recovery. Underneath the fragrance of flowers and plants were odors I recognized from before the accident. The faint remnants of cooking, the smell of polish—we had a lot of wood furniture—and the lingering essence of fabric softener from the laundry room.

The house also reeked of the familiar stench of cigarettes, another sign Caleb had been clinging to my lover.

Jon took my hand, leading me into somewhere that smelled of fruit and wax. I guessed the family room, where we had candles of all shapes and fragrances dotted around the room.

"We're in the family room right now," he murmured. "I've moved stuff around a bit, so you have an unobstructed path to most places," he explained. "I've pushed furniture out of the way, made sure the rugs won't curl up, that sort of thing. It took a while. Cal—" He stopped and I waited. "Well, anyway, we did what we could to make sure you didn't fall over anything. Marty's advice did come in useful, I suppose." He placed a flat hand on my chest, holding me still. "You're at the sofa now if you want to sit down."

Gingerly, my fingers reached out, grasping at air until they brushed the rolled edge of a cushion. My knees wobbled as I bent to lay my hands flat to support my descent.

Shit. Sitting was something I'd *never* thought about.

As I eased into the sofa, a gasp escaped my throat as my backside hit the soft cushion, and I leaned back with a sigh of relief. "Thank you. I appreciate everything you did. It couldn't have been easy."

Living in a single-story bungalow, with an open plan space that incorporated our family room, dining room and kitchen, I guessed things would become easier for me to get around. I was in familiar surroundings. And my memories of the space should help me navigate my home.

I hoped.

Sounds echoed off the wide walls, clear as radar as they bounced back into the room. That would come in useful too as I learned how to read them.

Jon sighed. "It needed to be done."

I ran my fingers over the sofa arm. Our family room couch was made of canvas and the fabric was smooth with slight ridges where the blue stripes lay against rich cream. It was strange to be "seeing" a familiar object with touch instead of my eyes.

"Why didn't you like Marty?" I asked. "You two seemed to have a bit of a bad vibe."

I heard the scowl in his voice when he spoke. Jon's voice seemed particularly expressive or perhaps it was me doing my new super Spidey sense thing.

"Marty talks bullshit. All that crap about you being able to sculpt again and telling you things will change, but not be as bad as you thought. I call bullshit because he was saying it to make you feel better. I thought it was unfair."

"You don't want me to feel better?" I was curious. "Have hope that I'll be like I was before only…different?"

A clock ticked, the one on the sideboard. It had always been loud but now it seemed clamorous. Outside, I heard faint honking and engine revving; the muted sounds of traffic.

Jon scoffed. "Nate, you'll never be the same. You're disabled now, we both know that. Now, in the kitchen I've organized stuff a bit differently so you can get easy access."

His voice moved away in the direction of the kitchen.

I didn't hear much more as he droned on about the condiments and the mugs and the placement of the tea and coffee. All I'd heard were the words that I was now classified as disabled in Jon's eyes.

He believed that I was less Nate than I'd been before. The very thing Marty had tried to tell me I wasn't had been blithely confirmed by my boyfriend.

Well, fuck him and the horse he rode in on. I might be feeling sorry for myself, but I'm not always going to be this way.

I wasn't disabled. Challenged, yes, but still the same person I'd been before, only without vision. I had no intention of letting the loss of sight take away the rest of my life.

Jon came back into the family room, his voice getting louder as he moved closer. "So what do you think?"

I nodded, biting back what I really wanted to say. "It all sounds great. You've given this some thought. Thank you."

The weary man in me told me to let it go. Battles took time to win and I didn't have the strength right now to be a warrior. I'd tried that once before and it had ended badly. Maybe tomorrow I'd take up the sword and argue, but in this instance, I wanted to lie down and absorb the fact I was home at last.

Spots danced before my eyes and I blinked. When I'd first seen them, I'd gotten excited, thinking it was my vision trying to come back. The doctor had told me that wasn't the case. It was simply my mind processing that it couldn't form pictures anymore.

The seat next to me sagged as Jon sat and took my hand in his. "I know this is all a lot to take in, but we'll be fine once we get you settled." He sounded as if he was trying to convince himself. Fingers brushed through my hair, which had grown longer during my hospital stay. "Do you want to take a shower or anything?"

I shook my head. "Maybe in a minute." I reached out and pulled Jon toward me, wanting nothing more than some physical contact. It had been so long.

His body stiffened under my hands, his breath hitched and I frowned.

"What's wrong? Do I smell or something?"

Jon shifted beside me. "No, well, maybe a little sweaty but that's all. I think perhaps a shower might make you feel a bit more refreshed. Then I can see about ordering us some takeout for lunch." He stood, and after a minute or so I heard the drawer open. Probably the one where we kept the fast food menus. "Do you feel like some Thai? Chicken Pad Thai maybe?"

Relying on the new things I'd learned, such as listening to voices, the timbre, inflection and emotions, I realized Jon was skittish about something.

Maybe my blindness turns him off.

My throat clenched at that thought. I needed some space to rest and think. I struggled to my feet, standing up straight and holding my hands out tentatively. "Fine, I'll shower. Can you point me in the right direction?"

"Oh don't be silly," Jon spluttered. He took hold of my elbow. "I'll take you there."

"No, it's okay." I shrugged his hand off gently. "I need to do this on my own. Just tell me there's nothing in my way and I'll get there. I remember the layout of our home. It hasn't been that long."

Jon sighed. "Fine." He turned me gently. "There, face that way. From here, it's about five steps to the door to the hallway, then turn left down the next hallway to the bedroom on the right. The bathroom—"

"I remember where the master bathroom is," I said tightly. My nerves pinged with tension, and I gravitated in the direction Jon turned me. My legs were longer than Jon's so I wasn't surprised when after only four steps I was gripping the door frame and moving into the tiled hallway.

I placed my right hand on the wall and started walking, lightly dragging my hand across the smooth surface. No sooner had I begun than my hand hit something that fell to the floor with a crash. I jumped, pressing back against the wall.

"What the hell was that?"

Jon's footsteps echoed behind me as he approached. "You knocked one of the canvas pictures off the wall. I haven't moved them because, well, I didn't think they'd be a problem. I guess I'll need to do that now." He didn't sound particularly pleased about it. "You're lucky they weren't the glass ones."

"Oh, sorry, I'll try to avoid them." I moved down the hall, my temper flaring. *Hello, blind guy here. What the fuck did you expect?*

Behind me, Jon sighed and I heard the sound of the hall closet opening and shutting. I guessed the picture had been relegated to dim confines.

I made it to the bedroom, pushed open the door and went inside, congratulating myself when I realized I was in the right place. I may know our home, but not being able to see anything was disconcerting, to say the least.

I bumped my knee against the bed, but managed to navigate to the en-suite bathroom on the other side of the room. With a sigh of relief, I pushed the door open.

Cool air brushed my skin, causing goose pimples to rise. The room smelled of aftershave, soap and the hair gel Jon used. The scent of smoke was prevalent in here too. I tried to push that unwelcome thought out of my head. If Caleb had been here, he'd probably used the toilet at some time, not fucked my boyfriend in the shower.

Would I care too much if he had?

I swore as again I knocked the same knee on the toilet bowl—I guessed I'd need to get used to sustaining bruises—fumbled around gingerly, pulled down the lid and sat. I stayed there, picturing the bathroom in my head, putting off the inevitable moment when I'd have to stand up, reach in and turn on a tap I could no longer see. Luckily Jon and I both enjoyed our showers steaming hot so the temperature setting was probably still the same and I wouldn't have to adjust it.

Sitting there, knowing where I was, yet unable to see the images I'd grown used to when I was sighted, turned my stomach to roiling nerves.

"Do you need any help, Nate?" Jon called from somewhere outside.

"No I'm fine," I called back. I stood and began unbuttoning my jeans, sliding them down my legs where they gathered at my ankles. My boxers followed and I pressed my palm against the wall as I pulled each foot from the clothing puddle at my feet. My shirt was next, dropped to the floor, then, using muscle memory to avoid hitting my naked hip on the basin, I fumbled for the glass door to pull it back.

It slid open easily, and silently I applauded myself.

The shower was large, the showerhead wide and generous, one of the luxuries I'd afforded myself when I'd bought the house. I liked the feeling of being in a space where water ran freely, and you could stay in and pretend you were caught in a rainstorm. Now, with the drought restrictions, taking an hour in the shower was a thing of the past.

"So far, so good," I muttered. "Now all I need is to turn the water on and to try not to slip on the soap." I stopped dead. "Maybe if I hit my head again, it might bring my sight back." The flare of hope was overshadowed by common sense. That only worked in the movies.

I had the water switched on in no time and once it was hot, I stepped in, closing the door behind me.

"God, this could almost be normal. If normal meant I couldn't see anything." I groped around for the soap, which was usually in the shallow dish attached to the wall. The dish was empty.

Fuck. Don't panic. Don't panic.

"Calm down," I whispered, taking a deep breath, using a technique Marty had taught me to stave off panic attacks. It didn't work. The water beat down on me, drowning the tears that welled in my eyes, joining them in sympathy and no doubt disappearing into the shower floor drain.

My throat choked up and I held the wall tightly with my hands and slid down to sit on the cold tiles, my knees raised. I laid my head on them and sobbed.

Who knew how long I sat there.

"Nate? Are you okay? Did you fall?" Jon's voice brought me to my senses.

I swallowed, and nodded. "I'm okay. Just needed to sit down. I couldn't—" my voice broke—"I couldn't find the damn soap."

"Oh crap, I forgot to pop a new one back in the shower. Hold on."

I heard the bathroom door opening, then fumbling with the bathroom cabinet and the crackling of paper as something tore. The shower door opened and something smooth and cold was pushed into my hand.

"Here you go. Do you need me to help you up?" Jon asked, his tone uncertain.

"I'm blind, not crippled. I can get up by myself." Slowly I climbed the wall with one hand, clutching the damn soap with the other and pushing myself up.

There was a breathy, resigned sigh as the shower door closed, and soon after, the bathroom door closed too. I stood there as the shower rained down and slowly I began to wash myself.

At least I can still do that.

Five minutes later, wrapped in only a towel, I'd managed to navigate my way to the wardrobe in the bedroom. It was a small triumph but one for which I'd given myself a mental pat on the back.

Now try to get dressed. This should be fun.

I felt my way around my clothes. I'd already had a makeshift system even if it was a bit messy—jeans on one shelf, tee shirts on another, formal shirts and trousers hung up. I was confident I'd look all right, no matter what I picked from my casual wear. I didn't care about appearance much anyway, not like Jon. He wanted everything color-coordinated with fabrics to match.

I needed to spend some time on detailing my wardrobe when I was up to it. Marty had given me some helpful tips: Use safety pins to indicate colors—one pin for blue, two for black, that kind of thing. Or there were iron-on tags with the first letter of the color. Marty had been a mine of useful information.

Yet another something to look forward to.

I took out a soft tee shirt and what felt like a pair of sweatpants.

Bearing in mind Marty's advice, I fingered the texture, familiarizing myself with it.

There were other ways to guess what I held in my hands. A denim texture and its unique smell indicated jeans. Silk could be used for shirts, and tee shirts might have emblems on them helping me differentiate. Buying trousers with a specific zip or set of buttons would enable me to recognize them.

I laid the clothes on my bed and grappled my way over to the bedside chest of drawers to find underwear. I heard a noise behind me as I bent down to pick up a pair.

"Nate? The takeout's arrived. I've set it out on the dining table. Are you ready to eat?"

I nodded. "Give me a minute to get dressed and I'll be there."

There was a murmured "Okay" before I was left alone. At least I thought I was from the way the room went quiet. I pulled on my clothes, made my stumbling way to the dressing table and ran a brush through my damp hair. I normally styled it a little with hair product so it didn't stand out all over the place. Now, I wasn't sure whether it was worth the effort.

After carefully navigating to the smell of food and from the memory I had of the layout of my home, I managed to get to the open plan dining room and kitchen.

Jon took my arm. "I've put your food over here. I got you the Chicken Pad Thai." He steered me toward a chair. "I took the liberty of getting you a fork and a spoon because I didn't think you'd want the chopsticks. The utensils are on the right of the food."

I'd once been adept at eating with chopsticks. Perhaps I'd get there again. I nodded, swallowing back the regret at not being able to use them now. The cutlery had been a thoughtful gesture, though.

"Thanks." I sat down, feeling around in front of me for the containers, one rice and one chicken, and finding the spoon, I tucked in. Across from me, a chair pulled out and something rustled as Jon began eating.

The meal was nothing like we'd had before. This dining experience was fraught with unanswered questions and heavy silence. In the past, our conversations would have held more animation despite the growing strain in our relationship well before the accident.

"So what happens now?" I asked as I set down my spoon. Sticky grains of rice clung to the underside of my forearm. I'd knocked the spoon once or twice against my lips when I'd missed my mouth. "I mean, we've both got to adapt to this new way of living. I'm not really sure what happens next." The words choked me but they had to be said. "Marty told me someone would be appointed to help teach me about living skills and coping with being blind."

"Yes, they've already been in touch." There was the shuffle of paper. "They dropped some stuff through the mail." More shuffling. "They've appointed a vision rehabilitation specialist to come in once a week and make sure you're coping, integrating back into society, that sort of thing. I have a brochure, hold on."

The reality of my situation hit home when Jon read out loud. With each word he uttered, my heart sank and I had to fight the despair rising inside.

"Daily Living Skills. Independent Living Skills Training. Provides all rehabilitation services in client's home and community. Personal management, Braille, handwriting, listening skills, typing, home management, and remedial education. In-Home Services include in-home rehabilitation teaching and orientation and mobility instruction."

Jon hesitated. "There are also various support groups you can go to, and groups for me too, to talk to people in similar circumstances."

We both fell silent. I didn't intend going to any support groups and I was damned sure Jon wouldn't either. I'd been lucky so far; my medical bills had mostly been covered by various insurances. I also had a healthy bank balance from my art sales, plus I owned the house outright. It had been purchased with the inheritance I'd gotten from my uncle.

That legacy had enabled me to get through college and make my own way in life. I'd forever be grateful to my Uncle Tim, even though I deeply regretted his untimely death.

I pushed away my food, no longer hungry. "So when does that start? This person coming in to help, tell me if I need a cane, or a dog, or to learn Braille so I can read?"

Apparently, there was a lot I could do to make my life easier. Canes, Braille, special gadgets—I knew I'd do anything to make sure I was independent. In my darkest moments, I'd thought about telling my lover he had carte blanche to leave me if he wished. I'd understand, even if it made me miserable. *But would it?*

I wanted to sculpt again. I wanted to do what I loved. There were people out there who could help me. But Jon didn't think it was possible, and that bothered me more than a little bit.

Jon cleared his throat. "The woman said she'd come around Friday to meet you. Her name's Suzanne. It'll be a regular thing." He huffed. "I don't think you'll need a dog, Nate."

Jon wasn't fond of dogs. They shed hair, crapped and peed all over the place, and in his book that was anathema to living his lifestyle.

Our home was beautifully decorated, and it was Jon's pride and joy. Not mine so much. That would be my messy, dirty and chaos-driven studio at the bottom of the backyard.

It was a solid white-boarded structure with picture windows that brought the light in, and it was the place where I felt most at home.

The memory of the sunlight flooding in, shining on the art spotted around the place, made me feel ill. I'd never enjoy seeing it again, highlighting the things I'd created.

I pushed away those thoughts before they drove me crazy.

Jon's chair scraped as he got up and moved over to me. "Are you finished with your food?"

I nodded. He came around, gathered my plate and, from the sound of it, the cartons, then he moved into the kitchen. The bin lid flipped and the sound of scraping followed. There was the plunk of water as Jon threw the cutlery into what must have already been a sink full of the liquid.

I marvelled that I heard all these sounds so clearly now. I'd heard Marty debating this with others in the hospital. He'd had the opinion that blind people didn't suddenly develop superpowers of hearing, taste and sensation. He said they'd always been there for each one of us and when one sense was taken away, we learned to adapt by using the others to the fullest.

I rather liked that premise. It made more sense to me than taking on superhero status and becoming Daredevil.

I stood and pushed my chair in. No way was I coming back here and falling over it. Using the sound of the water in the sink, I got my bearings to turn and face my way into the family room. I walked toward it, giving myself a mental pat on the back for getting this far. Until I fell over something. A sharp object sheared into my shin and

I yelped, reaching out a hand and finding nothing but air as I tripped and landed, winded, on my ass on the carpet.

Jon cried out in horror behind me. "Oh shit, sorry. I should have moved that. I forgot."

His hands pulled me to my feet, and I snapped at him. "What did I fall over? I thought you said you'd cleared this room of stuff I could trip on?"

One day home and I've already injured myself. And I can't even fucking see if I'm bleeding.

I tried to reach down and touch my throbbing shin but Jon's hands stopped me.

"I did, but I moved the table to pick up some fluff on the carpet and I forgot to move it back against the wall. God, I'm sorry, Nate. Let me see if you hurt yourself."

I closed my eyes in mortification as Jon's hands ran down my leg. My hands clenched tightly at my sides as I waited.

Finally, Jon spoke with relief. "No, I think you'll have a bruise. No blood. Why don't you sit down and I'll move the damn thing back where it should be." He hugged me, his chin pressed into my shoulder.

Once again he guided me to the sofa, and I sat, wincing. Jon's voice disappeared, the muttering dimming, and after a minute, he came back and sat beside me. He smelled good, really good. All male. An alluring aftershave, and the undercurrent of something vanilla. I needed physical contact, and not the kind that involved needles, therapy and sponge baths. I needed my man. I needed Jon.

He was a lifeline to my old world and I desperately needed to pretend things could be normal again.

Even if things haven't been great between us, he's all I've got.

I had to admit it wasn't the most charitable of thoughts. I reached out and grabbed what I thought was his arm, and pulled him closer. Again, he stiffened but relented and lay against me. His hair tickled my chin and I brushed it away.

"I can't even see where you are to kiss you," I muttered. "It's like Pin the Tail on the Donkey and Blind Man's Bluff going on all at once."

There was a smile now in Jon's voice when he answered. "Then I guess this will be like a birthday party. I'll try to make it a little easier. Here."

He reached up, warm hands pulling my head down, and his lips pressed against mine softly. It wasn't a passionate kiss, more one of reassurance. I wanted more so I delved deeper, pushing my tongue into his mouth and crushing his lips against mine. For the first time in weeks, my cock filled out and I wanted to shout in celebration. At last *there* was an element of normalcy.

Jon gave over, opening his mouth and dueling with my tongue, but I sensed hesitation. His heart wasn't in this and he wasn't the same man as before.

Or perhaps I wasn't.

I pulled away and stared in his direction, hoping I wasn't totally off course. "What's wrong? You seem different."

I sensed his shrug. "Nothing's wrong, apart from the obvious. I'm tired, I guess. I don't feel like sex right now."

"I don't care if we fuck or not," I said harshly. "I want my boyfriend to hold me. Is that too much to ask?" An uneasy thought drifted upward. "Or do I disgust you that much now I can't see?"

Jon's hands stilled. "No. Don't be so stupid. You don't disgust me. It's all so new, that's all. I need time to get used to this."

I heaved a shuddering breath. "So do I."

We shifted apart, sitting in silence. Jon's cell pinged across the room. He'd gotten a message. I didn't need to guess who it was from.

To his credit, he didn't stand to get his phone, but he remained still beside me. The atmosphere had thickened and whatever tiny bit of intimacy we had shared a minute ago had vanished.

I frowned. "By the way, what happened to *my* phone? I was at least expecting Cody to call me, see how I was. He didn't even come to the hospital today. Have you spoken to him lately?"

Jon took a quick breath. "I think it's in my satchel. I put it in there when we left the hospital. The battery had died anyway."

He stood up and I had a sudden vision in my mind of his face showing relief at getting away from me. I don't know why I thought that, but I didn't like the feeling.

There was the sound of Jon rummaging in something, probably his treasured Montblanc man bag. "Here it is. It'll need to charge though before you can use it. I'll put it in the charger in the bedroom."

"Fine," I said. "My iPhone isn't going to be much use to me now apart from taking calls and listening to messages. We're going to have to turn on the accessibility options, something called Voiceover. It reads out texts and stuff. Marty also told me I can get a Braille keyboard for it. I guess I first need to learn Braille though." I stood. "I'm going to the bedroom, have a nap. My head's full of crap and I want it to go away for a bit. Give you time to think too."

Jon was beside me, stroking my arm. "It will be okay, Nate. We both need some time. Go lie down, get some rest. I'll putter around, make doubly sure everything is blind-proofed."

I winced at that phrase, even though it was a part of my life now. "Yeah. All right." I turned and made my way to the bedroom.

It was only when I lay on the bed and pulled the duvet around me that I realized Jon hadn't answered my questions about Cody.

Chapter 4

Cody

It wasn't often I got pissed off. I was a pretty rational guy most of the time with a *comme ci, comme ça* attitude that served me well. Now though, sitting in my car, contemplating the beachfront and wondering why the hell I wasn't with Nate right now, to say I was ready to punch someone would be an understatement.

I'd taken the day off work specially to be with him. Thanks to Jon, it hadn't worked out, but I'd decided to give myself the day off anyway to brood. Rachel said I was a pain in the ass when I was broody and preferred to stay out of my way. It was a rare occasion but I tended to make them count.

I glowered at the bobbing dashboard figure of Yoda that Nate had bought me years ago from a head shop in Venice Beach. He said it reminded him of me since Yoda was calm and collected like me. Well, Nate should see me now.

Yoda stared at me with what I thought was a smirk on his face. I tapped it, making him bob.

"Stop that," I snarled. "It's enough that he didn't want me around today when he gets out of hospital. I don't need you silently sneering, trying to calm me down with your Yoda mind shit."

Oh yeah. I was definitely pissed off when I swore at Yoda.

I stared across the water. Why the hell wouldn't he let me be there? Jon said Nate didn't want me to see him "like that" at the hospital. What the hell did that mean? Like what exactly? And it's not as if I haven't seen worse with him. Like when he first woke up and was all messed in the head.

Scowling, I wondered why he hadn't responded to any of my messages. I eyed Yoda and narrowed my eyes at his wise face. "Jon would at least read them out to him or something, right? Do you think he's mad with me? Nate, I mean not Jon, 'cause he's *always* mad with me." The feeling of helplessness at not knowing what was going on drove me crazy.

Yoda stared back with knowing eyes and less of a smirk now.

I heaved a sigh, puffing out my cheeks as my phone rang. I decided to answer it. "Hey Dev. How are things going?"

Dev Wallis was a good friend—well, a fuckbuddy really—and someone I counted on to be there when I needed release of some sort. He knew about my feelings for Nate and was happy to play stand-in, which kind of sucked for him. The chemistry between us was great for sex, but had never been there to make our relationship more permanent.

"Hey, my friend. I wanted to ask if you wanted to meet up later? Maybe catch a drink and get a bit of action? I've been horny all week, and I need me some loving."

I stared into the distance. I didn't think I'd be seeing Nate today so why the hell shouldn't I have some fun?

"Yeah, sure. We can meet at Paulie's if you like, have a drink then we can go back to my place." Paulie's was a bar down on the beach that sold cheap alcohol and played great music.

"Sweet. We can catch up tonight. See you later."

The phone went dead and I threw it onto the passenger seat. I eyed the phone, reached for it, then pulled my hand away. Tapping the steering wheel, I watched as two seagulls fought over a piece of bread, only for it to fall into the depths of the ocean. The seagulls screamed in anger and swooped down like dive-bombing planes to rescue it.

I picked up my phone again. *Fuck it. I'm going to call again. He's not blowing me off like that.* I dialed Nate's cell number and waited. It rang a few times then cut off. I stared at the phone in disbelief.

"Did you cut me off, you bastard? No fuckin' way." I dialed again.

Just as I was about to give up, Nate's sleepy voice answered.

"Oh, you *are* alive." I couldn't keep the sarcasm from my voice. "I thought maybe you'd been abducted by aliens."

"Cody? Where the hell have you been?" Nate sounded angry.

I gaped. "What? I've been keeping away like I was asked. Where the hell have *you* been? And why did you cut me off?"

There was silence, then, "What do you mean, 'like you were asked'? I came out of hospital today, don't you remember?" It was hard to miss the hurt in Nate's voice. "And sorry about the cutting you off. I tried to answer and must have pressed the wrong button. I'm still getting used to the whole being blind thing."

I squinted at the seagulls, trying to see which one of them had won the food competition. It looked like the fat one with the tattered feathers was the reigning champion. I threw it a thumbs-up.

"Huh? Of course I remember. I've sent you loads of texts. And it was your boyfriend who told me you didn't want to see me today, and I should stay out of the way."

Nate went quiet again. I heard him shuffling around. "Jon told you I didn't want to see you? Why would he do that? He knows I wanted to see you."

I sighed. "That's why. I guess he wanted you to himself today. I can understand that." The tight feeling in my chest and throat must be heartburn, I reasoned. Not heartbreak. Nate *wasn't* mine and I couldn't lay claim to him like Jon could. And did.

"That wasn't his decision to make," Nate said fiercely, and I rejoiced at hearing my old testy friend back. "He didn't ask me what I wanted. Shit. I can make my own damn decisions."

"I hear you. I guess he was just looking out for you." Jon was probably keeping me away from Nate from sheer spite, but I wasn't going to tell Nate that.

"Well, he fucked up. I might be blind, but I'm not useless." He sounded truly pissed off and I sniggered. I loved Nate when he got riled up. It was a sexy sight.

I used my tank top to wipe the sweat off my forehead. "Of course you aren't. I'm glad to hear you weren't ignoring me. So what's it like being home?"

There was silence before Nate spoke again. "It's okay, I guess. Jon has tried to sort the house out for me so I don't fall on my ass every time I take a step. I'm figuring the rest out."

"You been down to your studio yet, checked it's still in one piece?" I knew I was pushing but I couldn't help myself.

"No. That's not in the cards anytime soon." Nate's tone was defeated and I hated that. "I need to get used to normal living before I even think about anything else." Knowing he needed it, even though he'd say differently, I pushed a bit more.

"Well, when you do—you should know that last week I spoke to a guy I know who teaches visually impaired people how to do art stuff. He's involved with that society that promotes art to the blind and he also teaches techniques and stuff to help people create their own. I told him about you and he says when you're ready, I should take you down to his place. I know that's still a ways off but, you know. When you're ready."

Marty had been adamant I push Nate back into sculpting somehow. I'd gotten in touch with people and found out what the options were.

I held my breath, knowing how Nate felt about his art now he was blind. He didn't believe he could do it. I knew he could. There wasn't any argument.

"Cody, you know I love you. And I appreciate what you're trying to do. I'm not sure I can."

Oh wow, did he say he loved me? My heart went pitter-patter. *I'm such a sap.* "Bullshit. Just because you can't see doesn't mean you can't use your hands. You have to look at things differently, that's all." I sniggered. "I didn't mean to say that."

"Yeah, you did," Nate bit back, but I could hear he was perking up. "Christ, I don't know what I'd do without you. You always make me feel better, not like such a freak. Thanks, man."

I could make you feel so much better. We'd be awesome together, like a fine oil paint on a primed canvas. Or like one of your pieces. I'll be your clay and you can mold me.

Memories of the movie *Ghost* flitted through my mind and I shivered, thinking of Nate's hands on my body, forming me into positions like those of a clay statue—touching me, stroking me, pushing his fingers into me and…

My lustful thoughts were interrupted when Nate barked down the phone. "Cody, you still there?"

I pushed my rapidly rising cock down with one hand and tried to answer without sounding like a dirty, breathless old man wheezing down the phone.

"Yeah," I said brightly. "Just moved on for a minute, but I'm back now."

"What are you doing? You sound out of breath. I hear seagulls, are you at the beach in your car?" Nate sounded suspicious. "Is someone with you there, am I interrupting something?"

"No, duh. Geesh, what's with the hundred and one questions? I called you, remember? I'm hardly like to do that while I'm getting a blowjob here."

Nate cleared his throat. "Car blowjobs all they're cracked up to be?"

I tried not to get excited at the yearning I thought I heard in his voice. "Oh yeah. You should try it sometime." I shifted in my seat, trying not to think of Nate and I having sex in my car.

"Jon doesn't like car sex," Nate said flatly. "I've suggested it but he's not too keen."

TMI, but I wasn't surprised. Car sex could get messy, and Jon's hair might get mussed.

"Tell him he doesn't know what he's missing. There's nothing like seeing the windows mist up while you're getting busy and wondering whether someone's going to knock and tell you to move on. The thrill of being caught in the act is a turn-on."

"Sounds like fun," Nate said, a wistfulness in his tone that made me want to go over, drag him down to the beach and ravish him in my car to show him how much fun it could be. That thought made me even harder and I took a deep breath to center myself.

Nate asked, "These guys you hook up with—do you know them all or are they strangers?"

I hesitated. "Not really. Well, maybe a little. They're guys I meet surfing, or at the diner. It's a mutual thing, getting each other off. Nothing serious."

"You're careful though, look after yourself?"

I rolled my eyes. "Nate, we use condoms, all right? I'm not an innocent anymore." I broke off as memories of my lost innocence pushed forward, and I swore I could smell Nate's musky sweat and hear his groans while I tasted his skin.

From the silence on the other end of the phone, I gathered Nate was remembering too. The incident we weren't allowed to discuss, those stolen nights when we'd been one were too painful to recollect and I pushed them back into their space beside my heart.

Clearing my throat, I asked, "So, do you need anything for the house?"

"You," was Nate's soft reply and my heart clenched. "Please come over for dinner. Forget what Jon said. I need my best bud."

I swallowed, my throat aching at those two innocent words that always destroyed my world. "Sure. I'll come over." I'd have to call Dev and put off our prospective night of debauchery. He'd understand. "I'll bring beer. We can hang out."

"Thanks. It's been a bit much, being home for the first time since the accident. I need things to be real, and you're as real as it gets."

I heard the affection in his voice and chuckled. "You with your compliments, making a man blush."

I glanced down at my tattered board shorts, sandals and tank top and grimaced. Maybe I should go home and change so Jon wasn't offended when I sat on his couch in my less-than-stellar clothing. Then I thought, nah, fuck him. He was the reason I wasn't at the hospital when Nate left, and I wasn't with Nate now. At the very least, Jon deserved to suffer my attire.

I messaged Dev to call off our date and set off to see Nate.

***

As predicted, Jon hadn't been happy to see me when I arrived around five o'clock. I smirked, waved a hand airily in Nate's direction as he sat on the sofa, and plonked myself down next to my best friend.

Jon muttered something about calling his agent, threw me a dirty look and disappeared onto the deck, shutting the glass doors behind him.

I placed a hand on Nate's knee, and leaned in and kissed his forehead. "So how are you *really* doing?"

He smelt like Nate—vanilla, mint and spice—but his beautiful brown eyes were distant with charcoal smudges underneath like dark sad smiles, and he'd lost weight. He was still my Nate though.

Thick brown hair touched with lustrous red tints, his pale skin freckled, and generous lips now being bit down in nervousness, which was new. His capable hands fidgeted in his lap; strong, hair-flecked hands that I loved to watch sculpt ordinary clay into sheer genius.

Nate shrugged. "I'm doing good."

In most ways, he looked as if the accident had never happened. If you hadn't known he couldn't see, it wouldn't have been obvious, apart from a fading scar on his forehead.

I'd done a lot of reading since the accident and learned that blind people show expression on their faces the same as anyone else; they didn't all stare fixedly behind or away from you. Their eyes could still show emotion. However, despite Nate's words, the tic at the corner of his mouth told me he wasn't okay.

"So, you fancy having car sex, huh? I'm sure you'd convince Jon somehow," I joked. We'd get into the serious stuff in a minute.

Nate snorted as he sat back. "Not likely. For some reason he has a bee in his bonnet about it. Thinks it's tacky." He cocked his head and his beautiful eyes looked at me. "So you're quite the expert, getting off with guys in your beat-up old Chevy?"

I laughed. "I'm not that much of a slut. But yeah, I guess I've done it a few times."

Nate's eyes narrowed. "You made it sound like a regular occurrence when we spoke earlier." I ignored his tone. It couldn't possibly be what I thought it was.

Nate reached up and his hands moved uncertainly in front of my face. "Can I touch you?" he asked softly. "I know your face so well in my mind but I want to see what it feels like now that I can't see. I want to feel if it looks the same to my fingers." There was no trace of self-pity, only a weary matter-of-fact flatness in his voice that broke my heart.

I swallowed and lifted his hands to my cheeks. "Sure."

Way to torment me, Nate.

Gently, Nate began to move his fingers and hands down my jawline, brushing the clipped stubble on my chin and upper lip with his thumb. I swallowed, and held my breath as Nate's hands traveled slowly across and down my face, touching me in a way he'd never done before. The movements were slow and sensuous, sending tingles over my skin, making my groin ache. My chest tightened at the rapt expression on Nate's face as he mapped me, got to know me through touch alone.

I blinked back hot tears, not wanting him to feel my wet cheeks. Then I closed my eyes, wanting to feel the sensation of those calloused and tender fingers without seeing what he was doing. Perhaps I'd get an idea how Nate felt using his other senses to explore his new world.

The way his hands explored my face reminded me of when he sculpted, how he made love to his clay. He'd always been tactile, and what he did now to my face left me breathless.

I couldn't help my cock pushing against my loose shorts and I picked up a cushion and held it across my lap in case Nate brushed his arm against me and caught my boner. That wouldn't be welcome, not to mention Jon was out on the deck still talking on the phone.

Nate's fingers found my lips, and I couldn't help parting them and finally letting out a pent-up sigh. I wanted to lick his fingers, suck them into my mouth and watch his face as I did it.

He paused, his eyes narrowing, and something, some indefinable current, ran between us. I ignored it. It was something I knew Nate didn't want or need, especially at this time of his life. He'd told me that a long time ago, and I'd tried to respect it ever since.

"Dude, this here is some serious personal space invasion." I chuckled as I moved away then stood as I dropped the cushion to the sofa. I tried to will my cock to deflate. "Am I still the same? No warts, moles or unusual hair growth?"

Nate dropped his hands to his sides and shook his head. "No." he said softly. "You still feel like the same Cody."

"Good, good." I glanced at the deck as Jon turned to look at us from outside. I waved at him and he looked away, and turned his back. "So, is the boyfriend treating you well? I see he's done some work moving things around. Does that make things easier?"

There was silence and I sat down again next to Nate, who'd gone paler. "Nate, what's wrong?"

"I don't think he wants me anymore, Cody." Nate's voice was barely audible. "He's…so cold. It's like I'm a freak and he doesn't want to touch me. I mean, things weren't great before the accident but now…" He looked dejected.

Ice trickled down my spine. I'd noticed something was off at the hospital. I'd even overheard a conversation between Jon and someone, no doubt Caleb; Jon had whispered he didn't think he could do this. The words that had really gotten me were, "How can I be with a man who can't see who I am? I'm wasted on him."

The only thing that had stopped me going over and drop-kicking Jon's ass down the hall was the presence of a little boy in his pajamas, wide eyed and pale as he sat with his family. I didn't want the poor kid to watch my ninja moves and be traumatized forever. He looked as if he had enough going on in his life.

At the time I'd chalked Jon's conversation down to the newness of the situation, to the fact everything had changed for everyone. Now, hearing Nate's agonized words, I wasn't so sure.

I wrapped my arms around him, taking care not to let any wayward body parts to get in the way. He sank into me with a soft sigh. I swallowed the need to have this comfort as a permanent thing in my life, and stroked his hair. This was about making him feel better, not me.

"I'm sure that's not it. He's getting used to the changes, that's all. Like you are. I mean," I drew away from Nate and framed his face in my hands. "Look at you. You're gorgeous. So you can't see. What the hell difference does that make? It means he can steal the biggest piece of steak first. He can grab that last baked potato without you noticing, and drink milk straight from the fridge." Nate hated it when I did that. "It means nothing else. You're still the same you that you were before." My hands traced idle patterns on his head, massaging his scalp the way he'd always liked. Nate gave a throaty groan, which caused my groin to flame hotter, and I suppressed the urge to adjust myself.

If I jerked off, he wouldn't be able to see me. He'd never know I came right in front of him. Yeah, but he'd probably smell it. Plus, I'm noisy, even when I'm by myself.

I gasped at the traitorous thoughts and ignored the image they projected.

"I'll never be the same me," Nate murmured into my chest. "You can't keep pretending that everything'll be the same. Jon's already used the word disabled, I nearly told him—"

"Oh hell no," I pulled back and snarled. Nate made a surprised noise as I stood. My hands left his soft mass of freshly shampooed hair and waved my arms about as I paced. "Jon is talking out his ass. We do not use that word in this house, or ever. That might be a word in a dictionary but it's not who you are." I put my hands on my hips and glared at him, hoping he'd feel the patented Cody laser stare.

Nate laughed loudly. "Calm down. Let me finish what I was going to say." The smile splitting his face made me feel better. "I didn't argue with him because to be honest, I was damn tired. If I hadn't been, I would have told him the same thing."

I squinted at him. "So we're on the same page?"

He nodded, as he grinned. "Yeah, Shaggy, we're on the same page."

"Don't call me that," I said, swatting his shoulder. "Good. As long as you don't let that douchebag call you disabled, you and I will be fine." I bit my lips. I hadn't meant to call Jon a douchebag, even though it was true.

Nate ignored it. He patted the seat beside him and I sat back down. As I did, Jon came in. He looked at us both and disappeared into the kitchen.

"As Cody is here with you, I'm going to go out and collect our food. I've ordered it, and the drive will do me good. I might be a while. I have to get some dry cleaning too on the way home."

Jon picked up his bag from the dining room table. "Anything else you need while I'm out, Nate?"

Nate shook his head. "No, I don't think so. I'm still figuring things out, but there's nothing I need desperately."

Jon nodded. "Okay. Well, I'll see you later." He bent down over the sofa and placed a perfunctory kiss on the top of Nate's head. "I'm sure Cody will look after you while I'm gone." Nate couldn't see the flash of petulance in Jon's eyes, but he also couldn't see the relief cross Jon's face. He looked glad to be going out and thankful he was getting away from Nate, which seemed to override his irritation I was around.

Me, I'd be glad to have Nate to myself for a little while. And longer.

We waited until we heard the front door shut then I poked Nate in the ribs. He squirmed. He'd always been ticklish.

"So what say you and I grab a beer, kick off our shoes, and you can tell me what's going to happen now that you're back home?" I asked. "I'm sure there must be plans and I'd like to be part of them, even if it's a just as a driver."

Nate frowned. "Cody, you have a business to run. A busy art gallery. You can't hang around and be at my beck and call."

I nudged him again. "Course I can. That's why I have minions. I'm the boss, I can do what I like. Just call me Despicable." I said the word with a Daffy Duck lisp, and Nate giggled. God, the man giggled. It had been a long time since I'd heard that noise leave his lips.

"You are too much," Nate said, his face affectionate. "You're like this force of nature I can't control, but in a good way. You blow in and make stuff better."

I stood and went to the fridge, where I retrieved two beers. "Of course I am. That's what crazy best friends do."

I came back and pressed the cold drink into Nate's hands. They were screw tops so I unscrewed mine and waited to see if Nate needed help. He didn't.

We sipped our beers and looked like two men without a care in the world.

"You heard from your folks?" I knew the answer already.

"No. They haven't been in touch at all. Not even a get well card." I heard the underlying pain. Losing his family had always messed with Nate's head even though he tried not to show it much.

"Bastards," I growled. "They're lucky they're on another continent or else I'd show up and give 'em a piece of my mind."

"It doesn't matter. I'm used to it. You know that's water under the bridge."

I did, although I knew the stream still trickled a little. Over the past twelve years, Nate had sent birthday cards, Christmas cards and anniversary cards to his parents and sister. Not one had ever been acknowledged. A few had even been marked "return to sender," but doggedly he continued to try to communicate with his family.

Phone calls he'd made were scarcely acknowledged and ended up in emotional outbursts. He'd given up calling them years ago.

Nate sighed. "No good stressing about it. I've got enough on my plate to think about." He gave a soft laugh. "Besides, I've got your folks. You know I'm their surrogate son."

My parents and siblings—Jessica, Levi and Daisy—had already visited Nate twice and offered to help in any way they could. They called every other day too.

"Jon's got this visual rehabilitation therapist coming in on Friday." Nate sat back and closed his eyes, his hands holding the bottle on his lap. "Her name's Suzanne. I guess she'll be talking to me about maybe using a cane to get around, following up on the stuff Marty told me about." He sighed heavily. "I don't really want a cane but it sounds as if they are really useful when I'm out and about." He frowned. "I also need to learn Braille. That's going to be fun."

"Ya know, canes can be awesome. You can get one that has a secret compartment in the top for your bourbon. And you can learn to use it like Obi Wan Kenobi did his light saber, like a weapon. Also, Matt Murdock. Just dwell on that for a while."

It was no secret I had a huge crush on the actor who played Daredevil in the TV series. Nate leaned forward and to my surprise, he ran a finger down my cheek without hesitation. I was floored he seemed to know exactly where I was. His other hand held his half-empty beer bottle between his thighs.

"You're the best, Cody," he murmured. "Everyone else has been treating me like spun glass, as if I'll shatter. Jon seems to think I need help with everything. But you act like nothing's changed. Like I'm still the same person."

I swallowed, thinking I definitely had an oral fixation as his finger reached the corner of my mouth and paused. I wanted to open and nab it inside my mouth, suck on it until Nate's eyes glazed over and he made that breathy sound when he orgasmed. A sound I'd only heard a few times in my life, and I'd probably never hear again.

"You make sense of all of this," Nate continued as his finger now traced my lips and I closed my eyes, wishing this was something else rather than a blind man getting familiar with my face. "I know things are going to be different, and I'm glad I've got you with me to help me make it through."

I sensed a shift in the air in front of me and opened my eyes. Nate leaned closer and for one heart-stopping, gut-wrenching moment, I thought he was going to kiss me.

Oh God, what's happening? Is he really going to do it?

Reality set in like a rush of frigid air to the skin when he stopped, looking confused, as he flopped back against the couch. The warm fingers on my mouth disappeared and Nate clenched his hands, dropping them into his lap.

"It's Jon's birthday next month. Will you help me plan a party for him? I want it to be a surprise. Maybe it'll make him happier, who knows." Well, that request grabbed me by the balls and made me realize how fleeting my dreams were.

Nate's voice was strained, and he looked down to his lap. Then he raised his beer bottle and took a long drink.

"Yeah, sure. Whatever you need." My fantasies had once again gone down the toilet, but I could do this.

"It's July twenty-first. He turns twenty-seven. I don't want anything big, an intimate get-together here at the house. Maybe we can have finger food, a bit of dancing. I need to make sure the food choices are healthy though, you know how he and his model friends are about their weight."

I nodded then realized Nate couldn't see it. "I'll ask Rachel to help out. She's good at stuff like that, getting menus organized for people's needs. Her family are a mix of vegetarian, vegan and cannibals."

I hoped Nate hadn't noticed the flatness in my voice.

Nate moved farther away on the sofa as if distancing himself. "Thanks, man, I appreciate that." He drained his beer and fumbled around at his side to place the empty bottle on the side table.

I stood. "Want another beer? I'm nearly done with this one myself."

Nate shook his head. "No thanks. I'm fine."

I grabbed another beer and downed half of it in one long swallow. "Want me to take a look at your iPhone, see if I can figure out how to get it to read texts? Maybe download whatever apps you'll need?"

"Sure, it's in the bedroom, in the charger still. Thanks, that'll be one less thing for Jon to do when he gets home." Nate lay back on the sofa and closed his eyes.

I rolled my eyes, not sure fixing Nate's phone would be on Jon's list of priorities. I chastised my inner bitch as I made my way to their bedroom. Nate's phone sat in the charger, green light blinking. I plucked it out and took a lingering look around.

It wasn't a place I'd spent a lot of time, but in the past, when Jon had been away on a photo shoot, we'd sometimes watch films in here, swathed in the floppy duvet, eating chocolate and drinking beer.

Neutral colors were bathed in natural light from the large picture windows. The bed was understated, king-size, of course, with a simple gray and blue striped duvet. It was Nate. Not fussy, simple but elegant and contemporary.

I caught myself in the dressing table mirror; light blond hair, deep green eyes and a few wrinkles in tanned skin stared back. I pulled a tongue, the gesture was returned. I sighed and turned away.

I left the room, switching on his phone and entering his numeric password to open. Nate was a hacker's dream. He used the same easy passwords, either 1792 or *Clayman17* for everything. I had no idea what the significance was. I'd told him countless times to change them because honestly, everyone knew his preference, his friends even teased him about it, but he'd always shrugged and said if anyone wanted into his stuff that bad, they'd get in no matter what.

"Nate, you really need to change your password, buddy. I—" I stopped. Nate was fast asleep, long lashes on his cheeks, hands loose and relaxed in his lap. His chest rose and fell evenly and his legs were splayed open in a display that made me want to cover him up like a prudish matron so no one else could see him. Nate had always had a pretty impressive package, and with his legs stretched like that, it was perfectly framed.

"Not cool, Cody," I muttered as I took out a blanket from the side dresser. "Perving over your best friend when he's sleeping. I need therapy."

I spread the soft blanket over Nate and sat down gently beside him, so as not to wake him up. My hands itched to push the soft strands of hair from his face, but I didn't dare in case I gave in and kissed him. Temptation was a bitch I wanted to slap.

I laid my head back too and contemplated the ceiling, watching the fan whirl around and around as it brushed air our way. Then turning my attention to Nate's cell, I managed to get the iPhone set up with all the accessibility options I could find then put it down on the side table.

"It's going to be okay," I murmured, half to myself, half to Nate in case he somehow heard. "This isn't the end of things. It's only the beginning of something new."

Chapter 5

Nate

A loud bang woke me. Startled out of sleep, I blinked and sat bolt upright. Somehow I was tangled in something and I swore as I fought to unwind whatever it was from around my legs. Next to me, there was a loud snort then Cody's voice echoed sleepily in the room.

"Wazzup? Where's the fire?"

"No fire. Just me coming home to find you two sprawled all over each other, fast asleep." The irritation in Jon's voice was hard to miss. "I brought dinner home in case you're interested. I'll put it in the kitchen."

I heard retreating footsteps as I pulled what turned out to be a blanket off me and threw it on the floor.

Cody protested. "Hey, that was keeping me warm, asshole. Give it back."

I grunted, my mouth dry. I'd probably been snoring. "Did you hear the man? Dinner's ready."

I leveraged myself to my feet and stood, legs aching from being in one position so long. "What's the time, bud?"

There was a grumble, a soft curse and the rattling of something on the table. "It's nearly eight o'clock. We've been asleep a couple of hours."

Cody yawned loudly and I imagined him stretching,

I frowned. "Jon took nearly three hours to fetch food and dry cleaning?" The familiar prickle of suspicion I'd gotten used to recently surfaced again. Where had he been for so long? More important question—did I truly care?

Mixed emotions made a soup of my insides but guilt, need, irritation and confusion was a broth I didn't need right now.

I held out a hand. "Up," I instructed. "We need to eat, I'm damned starving. And knowing you, you'll want to stuff your belly as well."

My hand was grasped by warm fingers as I helped pull Cody to his feet.

"Yeah, yeah, I can manage a little something," Cody grumbled, still holding on to my hand. I didn't want to let go.

I snorted to cover the unexpected emotion. "I don't know how you manage to keep fit with the amount of food you consume. You should be as big as Old Al."

Old Al was a new arrival—a gorilla at the Los Angeles Zoo Cody had dragged me to see more times than I cared to remember. He had a curious fascination with the primate.

Cody's hand left mine and gave me a light shove. "I'll have you know I have a killer metabolism. Sex, surf, dance and a good old-fashioned balanced lifestyle."

There was a patting sound. "That's how I keep this magnificent body of mine in shape. You could bounce a quarter off this stomach."

I tried valiantly to clamp down the memories I had of his lean, muscled physique, honed from years of surfing and swimming, golden skinned, and lean muscles. I wondered if he still tasted the same—sun-kissed, coconut and vanilla scent from the suntan oil he used and musky male.

I took a deep breath, trying to calm my wayward thoughts.

Shit. Where the fuck did that come from?

"Speaking of exercise, are you ever going to run again?" Cody's voice came from my left. "Maybe one day we can go out together, if you want to get back into it?"

Bile flooded my mouth, thankfully taking the tantalising thoughts of Cody's naked body from my mind. "No, I don't want to venture out onto the road ever again, even with someone. I did my last running the night that car hit me."

"Okay then, I'll say no more about it. What about surfing?" Cody's hand brushed mine. "If I took you out on a board, you think you might like to do that again sometime? I promise I'll look after you. I won't let you float away to China. Or get eaten by a giant jellyfish."

Despite my dampened mood, I smiled. "Maybe one day. It might be fun."

"That's a date, then." Cody squeezed my shoulder. "Right, food time. I'm hungry." Cody hesitated. "You need any help finding the kitchen?"

I shook my head. "I can get there on my own. I'm slowly learning what direction to go in once I get my bearings, how many steps it is to where I need to be. It'll take time but it's getting there."

"Good." Cody's voice was soft. "I'm glad you're not letting this get you down. That's my Nate."

"*His Nate*"? In some ways, I supposed I was more Cody's than Jon's, who'd humphed at the endearment. I sighed. The boyfriend's displeasure seemed a little out of place given his three-hour absence.

Resigned to a fragile peace, for the moment, I walked over to the kitchen and groped for a stool around the breakfast bar. I pulled it out, and sat as someone walked around to me.

"I plated you some food," Jon said. A plate slid over in front of me. "It's Mexican tonight. I got you a meat burrito and chilli cheese fries. You can eat it with your hands at least. Your beer is on the right, at about two o'clock to your plate. Don't knock it over. Cody, yours is in the bag. There's a selection of stuff, eat what you want. I've got mine already."

Cody cleared his throat. "Thanks. By the way, that's cool to use a clock to tell Nate where his stuff is. I'll have to remember that." I heard rustling from the bag on the kitchen counter to my left.

"Marty told me how to do it." Jon's voice was smug. "There's lots of stuff that can help Nate, you might want to read up on it, though. It's time-consuming making sure everything is easier for him."

And there it was. The condescension I'd already noticed. Jon was inconvenienced to the degree that he needed to mention it any chance he got.

Way to make me feel like a useless prick, asshole.

I lost my appetite there and then and laid my burrito down, staring down at a plate I could no longer see.

"Yeah? I guess you have a lot of time on your hands though, so at least helping Nate keeps you busy." Cody's tone was even but I heard the bite in it.

"What do you mean by that?" Jon asked frostily.

Knowing Cody as I did, he probably eye-rolled. "You haven't gotten a job in a while, your model shoots seem to be sporadic. The last one you did was about a month ago, for the underwear company, wasn't it? Anything happen since then?"

Cody must be past pissed to be bitchy; it wasn't his style. He knew the answer already. We'd already discussed it before the accident—Jon had been worried he was getting too old for modeling shoots, and the dearth of work the past few months had made him more insecure than usual.

There was a heavy silence that I tried to ignore, picking up the burrito I didn't want and biting into it. Juice trickled down my chin and I wiped it away with my hand.

Jon swore and a napkin was thrust into my hand. "Here. Wipe your mouth."

"Jesus, Jon, you are such an asshole," Cody snarled. "He's not a kid, don't talk to him like that. Do you always have to put him down?"

"I'm not putting him down; I'm simply trying to help—" Jon spluttered.

I stood up violently, my stool clattering to the ground.

"Enough," I shouted. "I'm here in the room, I don't need you two having a pissing contest over me. What the fuck is wrong with the both of you?"

As was his way, Cody was the first to apologize. "Sorry, Nate. I didn't mean to upset you. I was out of line." His stool scraped as he pushed it back. "I'd better be getting off, anyway, let you two have some space. I'm sorry we made you feel bad, man. It wasn't the intention."

I wanted to tell him not to go but I couldn't get the words out. My heart beat rapidly and I swallowed down bile.

Jon's tone was cold when he eventually spoke. "Really, Nate, we're not having a pissing contest over you. I care about you, that's all. I'm sorry if you don't see it that way."

"That's the problem, isn't it?" I whispered past the lump in my throat. "I *don't* see."

Cody gave a soft exclamation of distress and gripped my arm. "Nate, I'm so sorry—"

I shook my head, holding back hot tears of frustration. I was about to break down and I didn't want him seeing me lose it.

I turned toward Cody. "It's okay. Maybe you should go though. Thanks for coming by. Now if you'll excuse me, I've got somewhere else to be."

It was difficult to make a grand exit from the room, given the circumstances, but I liked to think I managed it with some dignity. Apart from once again knocking a picture off the wall. Obviously, Jon had not moved all of them.

I went into my room, and closed the door firmly behind me, disrobed down to my boxers, pulled back the covers, and crawled under them, shutting the whole world out.

Let it go on without me for a while. I need to think.

***

I didn't hear Jon come to bed that night and I wasn't even sure he had. When I woke, his side of the bed was cold. The house seemed empty. A frisson of fear swept through me.

Jesus, maybe he's left and I'm all alone.

How the hell would I *know*? I groaned, swung my legs over the side of the bed and stood. I needed to take a piss so I stumbled to the bathroom and reacquainted myself with the toilet seat, ensuring the lid was up. I aimed and fired. The sound of my pee hitting the water in the bowl was a welcome sound, rather than have it splash back on me as had been the case more than a few times in the hospital.

The shower wasn't such an ordeal today. The soap was where it should be and all was right with the world. I was busy washing my hair, lathering shampoo into a sudsy mess, when there was a knock on the shower door. I started, getting shampoo in my eyes, and yelped in pain.

"Sorry, didn't mean to scare you. Maybe I need a bell or something. Like a cat." Jon's voice sounded wry and I turned toward him in relief that he was still there.

"It's okay. No real harm done."

"Listen, about last night." There was the sound of the toilet lid being put down and I imagined Jon sitting down on it. "I'm sorry if you got upset. I didn't mean to do that, it's all so damn difficult for m—us, and sometimes maybe I mess up."

I shrugged. "It's fine. Didn't you come to bed?"

"I slept on the couch. Thought we both needed the space."

I washed the shampoo from my hair. I was glad he didn't sound pissed at me for the whole dramatic exit thing. I wondered what, if anything, he and Cody said to each other after I left. That was a phone call I'd need to make. Cody didn't hold grudges, and he'd been there for me and fought my corner. I wanted to make sure he knew I appreciated that, even though I'd gone off in a huff.

The shower door opened and I drew in a breath as a warm and naked body pressed itself against my back. It had been too damn long and my cock went from zero to hero in one second flat.

"Let me show you how sorry I am," Jon whispered as his hands encircled my cock and stroked. His balls pushed against the back of my thighs, the tip of his cock in my crease. "Maybe this will release some tension in us both."

I was both relieved and surprised. Like sex in cars, togetherness showers weren't Jon's thing.

Jon pulled me around to face him and I moaned as his hand stroked faster. Greedy fingers grasped me, stroking me to a point I knew wouldn't take long to reach.

Oh God, that feels good. It's been too long since I've had his hands on me like this.

I reached out to pull his head closer, to reach his lips. This time there was no resistance and Jon's mouth covered mine wantonly. I sighed into it as he jacked me off, water running down my body, the sensation of still being wanted flooding me like warm syrup.

From the hard cock prodding my own, Jon was as turned on as I was. *He must still want me.*

Water trickled into my mouth while sucking on Jon's tongue. His gasp of pleasure sent a shockwave to my already fluttering stomach. I groaned loudly, the heat from our bodies combined with the wet, slick skin rubbing against mine, making my body tingle.

Jon's hands on my cock grew fiercer, his thumb pressing into my slit. His thrusts between my cheeks grew erratic and stronger as he frotted against my willing body. The velvet sweep of his fingers over my hole was torture, and when I found my voice, I was going to beg him to fuck me.

Jon gasped against my ear, his thrusts getting weaker, and warm liquid flooded my belly.

I moaned in disappointment, knowing he'd come already.

"Let's finish this," Jon whispered huskily. His talented hands moved faster and stronger on my prick and the pressure built as my balls constricted. Despite the pleasure coursing through my body, I couldn't help the vision of a pair of dark green eyes covered with blond strands staring into mine, doing the exact same thing to me as Jon was now.

I tried to push the traitorous image from my head as my orgasm built. I bit my lip, terrified that when my climax ripped through me, I would say the wrong name.

Instead I focused on the memory of Jon's face and Jon's body, and when I came, in a mind-blowing rush of sensation and pent-up release, I made sure I said *his* name.

***

Friday morning the doorbell rang. I was sitting in the family room, listening to an audiobook that Cody had given me, a mystery and detective story I was enjoying. I had my coffee, a grilled ham and cheese sandwich Jon had made before leaving for an appointment he'd had in Los Angeles for a potential modeling job.

I heard the doorbell over the book narration. I paused the story and laid my phone down on the sofa beside me. I went to the door and yelled through it, "Yes?"

A cheerful voice rang out, "Hi, Mr. Powell. I'm Suzanne Ridley, your rehabilitation specialist. May I come in?"

She sounded young, but voices could be deceiving. Her accent was also unusual, more British with a slight twang. I debated whether I was letting in an axe murder or a rehab specialist then took a leap of faith. Opening the door, I said, "Sure. I was expecting you. And please call me Nate."

A waft of something clean and fresh hit my nostrils as Suzanne brushed past me. She stopped as I shut the door.

"You have a lovely home, Nate. Quite elegant and I see it's been arranged to make things easier for you. Your boyfriend did this?"

"Yeah, Jon worked out the configuration. We still have the occasional mishap when we both mess up, but other than that, I'm intact."

I moved toward the family room and motioned for her to follow me. "Please, make yourself comfortable."

When Jon had left that morning, he'd made sure to leave a pot of coffee on the machine, along with everything I might need.

I sure as fuck can manage to get a house guest a damn drink at least.

I heard Suzanne settle herself on the sofa as I went into the kitchen. "Can I get you a coffee?"

"Oh, not for me, thanks. I don't drink it. I'd love a glass of water if you have one."

"Sure." I took a deep breath, opened the cupboard, reached in carefully for a plastic tumbler—the last time I'd done it too quickly I'd ended up knocking a glass one out onto the counter. Luckily it hadn't broken. Now we had plastic ones. Jon had assured me they didn't look tacky.

I placed the tumbler safely on the counter then found my way to the fridge, and took out the iced water. Luckily it was always kept in the same place, something Jon and I were learning to live with as a life rule. I was proud of myself when I filled the tumbler and took it over to my guest.

She murmured her thanks and I sat down in the armchair, leaning forward.

"You have an unusual accent," I remarked. "Where's it from?"

"I was born in South Africa, then lived in England for a while, and came over to the U.S. about eight years ago. I guess I'm a bit of a hybrid."

I nodded. "So, what exactly is it you can do for me? Jon has told me all the hype about the things I need to learn, but how exactly do they translate to real life?"

What the hell can you teach me that will help? Convince me, lady, because I'm not sure anything will.

There was a warm chuckle. "Oh, you had the hype, huh? Well, let me see if I can clarify it for you. I'm someone who hopes to make your life a little easier, and helps make the transition from sighted to unsighted that little less scary. I'm here to recommend some useful tools for you to be independent, like using a white cane and learning Braille so you can read. Teaching you how to gauge your surroundings using sound. And, of course, showing you how you can acquire the information you need through hearing, taste, touch and smell, rather than through vision."

I sat back in my chair. "You make it sound so easy." I hadn't intended to sound snippy, but I wasn't going to buy the easy sell. "It'll probably take me years to learn all that stuff. In the meantime, I guess I need someone to accompany me every time I go out, like a damn nursemaid?"

She shifted in her chair and her voice got stronger. "To start with, that's a yes. You need to build confidence in getting out on your own and that will take time. The cane will take some getting used to as well. I've had people learn to use it after a few months, sometimes weeks, and others it takes longer. It also depends on your goals. Are you wanting to use public transport extensively, or is it simply for walking around locally?"

I drew a deep breath.

"For starters, it's more being out and about, able to walk down the road without someone there to hold my hand. Walking around my own or someone else's house, or in a park, without assistance."

"That's a great objective to start out with. As for the Braille—I believe you're a sculptor?"

I nodded as my throat constricted. I'd been pushing that part out of my life into the dark recesses of my brain since I'd gotten home. I wasn't willing to give it a voice.

"May I look at your fingers, Nate?" Suzanne asked gently.

I stuck out my arm and held my hands toward her palm up. Warm, small hands took mine and I imagined a bird of a woman opposite me, with warm eyes and a soft smile.

"As a sculptor, the tips of your fingers may be a little desensitized to reading Braille. Yours look undamaged, but rough, a little calloused. It may mean you might have to work a little harder than some to get it right, but I've no doubt you could do it if you have the motivation. You're young too, and that always helps. And of course, being blind certainly shouldn't stop you from sculpting. It's a tactile endeavor so using your fingers and base instincts to create something is already ingrained in you. Your sight loss shouldn't take that away from you."

My chest tightened with hope. Marty had said the same thing.

For the next two hours, I sat with the woman who fast became someone I wanted to know better. Suzanne's optimism, her compassion and her no-nonsense way of telling me to get over it when I whined were refreshing. Like Cody, she understood that I was still the same man I'd been before the accident.

Orientation and mobility, human guides, self-protective techniques and the different tools available for me to use—these words and phrases came at me like a slow freight train and I tried to absorb it all.

Suzanne's soft voice kept me company as she explained about special kitchenware, talking watches, and special phones. Apparently there are canes that have sensors and vibrate when things got a bit difficult, like navigating stairs. Hell, you could even get a Bluetooth Braille keyboard.

Wow. Who knew this stuff existed?

When Suzanne left with a waft of perfume and a firm handshake, I closed the door, went back into the family room, sat down, and for the first time in a long time, I knew hope.

"This is just a setback in your life, Nate," I muttered to myself. "Something you need to deal with. You can do it."

The fact I was starting to think of my blindness as a setback instead of a brick wall I couldn't climb lightened my soul.

I can do this. I can beat this damn thing. I know I can.

***

During the next two months Suzanne's rehab techniques were a rinse-and-repeat exercise in patience. She was a tough taskmaster who occasionally I likened to Genghis Khan.

Cody laughed and told me that, while he agreed with me on the personality part, she was far from it in looks.

I learned that my petite nemesis was twenty-eight, a little younger than me, yet looked even younger. She was tattooed and slim with auburn hair and a punk haircut. From the face-mapping I did with her, I discovered piercings in her nose and eyebrows. Her appearance was so at odds with her no-nonsense personality.

As part of my armoire of blind tools, my cane had to be tailored to the correct length for my height and stride and the fact I was right-handed. Protective techniques I'd been taught helped determine my location as I trailed my left hand down walls, while holding my right arm across my chest so if I bumped into anything, that would take the brunt first.

There were a lot of other techniques to learn, like staying in step, but with Suzanne at my side, I'd slowly gained some confidence in walking with the cane on the street outside my home.

I found the cane work tough going more out of a desire to fool myself into thinking this wasn't who I was, than an actual lack of technical ability to use it. Each movement, each sweep, each knock and bump and scrape told me I was no longer the person I used to be. I resented the fuck out of it.

Suzanne and I had some epic arguments, and more than one time I lost my shit and threw a tantrum. However, determination was my friend and I wanted nothing more than to show everyone that I could manage on my own without help.

But still, I hadn't entered my studio. I couldn't face it. The smell of my materials, the knowledge I was surrounded by my own work—some in various stages of completion—it devastated me to the point of a near panic attack.

Jon stayed out of my way, making excuses to go out when I had my lessons. At first it had rankled. After a while, it didn't matter anymore.

I'm more than capable of doing this on my own. I don't need him. Let him sneak off to see Caleb. I'm not fucking stupid.

In contrast to Jon's reluctance to participate, Suzanne and Cody made the journeys fun, with constant joking, sly wit and a lot of patience. And when Cody was around when I lost my shit, he'd been both supportive and a bastard.

My usual normal, easy-going Cody in his dominant, kick-ass mode was something to experience. Sometimes I wondered if I was doing it on purpose to bring out that side of him.

And didn't that idea confuse me. Every day I was growing more conflicted over how I felt about him. I knew we had chemistry—that had been proven over those sultry nights in the Keys when we'd thrown caution to the winds and acted out our lustful desires.

Whatever spark was there that hot and passionate weekend had been snuffed out when I told Cody we couldn't be more than friends. I'd had my reasons, and now, all these years later, the reasons didn't apply anymore. But it seemed the "us" ship had sailed.

We'd both moved on, gotten into relationships, become men. And right now I wanted to make sure I was ready to face life again, be my own man and learn all the skills that would make my life easier. It was my own personal mission to make sure I stayed independent.

What I hadn't factored on was those feelings of need arising once again every time I heard his voice or felt his touch on my body. They arose from the deep recesses of where I'd buried them for safety, and they taunted me with memories and unbidden scenes in which we did things that made me blush just imagining them.

I went to bed each night with those fantasies in my spank bank and woke up sticky with morning wood that wouldn't disappear until I'd rubbed one out in the shower.

I told myself to focus on my training—that maybe it would help me get rid of this urgent need I suddenly had for my best friend.

Right now I stood in a nearby office block that was empty. Suzanne knew the owner and used it for some of her training. It was the first time I'd gone out of the comfortable confines of my home, backyard and friendly neighborhood street to use my stick.

We'd gotten there early in the morning, so I'd only had one cup of coffee. I was grumpy and not looking forward to more bumped shins and elbows.

Suzanne stood at my left side, hand on my elbow. She grounded me that way, preparing me for what lay ahead.

"So, we're in a long hallway in an empty building. No one's around, the path ahead is clear, there's nothing to trip over. Remember that echolocation thing we've been working on?"

"Yeah, the human dolphin thing." I scowled. "I'm no Daniel Kish but I think I can manage the whole tapping my cane, stamping my foot and snapping my fingers thing to figure out where stuff is. Just don't expect to do the clicking thing. That's just not me. I'm no gray mammal."

Suzanne chuckled. "Fine. No marine mammal sounds. So, you've been out in the street listening to noises and you've learned to read your environment a bit, make yourself aware of what and who surrounds you. So you've done *some* of the dolphin stuff." She snorted with laughter as I grunted. "Now we need to make sure your ears manage to identify loss of sound as well as the cause of it. That's important in realizing what's around you."

"So what?" I muttered. "You going to put ear muffs on me or what?"

"No. Far from it. We're going to walk down these hallways and I want you to listen carefully. Tell me if you sense or feel anything different. It'll take a few minutes, but we've got time."

We began to walk down the hall together, Suzanne behind me and slightly to my left. We did this for what seemed like an hour but was probably only minutes.

"How long do we have to do this for?" I grumbled. "It's a hallway, nothing different about anything. Except some of the smells coming out of the offices." I wrinkled my nose. "Smells like old gym socks and curry."

Suzanne put a hand on my arm to stop me. "Okay. How do you know there are offices?"

I cocked my head and glared at her. "I don't know. I guess because we're in an *office building*?" I didn't mean to be sarcastic but I wanted—no, *needed*— another coffee.

"Nate, listen to your instincts. You know that there are offices, but I need you to understand how you do that. Walk up and down again. On your own this time. Use the wall to guide you."

I fixed my mind to the task as I set off down the corridor, stomach clenched with nerves. My cane tapped against the floor on what I assumed was linoleum. It didn't have the spring of carpet or the smoothness of tiles. My left hand trailed along the wall. As I walked I tried to focus.

Step one. Step two. After a while I noticed an emptiness between wall surfaces and the difference when I passed those certain areas. The sound changed, the air changed, and the smell changed.

I stopped. "I'm passing open doorways, I think," I murmured back to Suzanne. "The air feels different. I feel a slight breeze. The sound isn't as dead as when I'm against the walls and I guess the smells mean the door is open and I can smell inside."

"Oh Grasshopper, you have served Master well," was the only thing Suzanne said but I heard the pride in her voice. "That's exactly what I wanted you to figure out. Now keep going. Tell me what you feel when you get to the end of the next wall. Stop there. Don't go farther."

Feeling cocky, I sped up.

"Not too fast," Suzanne warned. "Slow down, tiger."

I smirked as I walked faster, gaining confidence. My hand dropped to my side and I lost contact with the wall.

Suzanne shouted something but I was too busy congratulating myself on getting this far in my training today. This cane work wasn't so difficult after all.

I forged ahead, forgetting Suzanne's instruction to stop after the wall ended. Yet stop I did. My cane hit something solid, pushing it back through my hand to slip onto the floor. My face collided with something hard. Suzanne shouted as I reeled back, warm fluid dripping from my nose.

Shit. That fucking hurt!

I yelled and barrelled back, losing my footing and crashing to the floor.

Suzanne rushed to my side, and her strong hands tried to pull me upright.

"Leave me," I snarled, wiping my hand across my nose and feeling the gush of blood. The metallic smell was overwhelming. "Why didn't you fucking tell me there was a wall there?"

Christ, I don't need this shit. I don't want *this shit.*

I struggled to my feet, shaking off the hands on my body.

"Nate, I told you to stop after the next wall." Suzanne's voice was even and a tissue was pushed into my hand. "It's a dead end with another corridor to the left, with another hallway. I wanted to see if you could sense it, the change in the layout."

"Well, it didn't work, did it?" I growled. I wiped my nose and threw the tissue down to the floor. Another tissue was pressed into my hand.

"Put your head forward. I'll go get some stronger toilet tissue and wet it. That should help. Don't move."

Suzanne's feet shuffled down the corridor, probably toward a bathroom somewhere. In an idle moment of clarity, I knew she was wearing sneakers. I'd learned to hear the difference between people's feet. Jon in his designer boots; Cody's flip-flops or combat boots. Everyone had a different footfall. I wondered dully whether this was my life, identifying people by their footwear. Maybe I should join a circus.

I stood there as angry desolation crept into me with insidious sly fingers.

Fuck, what the hell am I thinking? I can't do this. Be like this. I'm never going to be able to manage on my own.

Suzanne padded back toward me. "Here, lean forward," she instructed quietly. "This should help."

Something cold and wet was pressed to the bridge of my nose and we waited in silence for the faucet that was my nose to stop gushing.

"It's a glitch, Nate," Suzanne said softly as her nimble fingers pinched my nose shut. "You've done so well so far. Don't let this one little thing upset you."

I grunted, not able to speak. What the hell did she know?

I can't even stop a nosebleed without help. How the hell am I going to manage anything else?

When my nose finally stopped bleeding, we called it a day and Suzanne took me home to shower. I at least calmed down enough to get my coffee and sandwich.

By the time Cody came by that evening, my mood had improved. I basked in his concern about my swollen nose and snarled in mock anger at his jokes about looking like a prizefighter down on his luck. We listened to audiobooks of Clive Cussler and drank beer until it was time for him to leave.

Jon didn't even come home that night, citing an over-running photo shoot schedule as an excuse.

I was too tired, depressed and sore to give a damn. I wasn't even sure what we had could be called a relationship anymore. I'd kept up the pretense to the outside world that everything was fine, when in reality it was anything but. We hadn't touched each other since that one shower.

I craved the intimacy of the old days, feeling a man's body touch mine, and a hungry, wet mouth finding my lips, sending me into a thrall of passion and heat. All that was gone now, leaving a sexual wasteland. While what I'd had with Jon hadn't been my life's dream, we had been comfortable, and he was familiar.

Now, we hardly spoke; and when we did it was perfunctory, asking each other how our day had been, please pass the butter, do you want another glass of wine. It was conversation that was so mundane as to be worthless.

Jon had landed himself a new modeling campaign, which necessitated him being late often and away more than ever. When he was home, we'd lie in bed and I knew the man next to me was now a stranger.

I cursed the person driving the car that hit me then fled. The police still hadn't found the culprit. I didn't think they ever would. Sometimes I'd sit in solitude and wonder what they were doing now—if their lives had changed drastically as mine had. Pondering their fate had become a preoccupation I shouldn't have dwelled on, but one I couldn't help.

Too much introspection damaged my fragile psyche, and I tried not to give in to it too much. But damn, it was tough.

***

Despite my meltdown at the empty office building, I became better at learning how to use a cane. Apparently the secret was to let it become an extension of your arm. I was improving every day and Suzanne said I had a natural ability for it.

I'd always had a special sense of touch and feel, and the cane work had turned out to be an exercise in dexterity, remembering how to sweep and walk.

Suzanne preferred to teach her students with a normal cane to start with. She likened it to learning to drive a car with a stick first instead of an automatic.

Getting to know the terrain and movements on your own with no special help was critical in becoming independent. *You* were all you had when things got tough.

However, I'd now purchased a cane equipped with sensors, which made a difference to my mobility and freedom, and I was glad I'd bought it.

We'd had a few upsets of course, because nothing went smoothly all the time. I had tripped a few times, and had not listened to Suzanne on occasion and forged ahead again in misplaced confidence. Once I'd hit some poor old dear with my cane as I waved it around in frustration. Suzanne had placated her and I'd mumbled a terse apology. It hadn't been one of my better days.

I'd also bought a new phone, one that better met my needs and would enable the Braille keyboard later when I was more proficient.

Speaking of which…I scowled as my tired fingers ran over the teaching Braille flash cards once again.

Suzanne's voice interrupted my thoughts. "Nate, have you finished your homework?" The emphasis on homework was tinged with amusement at the fact I'd complained I felt like a damn schoolchild during what Suzanne called "session time."

I shook my head mulishly and moved my chair back from the dining table, stretching my legs. "No. My fingertips are tired, my head aches, and I wasn't much of a reader anyway so I don't really see why I need to learn this stupid dotty stuff."

The only reading I like doing is when Cody is here and we listen to audiobooks.

Suzanne chuckled. "That stupid dotty stuff is going to let you have choices. A choice to read a document or a book, to check out your TV listings or even better, read that program of your work when you start sculpting again and have an exhibit at an art show."

I scowled. Between Suzanne and Cody, I had a formidable and unrelenting team trying to get me to begin working again, or at least enter my studio.

"Stop your sly attempts to manipulate me into doing something I'm not ready to do yet," I muttered. "Christ, you're as bad as Cody. He thinks by getting me down into the studio, I'll have a miraculous breakthrough, smell the clay and become enthused with creativity and whoosh, look at who's the next Rodin. The dude is such a damn optimist."

Cody was such a loveable dork sometimes. Well, most of the time. He'd become my rock whereas Jon—I preferred not to think about Jon what had become.

Suzanne snorted, a most unladylike noise. "Cody is most certainly an optimistic guy. We had a conversation the other day where he said he didn't think piercings hurt. He talked about having 'mind over matter.'" She grimaced. "Did he tell you he was thinking of getting one himself? I told him about the one I had downstairs, and he wanted to know what it felt like. He seemed really curious about it." Her voice grew teasing. "Perhaps he's thinking about getting a Prince Albert."

I swallowed and instinctively reached down a hand to cover my crotch.

Hell no. Nothing sharp is going anywhere near my dangly bits. And yuck. Did she just mention her lady bits?

My distaste at thinking about lady parts was overtaken by the fact my cock liked the idea of Cody having a piercing in his dick.

Jesus. That's so fucking wrong on many levels.

"Hey, you little pixie woman. No letting out the Cody secrets. Nate doesn't want to hear about my rabid fantasies." Cody had just arrived, and his indignant voice echoed in the room like a familiar song, or a warm blanket over the shoulders. I grabbed a cushion to cover my groin. "You have all that steel in *you*, and maybe I'd like a little too…" His voice trailed off and he uttered a dirty laugh. "Of course, I do like a little steel in me sometimes."

I groaned both at the pun and the fact that the idea was making my chubby even worse. I didn't want to think of anyone else doing my best friend. "Hey, enough of the sex talk. There's a lady present."

Cody burst into a guffaw. "Suzie's no lady." His tone was affectionate and there was the sound of a slap and Cody's startled "Ouch" as Suzanne hit him. She was one tough character; she and Cody got on like mustard on a hot dog.

Cody's familiar scent came closer and I sensed him beside me as he dropped a kiss on the top of my head. "How's the dotty stuff going? Are you able to read Chaucer yet?"

He sniggered and I batted away the hand that rumpled my hair. "No. And enough with the hair already, you dork. It looks bad enough without you messing it up."

"I think it looks awesome, that cut suits you," Cody murmured as he brushed a strand off my forehead. "Suzanne is a great hairdresser. Another of her many talents."

I'd gotten tired of trying to put product in my unruly hair only for Jon to tut-tut and tell me it looked awful. Suzanne had offered to cut it shorter, so I could manage it better.

Cody's warmth disappeared as he no doubt went to the kitchen to find something to eat. There was the familiar sound of rummaging and muttering as Cody raided the fridge and I grinned.

"He makes you smile more than anyone I know," Suzanne said. "You might not realize it, but that man makes you happy."

"We're best friends. And he's Cody, so sure he makes me smile," I said guardedly.

Has she noticed something? Had I revealed something I shouldn't have?

There was a loud sniff. "You keep telling yourself that," she muttered. "I mean, you two are so in sync, it's scary."

I cleared my throat and fumbled on the table for the stress ball I kept near when my hands got tired of trying to read Braille. "Yeah, that's what happens when you spend a lot of time together."

Suzanne sighed deeply enough for warm air to blow past my cheek. "Uh-huh. Friends it is."

I ignored the knowing tone of her voice as the fridge forager in question came back to my side, eating an apple, from the sounds of it.

"So how are you doing now with the cane work?" he asked between crunches. "You stopped having hissy fits and falling over?"

I mock scowled. "I'm getting there, smart-ass. I'd like to see you try it. There's a lot to remember. Listening to sounds, recognizing open spaces, where there are doorways or alleys, how to hold the cane…it's all pretty overwhelming."

Cody nudged my shoulder and I inhaled his scent, musky sweat with warm spice and vanilla tones. The heat of his skin radiated against my bare arms. I tried to wear short sleeves and tank tops lately, finding it helped to recognize when people were near. Warmth of another person's skin and the static that made my hairs stand on end were good indicators of someone in my vicinity.

"You're doing great. The boss lady here said so." I loved the smile in his voice. Suzanne was right. He was good for me. "Apart from that nosebleed incident and the one with the fire hydrant and the dog shit…" he remarked slyly.

My head shot up. "What? Suzanne, you promised that would stay between us."

My traitorous lady friend chuckled loudly. "Did I? I don't remember making that promise."

My face flushed with heat as I recalled the ungainly way I'd stumbled over the fire hydrant right in the front of my house, while out on a cane lesson alone. I'd been determined to see if I could do it by myself. My fall had been broken by placing my hands in a lovely fresh pile of dog crap. Suzanne had been coming around the corner, and when she'd seen my predicament, despite being worried, she hadn't been able to hold back her laughter. I thought I'd sworn her to secrecy.

"Oh no. That was too good to keep to herself. Suze had to share, didn't you, my sweet?" Cody crunched the apple again. "So where's

Jon? Out at another underwear signing, or a business meeting?" I knew Cody had lost all regard for Jon.

"He's out with friends, then he has a fashion shoot later. He'll be late again, I guess."

Cody crunched his apple violently. "Really? You'd have thought he'd have had enough time with his friends, after being out with them for his birthday for two days a week ago."

I winced. "Yeah, I know. That didn't quite go as planned."

Cody huffed. "You're telling me. Dude. All that planning you put into his party just fizzled out because he decided he wanted to go clubbing and you said you weren't ready for that yet."

We'd had a silent, awkward dinner at home before he went out partying. I hadn't been ready to go into a busy club and put up with not being able to see anything, never mind trying to figure out where the bathroom was, but that didn't excuse him abandoning me.

He'd had no problem leaving for the club where he met up with his friends and it took him almost forty-eight hours to get home. Yeah, he'd messaged me to say he was wasted and was staying over at a friend's house, but still. And as if Uber didn't come to our neighborhood.

I rolled one shoulder. "It's nothing. It doesn't bother me."

I didn't need Cody to say anything to hear his disbelief. The way his breathing changed, the anger I could feel coming off him in waves made him a *wide* open book.

"Oh-kay. So once again you're alone tonight. Want me to stay? We can order takeout. Maybe you can show me a few moves with that cane of yours, give me a few pointers?" He cackled. "Get that, pointers? As in, your cane has a point—"

I rolled my eyes, hearing Suzanne's chuckle. "Yeah, I get it, it was such a bad one I hoped I could forget it. Yes, you can stay, and for a change we're having pizza. None of that crappy Chinese stuff you love, I'm tired of Wong Fuck Yu and Chicken Chow Whatever."

"What?" Cody was scandalized. "I'll have you know that's my patented speciality dish. Everyone loves a bit of Fuck Yu."

I couldn't help it, the laughter started deep in my chest and echoed in the room along with Suzanne's hearty chuckles.

"Well, I'm going to leave you guys alone to enjoy your evening. It's getting late and the traffic home will be a bitch." Suzanne leaned over and kissed my cheek. "Look after yourself, keep practicing the dotty stuff and if you get a chance, do some cane work. You know the old saying—"

"Practice makes perfect," I finished. "I know. Thanks for everything, Suzanne. I'll see you next week."

After she'd left, Cody ordered the pizza—double cheese-filled crust with pepperoni, meatballs, salami and chicken, topped with black olives. He grumbled about our arteries and the fact he'd have heartburn all night because of the dough, but I knew he'd enjoy it anyway.

Tonight, instead of playing movies with me listening to the audio version, we decided to listen to music. As it was my turn to choose, I wanted show tunes. I had a bit of a thing for them, loving the lyrics and the story they told.

I mean, who could resist "Cellblock Tango" from *Chicago*? Or "No One Mourns the Wicked" from *Wicked*? Only a heathen would be able to turn away a good show tune.

We hunkered down on the sofa eating peanuts and drinking beer or soda, singing along to lyrics that we knew. Cody hammed things up, making me laugh. He'd always loved air-guitaring and based on how many times he got up and danced around the room, I guessed he still did.

It was close to eleven p.m. when he finally stood up to leave.

"I'd better be off," he murmured, as I lay half-asleep on the sofa. "I've got an early start in the morning, I'm flying to San Francisco for an art show. I'll be out of town for a couple of days. It's a traveling fair theme with the weirdest stuff I've ever seen, like stuffed giant fish and bicycles with false sausages as spokes. For some reason, people are going crazy for Dwight's art. Me, I think it's horrible. But Rachel likes it, and it's making us money so..." He blew out air and I had a vision of him standing there looking adorably tousled, his hair escaping from his ponytail. "I'll check in with you, though, see how things are going. I don't like the idea of you being left alone like this."

I sighed and sat up. I was still a little groggy and I blamed my lack of clear mind on what I said next. "I'm not complaining. I'd rather Jon be out there than be here being miserable with me. Things have been shitty anyway lately, I'm better off on my own. So's he."

The air stilled. All sound stopped and I drew a deep breath. Shit, I hadn't meant to bare my soul like that.

I sensed the shift in air as Cody either crouched or knelt in front of me. "Nate, have things gotten that bad between you guys? I knew something was up, hell, he's hardly ever home but is that really how things are going?"

I rubbed my eyes. I didn't want Cody worrying about me when he should be enjoying his trip. "Nah, bud. I'm sounding off, that's all. I'm sure we'll get over the slump, heal the rift, you know, all those hippie kinda things you keep saying to me."

Who am I kidding? The rift between Jon and I is the Grand-fucking-Canyon.

I reached out and found Cody's arm and squeezed. "I'll be fine. Tomorrow we planned to go on a drive down to the beach, maybe have a picnic." That was such a lie. Jon had somewhere else to be tomorrow. "You go off and have fun with your circus and I'll catch up with you when you get back."

"Hmm." Cody didn't sound convinced. "Okay, but if you need me, you call, okay? I'm only a couple of hours away, traffic permitting. Oh, and remember the day I get back, I'm picking you up for that surf-off competition. I'll come over in the morning to get you."

"Okay. I'm looking forward to it."

"I'm gonna kick some butt out there," Cody said in satisfaction. "You wait and see."

He squawked as I shoved him. "Hey, you just pushed me over, bully boy."

I laughed. "You'll need better balance than that on your surfboard if you intend on kicking ass, surfer boy. Now go on, go home and get some sleep."

Cody grumbled but he left. I managed to clean up our pizza mess, and felt guilty I hadn't done any more homework. I went down the hall, washed up and fell into bed. I was already asleep when Jon came home, but the noise of his arrival woke me.

He smelled of cigarette smoke, aftershave that wasn't his and sweat. He disappeared into the bathroom. The shower ran. My gut wrenched. Jon normally fell straight into bed after a night out. I knew what he was trying to hide.

After he'd toweled off—yeah, I could hear that, too—he slid into bed and immediately turned on his side. There'd been a time when Jon would come to bed and spoon against my back, his hand drifting around to my cock to tease and bring me to release so I could do the same. Not anymore.

I tried to sleep but Jon's constant twisting and incessant fidgeting didn't help. Finally, he sat up, and the bedroom lamp clicked on.

"I know you're awake, Nate. I need to talk to you. About us." His tone was both challenging and apprehensive.

Here it comes.

I sat up, drawing the covers up to my chest like a security blanket. I felt my watch face. It was two a.m. "It's late. What's wrong?"

"I can't do this anymore. I need to move out."

Huh. Talk about frank speaking. I'd at least have thought he'd have led into it with the "It isn't you, it's me" speech. Except I knew that wasn't the truth. It *was* me. It was about the me he no longer saw as a whole man but as a chore, a burden to be borne. Until now.

"It's isn't you, it's me." Ah. *There* it was. He rushed on, his voice cracking. "I'm not afraid to say I'm ashamed of how I feel. I know it isn't right. But I need to be true to myself and say I can't be with you anymore. I need someone who can be with me the way I need them to be."

My throat tightened and my chest ached. "You mean someone who isn't blind." Despite the fact I'd been expecting this—hell, I felt relieved actually—my eyes prickled. Hearing someone you had cared about tell you he thinks you're defective, hurt. A lot.

There was silence. Then, "Yes I know that's the most selfish thing to say. I need someone who can see what I see, take pleasure in watching a great film, marvel at exquisite fashion. I'm a visual person, Nate. I need a partner who can share that with me." He drew a deep breath and I felt him leave the bed. "I need someone who can see *me*, appreciate me. You can't do that anymore."

I clenched the sheet as his words hit home.

Sure, I'd been expecting this but I was fucking tired of him throwing me away because he thought I was damaged.

"So because I can't see you anymore that makes you less? You think I don't remember what I'm missing not being able to see you? See anyone? You think it's easy for me facing life in darkness? Not being able to see your face when we make love, which is never by the way, or see the light in your eyes when you see something you like? You think it's easy not being able to see my art, and realize I'll never see it the same way again?"

Christ, you selfish bastard. It's not that you're leaving, I feel relieved about that. It's the reason *you're going that pisses me off. Throwing away someone because you think they're damaged.*

The closet door opened and something was dragged out. The suitcase no doubt. I held my breath as the familiar sound of hangers being pulled off the rod assailed my ears.

"I know it's tough for you, Nate. I can't even imagine what you're going through. And I guess that's the problem. I don't believe continuing this relationship is good for either of us. I'll grow to resent you every day a little more, you'll retreat inside yourself like you've done and together we'll become this toxic sludge. Believe me when I say after what we've shared together, I don't want that to happen. I don't want us to end up hating each other." He gave a humourless laugh. "I know this will be tough. But in the long run you'll thank me for being a selfish bastard and getting out of your life."

"So where are you going?" My words came out clipped with barely contained hostility.

There was silence, then Jon spoke again, defiance in his voice. "You know where I'm going. To Caleb's."

The bed dipped as he sat down. A soft kiss was planted on my forehead. "He'll take me in until I find somewhere to stay."

I gave a strangled laugh. "Please. We both know if you move in there you won't be moving out. Is that why you showered before coming to bed? Because you reeked of sex with him? I'm not stupid. Just blind."

My acerbic response must have triggered something in him because Jon stood up, and huffed. "I'm going to go before we both say something we regret and end up despising each other. Despite all this, Nate, I still care for you. I'd hoped we could be friends."

My gut churned. Temper flared and I didn't even try to quell it. I deserved this feeling, deserved this emotion rising in me like an exploding roman candle. Because once again I was watching a person I'd loved walk out of my life.

Hadn't it been enough I'd lost a whole family—been thrown away like fucking garbage because I didn't fit in with my family's idea of who I should be? That I'd never been able to nurture what Cody and I had the potential for all those years ago?

My eyes stung with the shame and the guilt of once again not being good enough for someone. Words poured out of me, all the frustration and hurt I felt coating them with bile.

"Just go then. Back to your old lover who threw you out like trash when he grew tired of you. As long as he can 'appreciate' you, I guess that's all that matters, isn't it? He can see you all dressed up and beautiful. He can pay you compliments about how you look, something I can't do anymore. I wish you all the best with that."

The suitcase snapped shut, a wordless reminder of the finality of the drama-ridden scene playing out.

"I'll be in touch to pick up the rest of my things." Jon's voice was clipped. "I'm going to deposit some money in your bank account to cover a few months' expenses on utilities and stuff. I know you don't need it but it will make me feel better about moving out. I've no doubt Cody will be around to see you once you tell him the news. That way at least I know you'll be looked after."

I didn't tell him Cody was out of town. I'd manage on my own. And with that happy thought, I fumbled for my plastic water glass next to the bed, picked it up and threw it hard in Jon's direction. I knew it wouldn't do much but I needed to throw something.

"I don't need looking after, asshole. And I don't want your money." Jon gave a startled yelp as the glass thudded against the wall. "So get the fuck out. Go!" There was a brief silence then the familiar sound of the suitcase being wheeled. The bedroom door opened then slammed shut. I flung myself against the pillows, exhausted.

My chest heaved and I lay down, curling into a fetal ball, pulling the covers over my head.

Angry tears fell freely now, the ache in my chest turning into despair.

As I lay there, my own insecurities and fears ate away at the confidence I'd felt earlier that evening. I had never felt so alone. I wiped my eyes fiercely and made a promise to myself to move on, no matter what. I'd done it when my family had discarded me. Losing my lover wasn't going to get the better of me.

I'd known this day was coming, but still, it cut me to my core.

***

Two days later I was still bleary-eyed and felt hungover from lack of sleep. I'd been managing okay by myself. I wasn't exactly Mr. Mobile, but I had plenty of audiobooks to keep me entertained. I'd switched on the television and kept up with the news, and I'd managed to feed myself.

I marveled at the way science and technology had made wonderful advances in assisting the blind. What with talking microwaves, one of which I now owned, kitchen timers and a plethora of other gadgets, I had become quite independent in the kitchen as long as I didn't have to cook anything too complicated.

More wonders, my phone featured a bar code scanner so online shopping was a breeze. Groceries arrived, I unpacked, scanned each item, and was told what I held in my hand. Everything went into its place, and my world became a lot more organized.

Of course, there was that time I'd messed up and spooned half a can of peas onto my tortilla instead of frijoles. I had no doubt there would be more culinary disasters in my future but I was ready for them.

Another morning alone, I forced my body out of bed, chose something to wear—my wardrobe had been completely reorganized, complete with safety pins that irritated my skin occasionally. It was a small price to pay for not wearing clashing colors, although to be honest, most of my clothes were muted shades anyway so it probably wouldn't have mattered.

Breakfast was a bowl of cereal with skim milk, a banana and a cup of coffee. I was now replenished and good to go. I wasn't sure where though. Or how.

I'd made good strides in learning how to wield my cane through countless walks outside plus a lot of training on my own. Fortunately, I'd turned out to be a quick learner but I didn't yet feel confident or adept enough to go out on my own.

"Huh," I muttered as I puttered about the kitchen, cleaning up. "Looks like my comfort zone is once again about to be challenged. I suppose I need to be able to get out there on my own quicker than I'd thought."

On the kitchen countertop I found Jon's cafétiere. It was something I didn't want knocking around, as I didn't use it. No doubt he'd come back for it since it was apparently a special and rather expensive one. In a fit of pique, I opened one of the seldom-used deep kitchen drawers to stash it in there. He could damn well hunt it down if he wanted it.

As I laid it down, my fingers touched a stack of paper. I reached in, fingering the bundle with the elastic band wrapped around it. My heart sank. So *this* was where I'd put them.

This bundle had to contain all the letters and cards I'd sent to my family. Christmas cards, birthday cards and letters all marked with a bold, black RTS: return to sender. It was a slap in the face from my father. He could have let me believe in all my naïveté that my letters had reached their destination, but no, he had to send them back—his way of telling me I was nothing and was unwanted.

I fingered the bundle, my chest aching as the familiar sense of loss crept in.

I shouldn't let this affect me anymore but damn, it's hard not to.

I shoved the package back into the drawer and closed it as the sound of the key in the door had me turning around.

My spirits lifted when I recognized the footsteps. Cody. He breezed in with what I knew would be a smile, the fresh scent of sea, sand and his trademark Davidoff Cool Water.

"Hey, Nate, I'm back. How've you been while I was away?" He pulled me in for a hug and I inhaled his familiar scent with a soft sigh of pleasure.

"I'm okay, bud. Kept myself busy while you were gone. How was the exhibition?"

He moved away, opened the fridge and took something out. "God, that trip was a nightmare, but we sold a lot of pieces. It was profitable, so I can't complain."

I heard the crunch of an apple or it might have been a pear. He really had a thing for my fruit.

"Of course, it would have been even better to have some of your stuff there as well." Cody crunched again. "Just saying."

I rolled my eyes. "Yeah, yeah. You're so damn transparent, you should be a pane of glass."

He sniggered and nudged my arm. "I try to get my point across. I know I'm not subtle." He came closer to me, as if to hug me again, then drew a startled breath. "God, Nate, you look like shit. What's wrong?"

I shrugged. "Bad night, couldn't sleep."

He jostled my arm gently. "That's tough. Have you got something for it, some herbal tablets maybe?"

I shook my head. "Nah. I'll be okay. It's temporary."

"Okay." He sounded unsure. "So are you ready for your excursion to the beach to witness the amazingness that is Cody Fisher become king of the sea?"

I frowned as I threw the cleaning cloth into the sink. "What?"

Cody's body heat warmed me as he moved closer, both affection and concern in his tone. "You forgot, didn't you? The big Holden House Charity Surf-off challenge is today. The one where I'm going to kick some ass on my board—do some tricks and make a lot of money? I hope."

I *had* forgotten. He'd spoken to me about it a few days ago—a sponsored surfing competition trying to raise funds for the struggling local homeless shelter. With everything going on, it had slipped my mind completely.

I gestured at him. "I'd forgotten. Sorry 'bout that. Give me a minute, and I'll grab my stuff, then we can go."

The soft caress of fingers on my cheek stopped me short. "Nate, wait. If you're not up to it, it's no big deal. You look bushed. If you want to sit this one out, I'll shoot by afterward if you like. We can go for a walk, get you some cane practice in. I'll make sure I leave before Jon gets home so you two can have your couple time. I assume he's out right now?"

The word "again" didn't have to be said. I heard the unspoken nuance.

I cleared my throat. "Yes, he's out. But you needn't worry about him being here later. He won't be coming home."

Cody touched my arm and squeezed. "Oh, okay, I take it he's staying out." Once more the *again* didn't need to be uttered.

I shook my head. "He's not coming back at all."

Cody gasped. "Wait—what?"

I took a deep breath. "He left me the other night. He said he'll come sometime and fetch his stuff. We're over. Kaput. Finished."

Strong, muscular arms wrapped around me and I reveled in the comfort offered in that simple hug.

"Jesus, Nate," Cody whispered. "I'm so damn sorry. Why didn't you call me and let me know?" He hugged me as only he could, without reservation; his warm body pressed against my front. I shifted carefully so he didn't feel what his closeness was doing to me. The last thing I wanted to do was scare him off with a boner.

"It's been coming for a while," I said as I basked awkwardly in the hug. "You know that. Jon and I had been growing apart before the accident and since, it's been worse. To be honest, it wasn't a surprise." It was a relief. "And I wasn't going to wreck your trip with my tale of woe."

My cock was enjoying Cody's proximity far too much, and I moved out of the haven of his arms.

"Anyway, enough of my shit." I moved toward the hall and my bedroom. "You have a competition to win and I want to be there when you do. I'll get my bag and my cane. Wait here."

I disappeared before Cody could say anything else. When I returned to the family room, he was uncharacteristically quiet.

"So he's not coming back at all?" he asked as I searched for my cane by the front door.

I shook my head. "I don't think so. He was pretty clear." I sighed. "Besides, I don't want him back. I'll be fine on my own."

There was a huff of startled breath. "Really? Okay. If you want to talk about this later, you know where I'll be. Here, with you. Because that's what best friends do when there's a breakup. Sit and drink beer and watch violent slasher movies, fantasizing the next victim is the ex-boyfriend."

My throat constricted. "Thanks. I appreciate that. You're a good friend."

Cody moved closer, tantalizingly near. "Nate, you and me, we're family," he said gently. "I'm always here for you. Except when I wasn't." His tone was amused. "You know, like the time we went away to different colleges at eighteen to do different things and didn't see each other much for four years. But it didn't mean I didn't think of you often. I'm always going to be here."

Leaving each other had been tough, and the reunion when we'd both completed our degrees and moved back to Los Angeles had been a joyful one. I'd missed Cody like hell when we'd both been studying, even if we'd met up when we could, it simply hadn't been the same.

I picked up my cane and waggled it at him, hoping to alleviate the heavy emotion hanging in the air.

"I get it, bud. You'll always be my wingman." I grinned at him. "Come on, let's go see you kick some butt out there." At least I'd hear the waves, smell the sea and the sweat and suntan lotion of the people around me—and I'd be rooting for Cody. I'd not be doing too much moving around at the beach, but I knew a lot of Cody's surfer friends and I'd no doubt they'd help me if I needed anything.

Things didn't quite go the way either of us planned. Cody didn't win but he came a respectable second, and the charity made close to five thousand dollars in tickets, raffles and sponsorships.

In the leisure surfing after the main event, one of the surfers disappeared. The scramble to find him, get him out of the water and into an ambulance took most of the night. The surfer had been hit on the head by his board and it'd resulted in all hands-on deck. I'd been left pretty much on my own, wondering what the hell was going on.

An exhausted Cody finally drove me home later that night after all the fuss and got me safely into the house with the promise of coming by in the morning to bring me breakfast. I was glad to tumble into bed, head pounding from too much sun and noise, and I slipped into the hazy solace of sleep.

Chapter 6

Cody

At eleven a.m. I let myself into Nate's house, fully expecting him to find him awake, up and about. It was a beautiful Sunday morning and I didn't have to go into work. I loved owning my own business and being able to leave it in the capable hands of Rachel when I needed time out. But with wanting to be with Nate more, I suffered guilt that I did it too much. Rachel had told me not to be stupid, she was happy to be the go-to girl. It still did nothing to assuage my fear I had been letting her down.

I'd spent a sleepless night alternating between two emotions: best-friend angst that Nate had been dumped, and best-friend-in-love-with-his-best-friend elation that Nate was single again. It had been an off-the-tracks roller coaster ride and my brain had been grinding in overtime.

Of course, the latter situation meant shit. I didn't think Nate and I would be pursuing any relationship or doing the nasty anytime soon even if he was single. Nate simply didn't seem to want me that way.

He hadn't spoken to me yet about Jon's reasons for leaving but in my uncharitable moments, I could guess. The bastard had always been needy and vain, so having a blind lover certainly wasn't top of his me-me-me happy-ever-after list of life accomplishments.

So, burdened with my mental tennis match, I wasn't feeling the usual Cody optimism when I put down the breakfast I'd bought—double bacon, egg, sausage and hot sauce all packed into a large pretzel. My favorite.

The house was oddly quiet, which was worrying. Nate was nowhere to be seen. There was only a strange, rhythmic sound emanating from down the hall—Nate's bedroom.

I frowned at the noise and started toward his bedroom door. A sudden sense of fear that he'd fallen and hurt himself, perhaps slipped in the shower, made my skin tingle and my step quicken.

I knew I should call out, warn him I'd entered in the house, but I was scared if I did, I'd startle him and make things worse. He could be shaving and I'd hate for him to cut himself. So, taking the middle ground, I said nothing and gently pushed open his bedroom door, fully expecting him to grin and tell me he was Daredevil and he'd known I'd been there all along.

The sight that greeted me was one I'll remember as long as I live. Nate lay on the bed legs spread wide, knees up, feet planted over the covers. His lithe, sun-kissed body glistened with sweat as he grasped his cock and jacked himself off. He had his earbuds in, and his eyes were half closed, lips parted, and the look on his face…

I nearly came there and then. I'd seen that look before twelve years ago when he'd lain beneath me as I'd thrust inside him. The memory made me feel faint and I pressed a fist into my mouth, stifling my groan of nostalgia and lust.

I should have turned and closed the door behind me. A better man would have left him to his pleasure and not stayed to watch the man he loved come to climax. I *wasn't* that better man and I'd challenge anyone that saw his fantasy playing out before him to turn and walk away.

So I stood and watched the scene play out.

Nate's strong fingers wound around his cock, slick with lube and his own semen, as he pleasured himself. The knowledge I'd once been granted entrance into the more private part of him, a part I could see now, nestled between taut ass cheeks that clenched as he moved—that memory was bittersweet.

The writhing man on the bed, the pervading smell of musk and sex, the faint tease of Nate's scent invading my nostrils, the erotic tableau before me was worthy of a classic film noir. Nate's breathless gasps and murmurs of satisfaction added to the scene, one of the most seductive I'd ever experienced.

Nate's moans grew in crescendo and I pressed my palm against my hardened cock, knowing I'd not be able to take much of this before I came in my pants. I turned to leave, hoping to make it to the guest bathroom down the hall, because even to me, orgasming here seemed a step too far.

But something happened that spun my world off its axis, and rocked my sanity.

Nate called my name as he came. *My name* uttered in a throaty cadence of sheer need and pleasure. His body twisted and jerked on the bed as he coated himself and the bed with streams of pearly come then his agonized pants slowly reduced to soft moans.

Chest heaving, I barely made it to the spare bathroom before ripping down my jeans and fisting myself hard, twice, facing the shower door. To be fair, I didn't even think I needed that second yank. I came fiercely, my balls tightening, my spunk hitting the glass with a spatter of white streams that slid slowly down. I bit my lip to stop the shout that built in my throat and buried my face in a towel to muffle any other sounds of pleasure.

Then, legs boneless and wobbly, I sank down onto the bathroom floor and wrapped my arms around my knees.

What the hell had just happened?

I didn't have much time. If I didn't want to be found pants down with come soaking my lower body and streaming down the glass, I needed to clean up quick and get into the kitchen before Nate knew I was there. Knowing him, he'd probably shower first so that gave me a little time.

I wiped off, frantically pulled up my jeans then used toilet paper and water to wipe the sticky come traces off the glass. Satisfied with the clean-up, I opened the bathroom door and peered outside. Guilt and shame washed over me, as if by becoming an unexpected voyeur, I'd tainted something Nate held intimate. I comforted myself with the fact that in some way I'd been present in Nate's fantasy and that gave me some sort of right to be here. That was my rationalization anyway.

As I slipped quietly into the kitchen and picked up the now cooling breakfast treat, I wondered with some smugness what the hell I'd done in his daydream to make him come so forcefully and with such abandon.

I heard the shower turn off and heaved a sigh of relief as I retraced my steps, slammed the front door and put the breakfast down on the counter and called out cheerfully. "Nate? I'm here with breakfast. Are you decent?"

There was a muffled shout from down the hall. "Getting there. Be out in a moment." He sounded normal, not like a man who'd been spied on during an intimate act.

I sagged with relief. I hadn't been noticed. He hadn't sensed me watching him or smelled my cologne. However, in case he caught a trace of it when he came out from the en-suite shower I stood in the hallway close to his bedroom and yelled back, waving my arms about, making sure my armpits sent out a scent signal. "It's getting cold, don't be long."

I could be a manipulative sneaky bastard when the situation warranted it.

The oven needed to be turned on to warm through breakfast. I unpacked the pretzels and popped them in on a baking tray. I made coffee, showing all the semblance of normalcy and not that of a man who'd only minutes ago watched his best friend jacking off, which caused me to blow my load.

Five minutes later, Nate appeared, toweling his thick, curling hair. He stood in the kitchen, dressed in loose sweatpants and a tight tee that showed off his toned body. I tended to ogle Nate a lot more now since he couldn't see me doing it.

"I'm warming up the food. Won't be long."

He flashed a warm smile in my direction and threw the towel on the kitchen counter. His hair curled in licks of dark brown against his cheeks, and he raised a hand and absently tucked a strand behind his ear. Remembering what I'd watched him do, I swallowed and looked away. My groin still tingled.

"Sorry about yesterday, it was a catastrophe," I confessed as I opened the oven door to check the food. "I really wanted to spend some time with you, see how you were doing what with, you know, Jon leaving."

Nate gave a deep sigh. "I'm doing okay. It's a little weird being here on my own after a year living with someone, but I guess I'll have to get used to it."

He reached out, searching for a kitchen stool. I watched as he found one, pulled it out from under the counter and perched his ass on it. He reached into his pocket and drew out his phone, placing it on the counter. He'd bought one of those special cell phones Suzanne had recommended. It was simple and basic but did everything that a visually impaired person needed. It was also his lifeline if he got lost or fell. Both Suzanne and I were programmed in as emergency contacts.

God, it had only been a few months and Nate was doing so well at managing his blindness. I was so damned proud of him for not letting it take him over and for him not giving in to the darkness. The man was an inspiration.

"Have I told you lately you're my hero?" I said as I took out the warmed food from the oven.

"I am?" Nate said in amusement. "How come?

I stood and took in his brown eyes filled with affection. Nate never looked over my shoulder or at my chest as I'd seen happen with some blind people.

Nate always seemed to see straight into my soul.

"Because despite life throwing you this ugly curveball, you're coping as best as you can, and in my opinion, you're doing one hell of a job. I mean, you're not bitter—much," I qualified that as there were the odd times he got down about his lack of sight, "you try so damn hard to be you. That's really cool, dude."

Nate's face flushed. He looked pleased, but I knew there was some sort of self-deprecating remark coming. "Oh yeah? Thanks, bud. I don't have a choice, though, do I?" He pursed his pink lips. "This is the hand I've been dealt and I have to learn to live with it. I'm lucky I have you and Suzanne. You guys are the ones who keep spurring me on. I feel I can get anywhere if you're both around."

I noticed he hadn't mentioned Jon. I thought now was a good time to bring that up. "And Jon—how do you really feel about him going?" I asked as I placed Nate's breakfast in front of him and nudged his hand. "Plate in front, coffee at one o'clock."

I sat next to him and took a sip of coffee.

Nate's fingers toyed with the handle of his coffee mug. "Like I said yesterday, I knew something was going on. Things hadn't been the same between us and Jon slowly drew away." He sighed and picked up his pretzel. "It was like a boat in the water, slowly drifting out of reach until it was so far gone you couldn't catch it anymore." His voice held both relief and resignation. He took a bite of his breakfast and we sat in silence for a bit.

A few minutes later the silence was broken by Nate's phone ringing. The phone announced the caller in a robotic monotone as Jon Roland. Nate ignored it and carried on eating.

"I don't feel like talking to him," he said softly amidst chews. "He's made his decision. We've nothing to talk about anymore."

One of Nate's sometimes less endearing traits was the fact that when he made his mind up about something, there was no changing it. He was the most stubborn man I'd ever met, and we'd had plenty of disagreements over the years because for him it was either black or white. There was no gray in his world. It was also probably the reason he was coping with being blind far better than I thought I would ever do. He'd done the same thing when his family had kicked him out.

Nate flapped a hand in my direction, a hand covered with oil from the pretzel. "So what's on the agenda for today? Have I got more blood and gore beach excitement to look forward to?"

Deep breath. I'd planned this carefully and I wasn't sure how it was going to play out. I hoped I wasn't about to get thumped with a cane by this stubborn man. But I had to try.

It was time Nate got his head out of his ass about this particular topic.

"Actually, I do have something different planned. And for the first part of it, we don't even have to go far."

Nate's ears seemed to perk up. "That sounds interesting. Tell me more."

"Well," I drawled, "I was at the gallery and I met this guy."

Nate's eyes narrowed. "You met a guy. You mean, like an 'I'm going on a date' guy? How is that relevant to me?" There was a bite in his tone.

After what I'd just heard and saw, my pulse raced, and I wondered if he was jealous. God, I was so delusional. And hopeful.

"No, nothing like that." I hastened to explain. "I mean, I'd *like* to meet one of those kinda guys, because, to be honest, things have been a little dire in that department, if you know what I mean, but so far, nuh-huh. The well is dry." I realized I was rambling.

Nate's face darkened. He gripped his cup with white knuckles. My stomach gave a little squirm and I licked my lips.

"Anyway, enough of my non-existent sex life. No, I mean I met this artist guy, a sculpting teacher. He's one of the people Marty recommended on his list. This guy swung by to see me."

Nate's fingers curled tighter around his coffee cup and his lips thinned.

I ignored the warning signs and went full steam ahead. "He's had a few people in his classes over the years, well, a lot of years I guess, because he's pretty old. Mr. Miyagi old, you know?"

Nate's brow furrowed but I plowed on. "Anyway, he's taught quite a few people like you, and he says because your art is so tactile, he's seen some great results with artists creating their pottery and sculpture. He's even had one student win an award at some special exhibition—"

Nate pushed himself off his stool, stood up and slapped his hands on the counter. "Let me get this straight. 'Like me'? You mean blind? As in, can't see a damn thing?"

"Well, yeah. Just like that." I mean, what else could I say? It was the truth.

Nate glared. It was disconcerting, but oh boy, he still did it so well. I had a fleeting thought of the mutant called Cyclops from X-Men shooting fiery laser beams from his eyes and saw myself combusting into flames and ashes. "Anyway, I told him about you. He recognized your name from the stuff you exhibited before and he said he wanted to meet you."

"What, here? At the house today?" Nate's voice rose an octave.

"No, dumbass. Not here. Next week."

"Then what's happening today that isn't far away? Cody, damn you, I swear, if you don't stop talking in riddles…"

I clapped a hand to my forehead. "Your studio, you idiot. I wanted you to go back into your studio. I want you to remember how it used to be, get the old creative juices flowing." I gestured to the open back door and the studio beyond, before I realized he wouldn't see what I was doing. I dropped my hand and stared at him in frustration.

"No." Nate shook his head vehemently. "Not going to happen."

"But, Nate," I wheedled. "Hear me out, please." I played the best friend card. "You owe me for that time I saved your skinny ass from those pelicans that attacked you down at Grotto Bay. I took a bite for you. And for the time I let you win on all those stupid fairground games because your aim was shit and you were about to cry because you wanted a stupid Cabbage Patch doll. So I won one for you. Remember that, hot shot—not?"

"Cody." Nate's lips were twitching. I took that as a good sign. Maybe it was a smile and he wasn't about to attack me and tear me apart with his teeth. Have I mentioned I'm a glass-half-full kind of guy? "We were ten years old. And it was a Furby, not a Cabbage Patch doll."

"Whatever. Anyway, you owe me this one. If you do this for me today, and agree to meet Mr. Miyagi next week and hear him out, I'll waive all the other debts you owe me from before and we'll be even. And boy, that's a lot of favors I'm not going to be cashing in. I'm going to end up the loser here." I laid it on thick. "Think about it."

I finished my pretzel and watched him, hopeful. The seed had been sown. All I could do was see if it grew.

Nate sat and took a sip of his coffee. "Why is this so important to you?" he asked finally. "How is me getting back into sculpting going to make you happy?"

Wow. Had it really been that easy? I'd been expecting angst and denial, not a Nate who seemed to give a damn about what I was saying.

I got off my stool and knelt beside him, my hands resting loosely on his knees. I was at eye level with his groin and I tried not to think of what I'd seen earlier. That would lead to madness.

I swallowed, my throat dry. "Because you and me, Nate, we've been best friends since we were kids. We've been through some shit together and we've always looked out for each other. This accident didn't only happen to you. It happened to me too. I want to be the one making sure your life is as much the same as it could ever be. Because if I don't, I've failed as a friend." I gulped. The look of affection on Nate's face brought a lump to my throat. "And because I need some shit to display at Artisana and I think you're the man for the job."

Nate gave a soft chuckle and cupped my face in his hands without even fumbling. Again—how the hell did he do that?

"That was some intense shit. I feel all warm and fuzzy inside." I didn't miss the tremor in his voice. "I'd be a complete bastard to say no after all that, wouldn't I?" He lifted one hand and tugged at my ponytail. "I know you can be a manipulative little shit but somehow, right now, I don't think I've been played." His hand hovered over my cheek then pulled away. "Fine. Let's go see what's happened in the studio since I left it."

He rolled his shoulders in that move he had when he got agitated but he didn't let it stop him. I whooped and got to my feet. "Yeah!" I fist pumped the air and did a little shimmy.

"You're dancing right now, aren't you? Did you do the whole fist-pump thing as well?" Nate said drily.

I laughed. "You know me too well. Right, come with me. We have a quest to finish. Do you need your cane?"

"No, not if you're there with me. I haven't been down the path for a while. Too many obstacles and nooks and crannies. I really should look at getting it fixed." Nate puffed out his cheeks.

Secretly I was thrilled. Nate considering fixing the path meant perhaps he was seriously considering using the studio more.

He allowed himself to be dragged from his stool and out through the back door.

"His name isn't really Mr. Miyagi, is it?" Nate asked as we navigated our way down the stone path. I liked holding Nate's hand. Any excuse would do.

"Nah. His name is Michael Mitchell. I said I'd speak to you and if I was still alive, I'd drive you over there next week." I cackled. "Guy looks like a little rooster. Tiny, with this mohawk thing on his head. His eyes stare right through you. I expected him to start pecking for chicken feed at any moment."

Whenever I could, I tried to paint pictures in words so Nate could visualize what he'd lost. He said it helped and I'd seen the appreciation on his face when I did it.

Nate laughed loudly. "Christ, that's one hell of an image to process. How am I going to talk to the guy next week without bursting into laughter?"

We reached the studio and I tried the handle. It was locked. "Damn, have you got the key with you?"

Nate shook his head. "Crap, I forgot. It's still on the hook in the kitchen, I hope. Unless Jon moved it."

"Stay here, I'll go get it." I patted Nate on the shoulder. "Don't go anywhere."

"Where the hell would I go?" Nate remarked testily. His shoulders tensed and he glanced at the studio, his face filled with apprehension.

I sped back to the kitchen, found the key easy enough and was back at the studio in time to see Nate with his palm against the door. I could swear he'd been stroking it.

"Were you getting kinky with the door?" I unlocked it, smiling at Nate's scowl. "It's okay. We all need a little wood in our lives occasionally."

"Hah-hah," Nate said as he gave me the stink-eye. I took his arm as he stepped inside his old haven. Because that was what it had been to him. A place he could come and lose himself in the passion of creating some of the amazing pieces dotted around the wide-open space in front of me.

I hoped it would be that place again for him.

He gazed around, his face shadowed, eyes narrowed. His nostrils flared as he took in the scents of the studio he'd last been in a few months ago. His nose wrinkled. Mine did too. It didn't smell particularly fresh in here.

"The place reeks of old clay," he muttered. "It needs to be thrown out. Dude, help me navigate around so I can remember where everything is."

I held his elbow, moving things as he walked around. Later, if he wanted to work here, I'd try to create a safe space for him, making sure everything was in easy reach and accessible. I was sure Suzanne would help with that, too.

The studio was large and airy with a bright yellow kiln on one side that Nate used to fire all his pieces. Various workbenches and tables were scattered around, all sorts of tools and things I had no clue what they were dotted the worktops and the floor.

A potter's wheel stood on one surface, looking forlorn and unused. Shelves were littered with items of Nate's trade, including various colored and sized plastic containers with labels like lead basilicate, ball clay, and soda feldspar. In one corner was a small stack of shelves holding plastic bags tied with different color pegs. Each peg had a nametag attached.

My heart swelled when I remembered the class Nate had held for a local school. The kids had come here and he'd taught them to make a rudimentary pinch pot. The results of those endeavors still lined a small part of the wall. Clearly Nate hadn't had the heart to throw their hard work away.

Sunlight shone through the large picture window running one side of the place. I remembered how Nate had loved to sit there, basking in the sunlight, as he contemplated his next steps on a piece.

He said nothing as he explored his space. He ran his hands over his tools and along the surfaces of his worktops. His fingers trailed lovingly over some of his finished and unfinished pieces and I didn't miss the fleeting look of pain as he did it. I was beginning to think this hadn't been a good idea, seeing the anguish on his face at the realization this had been his old life and now he needed to create a new one here at the bottom of his backyard.

He took a deep breath. "What the hell am I supposed to do, Cody?" His voice cracked. "I can see the place in my head as I left it but I've no idea what I should be doing now. How do I—" He gestured helplessly around him. "How do I move on with all this?"

"I guess the answer would be slowly," I said as I looked around. "You've got some amazing pieces here, Nate. I know some of them you'd said you'd finished but you weren't sure what to do with them. The others, the ones not yet completed—maybe Mr. Miyagi can help you make sense of them. It's worth a try." I hesitated. "Maybe you simply start over with making new pieces from scratch."

He looked over, his eyes tormented. "I don't know," he whispered. "I don't know if I can do this."

He moved away from me, almost stumbling over a box of tools left on the floor that I'd missed. Nate shouted out in panic as he toppled forward and I moved swiftly to catch him. He clung to me, arms around my waist and head burrowed in my shoulder.

"Take me out of here," he murmured. "Please. It's enough."

I nodded then murmured my acquiescence because, of course, he couldn't see. *Dumbass.* We walked slowly back to the house.

In the kitchen, Nate sat on a stool and stared into space. I waited, wondering if I'd messed things up for him with my meddling insistence. I busied myself washing up the coffee cups. Finally, he cleared his throat and I turned to look at him.

"I'll go see your Mr. Miyagi," he said quietly. "I owe you that. But I'm not making any promises."

I closed my eyes, relief flooding my body. "That's all I'm asking. I'll take you to see him next week."

I'd won this battle and for that I was grateful.

Chapter 7

Nate

I was not going to tell a lie. I was nervous. Truly butt-clenching nervous. Good to my word, I'd met Michael Mitchell, Cody's contact, and I'd seen him a few times since our initial meeting.

I'd liked Mike from the start. He was an easy-going, affable man with a deep belly laugh and the ability to challenge me. More than anything, it was what I had needed. I did have to choke down a chuckle when I thought of the way Cody had described his hair.

I'd learned some valuable lessons about working unsighted in the classroom Mike laughingly called Pottery Perversion because of the number of strange items apparently ending up resembling penises or breasts created by his eager but inexperienced students.

I was lucky. I already knew what I was doing despite my lack of sight. I knew the tools, the method, techniques and the creative process. I was an old hand at the steps to produce a piece, unlike some of his students who had been blind from birth and were learning the process from scratch.

"Use every sense you have," Mike had directed as he guided me through the first stages of my lessons, or rather, his mentoring. "Visually impaired people often have a more tactile sense. They can feel what they are doing while seeing it in their mind's eye. Use that fertile imagination you have. Caress the clay, make love to it. Use that muscle memory, let it guide you and become an instinctive process."

He'd laughed. "You have an advantage actually. You'll probably be quicker in shaping what you want because you're not distracted by sight. You don't spend unnecessary time checking it out every few minutes. You simply *feel* it develop."

I'd found it easier than I'd thought to get back into it. The memories of my old life had flooded back and I'd realized, with a start of surprise, that even when I'd been sighted, I'd often shut my eyes and molded the clay into what I wanted using the sheer power of my fingers and the picture in my brain.

The vision I'd had in my head of what I wanted to create had been a blueprint to its creation, my hands and eyes the physical tools to bring to life. The only difference now was that I couldn't open my eyes and see what I'd created. Now I *had* to feel it.

The last few weeks I'd been itching to begin something new that had haunted me in my dreams. I'd never seen the details, only the indistinct image of a man's head, his features blurred and unformed. It was hazy but I knew that when I started sculpting it, it would all become clear.

Old projects would have to wait until I got this burning need out of me to create this face that haunted my dreams. I knew my hands would show me the way.

I was ready to create my first real piece now, in my own home studio, armed with my memories, my hands and the common sense advice Mike had given me. I'd even called Marty and told him what I was up to.

He'd given a booming, pleased guffaw. "That's great, Nate. See, I told you you could do it. Don't let anyone tell you otherwise. I'm damn proud of you, man."

Cody and Suzanne had come over to the studio and between them they'd created a space where I could work safely. Where everything I needed was in easy reach, where the things I'd held dear like my kiln and my pottery wheel, my work surface and my tools, were instruments of creation now and not obstacles to my own self-perceived limits.

It was time.

My fingers slid over the rough shape of the clay I'd just worked and kneaded in front of me. My fingers ached but it was a good ache. A familiar one.

I'd already placed what clay I needed over the armature, molding it into what I hoped was a reasonable facsimile of a head and shoulders. Now the real work began.

Hours later I wasn't so sure this had been a good idea.

Fuck. Fuck. Fuck.

My fingers were sore. The skull I'd started simply didn't *feel* right. I'd not been able to get the head right and in my frustration I'd knocked something off—probably a damn ear— and that piece now lay somewhere on the floor beneath my feet.

Shitfuckcrap.

Blinking sweat from my eyes, I raised one clay-smeared finger to wipe my eyes, and nearly poked my eye out. The stinging sensation and resultant floodwaters opening in my left eye caused the air to turn blue.

"Fuck. I can't even clean my eye without damaging myself."

I fumbled for the rag I always had on my worktop and finding it damp and clammy, raised it to my weeping eye. My other one had started tearing up now in sympathy.

Once I'd finished drying my eyes, the rag was consigned to the waste bin beside me, together with the skull, complete with armature. The thump it made as it hit the bin was satisfying and I snarled.

"Fuck. You. You messed with the wrong person today."

It was childish, even pathetic, but it did make me feel better. Someone whistled behind me and Cody's familiar scent assailed my nostrils.

"Bro, you are such a badass. What the hell did that thing ever do to you?"

The joy I always felt when Cody visited—albeit unannounced— rose unbidden. His being here was instant good mood in a bottle.

"Did you bring coffee? Bear claws? Donuts?" I growled. "If not, get the fuck out."

Cody punched me in the arm. "Dude, so rude." He moved around to my side. "Yeah, I brought you coffee, black and sweet just as you like it. And the bakery was out of bear claws, so you got a custard donut instead."

Something was placed on the table on my left. Cody nudged my shoulder. "Ten o'clock. Coffee's hot, so careful. The lid's on though."

I was already searching out the donut, my sweet tooth craving Benny's Bakery's delicious pastry. I took a mouthful, uttering a soft moan as I closed my eyes in pleasure at the taste of pure goodness. "God, this is good. It gets better each time I eat one of these."

"Uh, yeah." His voice sounded strange and breathless. "Looks good to me too. I mean, tastes good…" His voice trailed off and there was the sound of paper rustling. It sounded like it was coming from my bin.

"Why'd you throw this away?" I guessed Cody was holding the unfinished bust. "It looks pretty cool."

I shrugged as I shoved the rest of my donut into my mouth. "It didn't feel right. I'll do it again until I'm happy with it."

I need to get it right. I've got something special in mind and I can't afford a half-cocked sculpture spoiling the surprise. OCD it's-got-to-be-perfect Nate, that's my name.

My need for absolute perfection seemed to have gotten worse since I'd lost my sight. Yep, a classic case of overcompensation.

He chuckled. "It'll double as a hat stand. Maybe I can take it into the gallery and we can market it as such."

His words struck a chord.

"Don't you have a family member with alopecia?" I asked as I slid the lid off my coffee. I'd vaguely heard him mention her previously. His family was legion. "Does she wear wigs? Maybe she can keep it for that."

Cody gasped. "Dude, that's an awesome idea. Sandstorm Dune will love this."

I blinked. "Sandstorm Dune? That's a new one, I don't think you've actually mentioned her name before."

"Yeah, she's a distant cousin on my dad's side. She'll get a real kick out of this head."

I sniggered. "Don't we all. Get a kick out of head I mean. Not that I'd remember, it's been too damn long since I got any."

He moved closer and I breathed in his scent, ignoring the stirring in my trousers. I was horny, that was all.

His breath warmed my ear. "Maybe you need to get out more. You've become a bit of a hermit, you know."

I bristled at the comment. "I don't have a lot of choices, do I? Hello. Blind guy. Action tends to be a little limited when people see that."

"Don't talk such shit." The table shuddered as he leaned against it. "You're just damned scared to go out and be sociable is all."

He was right, but measures had already been taken to address that. I sighed and drained my coffee, throwing the cup toward the bin. It hit the floor and I snorted. "You moved the bin, dickwad. Put it back so I can find it later."

There was the sound of the metal bin being dragged back no doubt to its original position.

"Sorry, I only moved it a bit when I was rummaging."

"Don't worry, bud. I forgive you."

He squeezed my arm. "So, you planning on going out anytime soon, having some fun?"

I nodded, wondering why I wasn't more excited about the news. "Already in place. Suzanne's taking me to a club next week."

Cody's breath hitched and the air in the room thickened.

"Oh yeah?" He nudged his shoulder with mine. "Way to go, get back on that horse." The element of forced cheer in his voice didn't escape me. I wondered whether it was because I hadn't invited him.

"Suze got tickets for the VIP room, and it just so happens to be the night you have your next big gallery opening. I knew you'd want to be there for that, otherwise I'd have invited you to come with—"

Calloused fingers touched my lips, shushing me. "Nate, it's fine, honest. I don't expect to go out with you every time. Suzanne and you deserve some party time together."

I huffed, feeling that somehow I'd let him down. "I wasn't sure I'd go, but you know Suzanne. She's a damn bully."

He snickered. "You got that right."

The room fell silent, the atmosphere between us awkward.

Did I say something wrong? Christ, I wish I could see his face. He always showed everything there. I hate having to interpret everything through tone and innuendo.

I tried to fill the silence. "I forgot to tell you. Jon came by last week and collected his stuff, and he paid money into my bank account to 'compensate' me. It was fucking guilt money and I asked the bank to send it back to him. He hasn't been in touch since."

In recent weeks, I'd heard from friends that Jon's relationship status had gone from "in a relationship" to "single" then back to "in a relationship" again. According to my sources, Caleb looked damn smug with his arms around Jon in every photo that appeared on Facebook.

To be honest, although I regretted what had happened, I wasn't as gutted about it as I would have thought I'd be.

Cody shifted, his footfall moving over to the other side of the room. "I've seen it all on Facebook," he muttered. "He's a dickwad and you're better off without him."

True. I wasn't sure why I'd put up with all his shit when we'd been together as a couple. Especially when Caleb had been around. The last six weeks since he'd left me had been tough only as it applied to learning to live alone unsighted. But I was happier now than I'd been in over a year.

The little fridge opened—Cody was probably helping himself to the fruit I kept in a bowl in there. What was it with him and my fruit?

"Anyway, I need to get off." He closed the fridge. "Rachel's expecting me back to meet a client. I just wanted to bring you your donut and coffee fix."

Disappointed but I understood. Work was work and Cody had sacrificed a lot of work time to babysit me.

Warm arms wrapped around me in a hug. "Try be a little more patient, and let that muse on your shoulder do his thing. Stop beating yourself up when it doesn't go how you want it to at that moment. You're awesome, dude. Remember that." A warm hand caressed my cheek. "Believe in yourself, Nate. I do."

Another squeeze of my arm and Cody was gone, leaving me with a deep sense of loss.

***

Later that week, while I worked down in the studio, I considered the new club Suzanne was dragging me to called The Empty Closet. It had opened a few months ago amidst great fanfare and celebration, and was apparently the "in" place for any self-respecting gay man to be seen. I wasn't so sure I was ready, but I'd promised Suzanne.

Perhaps I might find someone who I'd want to start a relationship with and put my recent obsession with Cody out of my head.

I wasn't a one-night-stand kind of guy. I preferred to date and see where it took us rather than have sex with strangers. I wasn't looking for anything special, but I was tired of jacking off to the porn film track in my head.

My inner voice sniggered.

Yeah, a porn track that involves a certain someone who makes you come like a rocket.

Go to hell. I'm going out to have fun and to forget about him.

More fun than when you think about him naked, sweaty and pounding your ass?

I swatted the voice away with a mental hand.

Shut the fuck up.

I'd lost track of time working the clay, and it was only when I heard a knock on the door that I was roused back to the real world. I ignored the knock, intent on getting the curve of the face right. The door squeaked open and a soft voice insinuated itself into my musings.

"Nate? You in here?" The light switch clicked on and I turned at the sound of Suzanne's voice.

"Yeah." My voice was husky from disuse and I let go of the clay and stretched. My fingers tingled, my hands ached and the old familiar dull throb of a pain in my shoulders made itself known.

Soft fabric brushed against my bare arm. "It's late already," she said. "We're supposed to leave for the club. You're not even dressed yet."

I reached out and moved my hands over the head I'd been shaping. "Give me a minute and I'll get changed. It won't take me long. Sorry, I lost track of time."

"It's almost nine p.m. How long have you been down here?" Suzanne brushed something off my cheek. "You're covered in bits of clay. You're probably going to want a shower."

Once again I ignored her, and made a few small adjustments to my creation. Then I sat back with a satisfied sigh. "Huh. I think I came down here about lunchtime? Not sure." I grinned tiredly. "No idea when day starts and night begins, you know? I get a bit lost with it all."

I stood and grimaced as my knees cracked and my lower back complained. I supposed begging off was a no-no. She'd been looking forward to it.

In the confines of the studio, she smelled good; her favorite perfume, White Linen, filled the room with notes of summer rose and violets. It drifted like a soft breeze over the earthier scent of clay, sweat and the coffee I'd been drinking. "Uhm, I don't suppose we could, like, do this whole club thing another day? Because I'm really tired and—"

My plea was cut off by the soft press of a fragranced finger to my lips. "Uh, no. We're going. You need to get out and live a little, and I've been looking forward to all those hot, sweaty dancing bodies. Plus, friends are meeting me there to say hi. So, no. You committed, baby."

She slapped my rear and I moved out the way. "So get yourself dressed up, put on your dancing shoes and let's make a move."

"I doubt I'll be doing any damn dancing," I grumbled as I locked up and we made our way up the footpath to the house. "I didn't dance much when I could see, so why should I start now?" My favorite pastime when I'd gone to clubs with Jon had been people watching. I got off on the writhing bodies and the dynamics of people trying to hook up. Some of their dance moves had found their way into my sculpture. Now, I guessed I'd have to imagine their interactions and drink in their movements through the smell of testosterone, sexual arousal, semen and sweat.

Hmmm. Going to the club was beginning to sound like not such a bad idea. I grinned when she bopped my hip with hers.

"Shoo, grumpy. Go shower, and I'll wait for you."

I showered and dressed in whatever I could find that I thought would constitute "clubbing clothes." I was finding the safety pin thing a great addition to my day-to-day life. I hadn't yet gone to the trouble of ironing little Braille tags with the letters denoting color onto my clothes. I spent a lot of money on safety pins.

I found a tight black tee shirt, and teamed it with a loose fitting, soft burgundy button-down with long sleeves that I rolled up to my elbows. I put on my tightest jeans, because I was a *little* curious about whether I'd be able to attract someone, and my favorite pair of black combat boots. It was an easy choice. I only had two pairs of boots and three pairs of shoes and every pair felt different.

I hoped I looked as good as I thought I did and was gratified to learn I'd done myself proud when I made my way into the family room.

"Oh my God," Suzanne squealed as I walked in. "You are so going to get the guys hot tonight. You look like sex on a stick."

I chuckled. "Good to know. Let's hope the guys think so too instead of just seeing a blind guy." Suzanne's breath hitched and I frowned. "What, is it too much?"

"No." Her voice was hesitant. "I hadn't thought—you do want to do this, right? Meet someone new?"

I was bemused. "I guess. Why?"

My cock needed some sort of release soon. I was tired of jacking off and tired of my Fleshjack or sticking a dildo up my ass. It'd be nice to have some real live human one-on-one action once I had gotten to know another man.

"It's only, you know, I thought…" Her voice trailed off. "Never mind, it doesn't matter."

Now I was burning with curiosity. "Woman, for God's sake, spit it out. What did you think?"

"You'll be mad," she said in a small voice, and I felt like shit that somehow I had made her feel bad.

"Sweetheart, I could never be mad at you. Haven't we become good friends?" There was silence. I scowled. "What now? We're *not* friends, and you have to think about that statement?"

"No," she said hurriedly. "We are friends. Definitely." Her next words came out in a rush. "And so is Cody. You know, the guy who's always there for you?"

Ah. So *that's* where this was going. I should have known that someone as astute as Suze had picked up on my growing attraction to Cody. I obviously hadn't hidden it as well as I'd thought.

Shit, I hope no one else has noticed. I need to head this off at the pass, quick.

"Suze. Cody and I are good friends, but just friends." The words sounded hollow even to me. *You're going to hell for that lie, Nate Powell. Deep down, you know he's more than that.* "Yeah, sure we spend a lot of time together. But we're not romantically involved. Anyway, he's seeing Dev now, they seem to have hooked up again."

My chest tightened. I'd heard via our mutual grapevine that Dev had become something more than an occasional bump-and-grind in Cody's life. The pang of whatever the hell it was that went through me when I thought of Cody and Dev together was unwarranted and yet I begrudged Cody his relationship. Dev, with his pitch black hair, winning smile and blue eyes, who could see, who could surf with

Cody anytime he wanted and it didn't take a mission to arrange an outing so he could go out on a board and still be safe.

I liked Dev, which made it worse.

"Oh," she said. "I didn't know he was seeing someone."

"They've been on and off fuck buddies, but lately they seem to be seeing a lot more of each other. I guess time will tell." I swallowed down the sudden tightness in my throat and went to fetch my stick. "Anyway enough about Cody's sex life. I need to get back to sorting out my own. Shall we go?"

***

According to Suze, The Empty Closet was garish with red and copper neon blazing in the shiny downtown street. The logo above the club, an actual door that opened and closed, revealed the silhouette of a man. I shuddered. It sounded more tacky than trendy and I wondered what the hell I'd let myself in for.

Suzanne held tightly to my arm as we walked in. I wasn't sure if it was for her benefit or for mine. She uttered small gasps as she steered us over to what I hoped was a table.

"Right, we're at the table now, Nate. Take a seat, I'll try to find my friends and get us a drink. You want your usual beer?"

I hated that she needed to do that for me. In the past I'd be the one at the bar.

I nodded my agreement, felt for the back of the chair then sat. Within moments, bodies began brushing my arms and the heat radiating off them, sweaty, some smelly and all of them sexually charged, told me our table was close to the dance floor. The pulsing music was an assault to my senses, the noise throbbing through my brain. Even when sighted I hadn't been all that fond of the jostling and raucousness of clubs. Dancing hadn't been one of my favorite things; I did it, but I had to be in the mood.

Why had I agreed to come here tonight? I knew I'd joked with Suzanne about needing to get laid, but casual sex wasn't me. I liked to get to know someone before jumping into bed with them. So I supposed I was here being sociable. A couple of drinks might loosen me up so I could chat with other people —potential relationship material—and that wasn't such a bad idea.

Tucking my stick under the table, I made sure I could feel it resting against my thigh. It wasn't particularly club friendly and I'd be mortified if I swept some guy off his feet in a non-romantic sexy way.

Suzanne's perfume hit my nose before she sat down beside me. Glass clinked against the glass on the table.

"I got you a beer. It's at your one o'clock," Suzanne shouted above the music. "I have to say, this place is pumping. I never expected it to be this busy." She leaned in close; her breath tickled my ear. "If you want to leave after one drink, I'll understand. This is your evening, Nate. You set the pace."

My instinct was to gulp down my drink and rush back to the quiet of my home. I clamped that desire down. Suzanne had brought me here and bought me a drink. The least I could do was stay a while to see how I coped. I'd done street theaters and music venues with Cody by my side. I could do a vibrant gay nightclub.

"It's fine," I said, raising my voice. "I'll sit here and get a little tipsy and enjoy the music."

I'd made my expectations for the night clear, and one of them was not to be hovered over; she was here to have a good time too.

She nudged my arm. "Cool. Okay, so I'm going to hit the dance floor with a couple of friends. I won't be long. You sure you don't want to come dance with us?"

"Nope. Go enjoy yourself. I'll sit here and see what happens." I heard her leave and I sipped my beer. It was cold and refreshing with a hint of citrus. I enjoyed flavored beers. They teased my palate, made me think of summer days, warm nights and those times Cody and I had sat together out on the patio and enjoyed each other's company.

I wondered idly what Jon was doing now. Wouldn't he be surprised to see me at a place like this? Interestingly, I didn't feel nostalgic about our past and that bothered me a little. How could you be with someone for almost two years, live with them for one and when they leave, not feel it that much? Did that make me shallow and fickle?

I'd finished my beer and was wondering where the toilet was when someone plonked down next to me. Someone decidedly male with the tang of sweat, some earthy and spicy cologne, and a body that radiated a furnace of heat.

"Your lady friend told me to bring this over when yours ran dry. She also said to bring it over personally and still capped?" I heard bemusement in his voice. "I said I'd be glad to. It's criminal having a guy like you sit all alone here." His voice was husky, slightly Southern, and I smelled cigarette smoke on his clothes.

The glass was plonked somewhere on the table and I sighed. I'd have to figure out where it was and hoped I didn't knock it over in the process.

"You see a lot of action with a pick-up line like that?"

He laughed loudly and for some inexplicable reason I pictured a cowboy. Rangy, lean, wearing a Stetson and tight, worn blue jeans.

"I can't complain. But I wasn't trying to pick you up. Well, maybe a little. I'm the bartender. Name's Blu." He shifted and I waited for the mortifying offer of a handshake I couldn't see.

He cleared his throat after a couple of awkward moments. "Okay, no handshake. No problem."

"I'm blind," I said quietly. "So not too good at doing stuff like that."

His stillness in the throb of the music and the sighs and pants of people dancing around me was telling.

"Ah, the capped bottle makes sense now." He exhaled in a long, drawn-out whoosh and I smelled peppermint and cigarettes on his breath. Sexy. "Sorry. She didn't tell me that. Okay, well, your drink is on your left, about a forearm distance away. Or ten o'clock if you prefer. It's the same beer you had. I brought an opener with."

I was surprised at the time position reference. "You've had experience with blind people?" If so, perhaps it explained why he wasn't running for the hills when he'd discovered I was.

He stilled, and must have been holding his breath because the exhale was noticeable. "Yeah. My little sister was blind."

I heard pain and guilt in his voice at the use of the word "was" so didn't push. Instead, I reached over, picked up the bottle and waggled it at him. It *was* still capped. If it hadn't been, there would have no ways on earth I'd have accepted it. "Okay, well, you can open my beer for me, and I'll toast you a thanks for the exceptional bar service here at The Empty Closet."

Blu chuckled. "That works for me." He took the bottle and I heard the pop as he opened it. He placed it back in my hand and squeezed mine gently. My skin tingled at feeling another man's hand on me. It had been so long since I'd had any sort of skin-to-skin contact. "There you go."

"Thanks." I raised the bottle in his direction and tipped my head. "To the bartender who goes above and beyond the call of duty for his patrons."

Blu laughed again. "*Salud*, my friend. It would be nice to know your name."

"Nate Powell." I reached my hand out this time and found it grasped in a warm, calloused hand that lingered a little bit longer than the norm.

The nightclub was loud, the music resonant and the smell of testosterone, sex and male bodies was overpowering, but during the next half hour I enjoyed myself tremendously. Blu was entertaining, funny, irreverent and easy to talk to. He reminded me of Cody.

It was a pity he hadn't been able to make it tonight. Cody loved clubs, got off on the vibe and the hype and was a marvel with those hips on the dance floor. He would have every man in the club drooling and wishing they were between those swivel hips. He could be quite the slut when he wanted.

A pang of regret swept over me thinking about what I'd lost in that fucking accident.

I'll never see Cody rip his shirt off and throw it into the crowd. I'll never dance with him, body to body, and see the sweat glisten on his skin, or that wide smile he had when he was happy. All I have now are memories.

I clenched my fists, body tightening. A loud cough brought me back to the present.

"Earth to Nate. Where the hell did you go?" Blu's amused voice broke through my reverie and I blinked, coming back to the raucous club.

"Sorry. I zoned for a bit there. It's not the company, honest." I frowned. "Wait, how long have we been sitting here? Shouldn't you be back at the bar?"

I sensed his shrug as he leaned forward and picked up something off the table. "Naw. I've got underlings taking care of that. What's the point of being bar manager if you can't slack off to meet an attractive guy?"

I heard the distinct pop of a bottle and the sound of Blu swallowing. Someone must have brought him a drink. Probably one of his underlings.

"So, you're a sculptor. How's that working for you? I imagine you let your hands do the talking now? Do you visualize it in your head and work it into the clay or whatever you use?"

I nodded, tilting my head down to the table. "Yeah. It's been a bit tough to transition to the whole 'not seeing what I'm creating' thing, but I'm getting there."

"Can you tell me what you're working on right now?" he asked.

I hesitated. My art was private and I wasn't keen on revealing it to strangers, even people as easy-going as Blu. He must have sensed my reluctance because a rough hand covered mine.

"Hey, no sweat if you don't want to tell me. I know that you creative geniuses don't like to show your hand too soon."

"Cool, thanks for that. It's not a big thing, but I prefer to keep it to myself until it's finished." I grinned. "And not really a genius. Just an artist."

We talked for what seemed like ages and when the music changed and RuPaul blared throughout the club, my ears pricked up. I loved RuPaul. Under the table, my feet began tapping to the beat.

"Does this sculptor dance?" Blu leaned in, his breath ghosting my ear. The hairs on my forearms prickled with static and my groin grew warm. He smelled so damn good.

"I have been known to but it's not my favorite thing. I haven't danced in a club since the accident. I don't want to poke someone's eyes out with my fingers."

"I'll get you in the mood and keep you focused. Come on."

Blu scraped his chair back, and I had a vision of his crotch close to my mouth. My face flamed.

"I'm not sure," I hedged, while my feet tapped below. "It's been a while."

Blu leaned down and whispered in my ear. "Then let's stop the dry spell and get you going again." The double entendre was plain, and my cock stirred and inflated.

Okay. Caution to the wind; I stood up. "You'll have to help me," I muttered. "Best for me to hold your arm."

Blu took my left hand and placed it on his impressively muscled bicep. "There you go. Stay with me and I'll get us into the party. Don't worry, I won't lose you."

"I might need to pee soon," I said as I followed him onto the heaving dance floor. "In fact, after this dance, I'll definitely need to take a piss. For no other reason than relieving myself," I added hastily lest he think I was offering him a bathroom blowjob or a quick fuck.

He laughed and pressed a hand around my waist, navigating me skilfully through the hands that flew past my face, causing waves of air, and feet that knocked mine as we entered the fray. The scent of sweat and perfume mixed with sexual arousal was intoxicating.

"No worries." Blu chuckled. "I promise I'll show you where it is after this dance. No strings attached."

Part of me was disappointed by his comment. Perhaps a one-night stand was exactly what I needed.

For someone who wasn't all that fond of dancing, I outdid myself. I danced with abandon with a man who wasn't Jon or Cody. A man who was careful of my needs, and every now and then squeezed my arm to let me know he was there. I knew where he was though; the distinct scent of Blu and sandalwood was signature.

I had no way of knowing whether the hands roaming my backside and occasionally hitting my crotch were Blu's or whether the tongue trailing down my collarbone was his amidst the overwhelming scent of other men's sweat and cologne around me, but I didn't care. It was good to be wanted, even if it was by random men or women. There'd been a few of them goosing me, their perfume unmistakeable, their soft hands brushing my arm and the bare skin of my throat and chest.

"You are so sexy," Blu murmured in my ear as his hand slid over my belly, its heat and caress causing my cock to reach the near-exploding point. "You look fantastic. All eyes are on you. They want you, Nate. So do I."

"Yeah?" I managed to pant out in between hard breaths. "Well, all good things come to those who wait. Now, dance with me some more."

I lost myself in the rhythm of the music, flaunting my body and basking in the knowledge I still had "it" made this seem like old times. It was a welcome reminder that things could be normal.

Finally, when my bladder could last no longer, I reached out for Blu, hands searching, and found myself pressed against a highly aroused male form. Corded arms encircled my waist and pulled me closer, the smell of male sweat intoxicating.

"You okay?" Blu shouted over the music.

"I need the can desperately. Would you take me there?"

Within seconds I was being hustled off the dance floor, through clutching hands, ribald comments and jokes as Blu no doubt hauled me in the direction of the bathroom. I guessed the dancers thought we couldn't wait to get there for another reason.

It took a while to move away but finally the music faded, the air got cooler, and a door squeaked.

"We're in the bathroom," Blu said. "There's an empty stall. You want that or the urinal?"

"Stall, please." I didn't pee in front of people in case I missed the basin.

I held Blu's arm again and he stopped, and there was a waft of air as a door was pushed open. "There you go, all yours. I'm going to wait outside, if you like, then we can go back to the table, have another drink?"

I nodded, found the door and closed it, slipping the lock. I unzipped myself with a sigh of relief, and felt around for the bowl with my foot, then I aimed and fired.

True to his word, Blu was waiting for me when I walked out and soon we were seated once again at the table.

Another beer found its way into my hand and I drank from it thirstily. I wiped the sweat from my brow and smiled over at Blu, who was seated next to me, much closer than he'd been before.

"God, you're gorgeous," he whispered as his hot tongue lapped at my ear. "Sorry, I can't help myself. I had to taste you."

I closed my eyes and gave over to the sensations of lust and desire coursing through me. I was about to break my own rule about no sex on a first meet. I needed sex tonight. A blowjob would be good, but even better would be someone pounding me into the mattress. I had no problem returning the favor. It would be fun having someone's hand guide me inside them; the sanctity of that place invaded through nothing more than touch.

"You want to come home with me?" I breathed out the words as Blu nibbled on my ear. "Suzanne will drive me home, you could follow. Spend the night."

His hand caressed my chin and then my lips. "Nothing I'd like more," he said softly. "But I think I'm going to take it easy with you. I like you, Nate. I don't want this to be another sex-fueled evening. I think I'd rather wait, and ask you out on a date."

I opened my eyes and stared at him indignantly. "You're turning me down? You know how horny I am?"

He chuckled, his lips brushing my cheek. "I know because I feel the same. Blu has blue balls, buddy, blue balls. But think how good it will be after dinner and some wine, and getting to know each other a bit more." He laughed huskily. "Plus your lady friend threatened to cut my blue balls off if I took advantage of you. So you can stop pouting, even though it's adorable."

Halle-fucking-lujah. I still have it. Sex appeal.

"I'm not pouting," I denied, and a smile curved my lips. "Well, maybe a little. And Suzanne talks too much. If I want to get laid, I'll damn well get laid."

Blu laughed. "So how does Saturday sound for date night? I'll come over, pick you up and we'll take it from there."

"I suppose it'll do."

My Fleshjack will get a good workout tonight. It's crap I have to wait until Saturday to get laid though.

Something inside me twinged—a sudden snap of guilt, a feeling of regret of something not quite right. I liked Blu, but something was telling me I was rushing things. I quashed the feeling and ignored it. I was single, and a healthy sexual man. There was nothing to feel bad about.

A soft bosom pressed against my back in a hug. "Nate, you looked like you were having fun for a man who didn't want to dance. You both looked great out there." Suzanne flopped down on my other side. "Whew, I'm done, it's one a.m. Do you think you're ready to leave yet?"

I drained my drink and nodded. "I'm fine with that. Just show me the way out when you're ready."

There was the usual flurry of female good-byes, tracking down handbags and popping to the toilet. We stood up to leave and Blu reached over for a hug.

"Is it okay to kiss you?" he murmured.

Fuck yes.

I nodded. His lips found mine, his breath beer-scented, and I closed my eyes as he kissed me. There was no rabid entry into my mouth, simply a hint of tongue and he was gone, leaving me wanting more. It seemed to be the bastard's modus operandi.

After he released me and exhaled a breath, I opened my eyes.

Some guy in the room called out, "Hot kiss, man, do it again."

Blu let out a loud laugh. "If you think that's hot wait 'til Saturday." I could hear the grin in his voice. "We have a date."

"Ooh, a date. I knew you two would hit it off." Suzanne punched my arm. "Okay, lover boy, let's get going. Blu, lovely to meet you. No doubt I'll see you around."

I managed to say good-bye to Blu before my hand was grasped, placed on Suzanne's arm and I was manoeuvred through the crowd once more.

Despite my earlier reservations, tonight had been good. I'd made a new friend, a potential lover and had a good time.

What more could I want?

Chapter 8

Cody

It sucked being a coward. My cell phone rang again and I glanced down at it guiltily.

Nate Powell calling.

I ignored it, as I had the previous calls the past few days. So it didn't look as if I was ignoring him completely, I'd briefly texted Nate back, telling him work was busy and I had some things to sort out so I'd be in touch. It was easier than hearing his voice or details of his evening at the nightclub with another man.

It had been a bad few days. I hadn't been lying to Nate. Work had been frantically busy, and a shipment of surreal canvas paintings from a young artist known only as *Ug* had gone missing. Rachel and I had finally tracked it down to an art gallery on the other side of town. The delivery guys had fucked up again. I'd already instructed Rachel to find another service.

I'd also learned from my older sister Jess that my mom had gone into the hospital for some tests. The words "checking for breast cancer" had been said quickly, as if dwelling on it would make it true. Jess had sounded scared.

My dad had tried to sound upbeat, but I'd heard the fear in his voice. My mom was his world; she was mine too, and I didn't want to think about what might be happening. I'd offered to go home and be with them, despite the fact I had an event and it wouldn't look good if I wasn't there, but I was prepared to do it.

My dad had talked me out of it, saying it wasn't necessary, it was tests, and anyway it was all going to be fine. It was only a precaution.

I hoped so.

Ordinarily I'd be lamenting on Nate's shoulder, letting him know what was going on in the Fisher family. They were his family too, and he'd want to know. But not right now. I'd asked Jess and my dad not to tell him just yet. Why have him worry over something that might not be bad news? He had enough on his plate.

The pictures on Suzanne's Facebook page of Nate cozying up to some gorgeous guy in a nightclub, some man with a killer smile, a body I could only wish for, and a thatch of messy dark brown hair, had made my stomach roil.

It wasn't helped by the pictures of them kissing at the table. Nate had his eyes closed but the other man's were wide open. Usually I would have found that hot but not this time. That was *my* Nate this guy was making a meal of.

Then seeing on the same post that Nate had a date with this guy tonight—his name was Blu and from the comments, both were looking forward to it—my spirits had ebbed lower and I'd shut Facebook the hell down.

Obviously, Nate was moving on. I was a little surprised it was so soon because Nate was a slow-motion kind of guy. He deliberated everything before he did it. With a heavy heart, I guessed this other man was special enough for Nate to dive in to dating right away.

God, I was such a hypocrite. I hadn't exactly been a sexless hermit.

I stared out at the sea, watching the surfers and swimmers. Manhattan Beach was my favorite place to watch them. Since they'd built that damn breakwater at Long Beach, the waves had disappeared and the once-named "Waikiki of the West Coast" surf paradise was now a memory. I hated what they'd done to my coastline.

Someone kicked sand in my face and I shouted, "Hey! Watch what you're doing, asshole."

My friend Dev plonked himself down next to me, an amiable shit-eating grin on his face. "Hey, surfer boy, what's happening?"

Dev and I had gotten together lately more than usual—a couple of times for blowjobs, and the rest to simply to hang out, see a movie, go to dinner. I wasn't sure why, but I had the guilty feeling it was to take Nate off my mind.

So what was I doing agonizing over Nate's date? Dev and I were simply guys hooking up to get each other off. But Nate? In the pictures I'd seen of him and Blu sucking face and being handsy on the dance floor, it looked to be the start of something more.

"Nothing," I said moodily.

Dev sprawled down on the sand, tanned legs stretched out, hands behind his head as he regarded the sea thoughtfully. "So, I saw the pictures on Facebook. Are you okay?"

I glanced over; he continued staring out at the waves, but a muscle in his jaw twitched.

"What pictures?" I knew which ones he was talking about.

He snorted. "The ones of Nate and his new boyfriend."

"He's not Nate's damned boyfriend. Yet."

"Oh yeah. My boy has it bad." Dev sat up and drew his knees up, his eyes searching mine. "Cody, you know I love being with you. But why the hell aren't you going after Nate with everything you've got? What's holding you back?"

"Nate isn't into me that way. I told you. It's a one-way street." I picked up a shell and toyed with it, then threw it angrily across the beach.

"I'm not so sure," Dev said thoughtfully. "I've gotten this vibe from him that says something else."

I laughed harshly. "Yeah, you think that. I've got the old scars to prove he only wants to be friends."

Dev was the only person who knew about what had gone down between me and Nate during those few sultry nights in the Keys.

Dev's gaze narrowed, his bright blue eyes assessing me. "You sure about that? Because I've got twenty dollars says otherwise. I mean..."

I couldn't take it anymore and my resentment pushed through.

"Dev, he was clear about it back in the day. We'd spent three days doing things to each other that blew my mind. It happened just that weekend and no one was more surprised about it than me. Then two days later he told me he didn't feel anything romantic for me, the sex had been a mistake and we needed to cool it. There was no confusion about what he said, believe me. Not when you're seventeen years old and crazy about a guy you hoped you might be with for the rest of your life. We didn't even get a chance to take it further, see what might develop."

Dev's face crinkled. "Huh," was all he said. He reached inside his board shorts and drew out a packet of gum, tilting the pack in my direction. I declined. I'd probably choke on it the way my throat had tightened remembering that conversation when the world as I knew it stopped turning.

Dev picked out a piece and chewed on it. "And then what? You both went off to college and forgot it ever happened?"

I lay back and shielded my eyes from the sun. "Basically. When his folks kicked him out and he came to stay with us, he was a bit withdrawn. I thought it was losing his family that made him that way. We spent the next few months tiptoeing around each other, pretending we hadn't had raunchy sex in his folks' boathouse in Florida. I tried to forget I'd ever thought I loved him, and we managed to stay good friends. He got over his reticence eventually and things went back to normal." I sighed. "It was a tough situation, but it was either that or lose him altogether, and I didn't want that."

I closed my eyes and laid my hands on my chest as the sun warmed me. "Then we both went off to study, saw each other in between and when we finished, we both came back to L.A. Nate was seeing some other guy, I had a boyfriend…" I shrugged. "That was the way it was. The way it's been ever since."

"But you never got over him," Dev remarked softly.

Silently, we lay together on the sand, basking like lizards.

"He's hot though," Dev finally muttered.

"Who, Nate?" Nate was hot, no doubt.

"No. The other guy. Blu."

"Well, go down to the Empty Closet," I retorted. "Perhaps I'll get you an introduction and you two can be a thing," I said acerbically. "Maybe you can steal him away from Nate, I'll declare my undying love, which Nate will reciprocate, and we'll all live happy ever after."

Dev cackled and shoved a handful of sand down the front of my shirt. I returned the favor by pulling the drawstring out of his shorts and throwing it to one side. We play-wrestled for a minute and finally lay, panting and exhausted, on the beach, staring up into the sky.

"Jeez, I'm wiped and we didn't even have sex," I joked as Dev turned onto his side and regarded me warmly.

"You're a great guy, Cody. He's a fool not to see you as anything other than a friend. But maybe it's time to let go. Find someone else." He waggled his eyebrows. "Someone like me."

I chuckled loudly. "You and me will never be more than we are, and you know that." Dev knew I was right; there was no real spark there.

"Yeah, but maybe I should convince you." Dev's eyes sparkled wickedly as he pinned me to the ground. "I'll make you a believer with a kiss."

The kiss was sweet and later that night Dev helped me forget about Nate, Blu and my mom.

***

The following morning, I showered at Dev's then left, ready to spend Sunday at home cleaning up and answering long-overdue emails. Finally, unable to bear it any longer, I changed out of my Star Wars Jedi dressing gown and into grown-up clothes. I left the house mid-afternoon and drove down to Nate's place, hoping he was home. I had to get over my hissy fit and get back on track with him.

The fact he was moving on would not wipe out over twenty years of friendship.

When I got to his house, I let myself in. Remembering the last time I'd walked in on him, I made sure to holler out when I went through the front door. I wasn't going to lie and say I didn't want to see him jerking off again, but I didn't want to be a stalker.

"Nate. I'm here. Are you decent?"

The house smelled of pot and I frowned. Nate indulged occasionally, as did I, but this smelled pretty rank. I wrinkled my nose in disgust.

"Nate, where are you?"

As panic built, I searched the house. I found him lying on the deck, earphones in, stark naked and looking stoned. I wasn't ashamed to admit my eyes were drawn to the delicious cock lying among a clipped bush of dark hair. I picked up a towel from a deck chair and threw it over his groin. He sat up hurriedly, dislodging the towel, and squawked in panic as he removed his earphones.

Shit, there was that cock again. I picked up the towel again and shoved it into his hands.

"Who's there? Cody, is that you?"

"Yeah, you idiot. Put something on for God's sake. What the hell is going on? The place stinks of pot. Did you smoke a whole damn dime bag?"

Both relief and disappointment pinged when Nate stood and wrapped the towel around his waist.

"Uhm, no, not the whole thing. I've got some left if you want, bud. It's in the kitchen."

"No thanks. I'm not in the mood. What's the matter with you? You could have fallen and hurt yourself or something."

He burst into laughter and fumbled around, looking for the deck chair. He found it and flung himself into it. The towel shifted but didn't reveal anything. Fate was smiling on me. Or not.

Yeah, I'd been miffed at him for being a little stoned, because he could have hurt himself—but there was something on his face that jabbed straight into my heart. His eyes were bloodshot, but the look of despair in them was unmistakeable. His hands fidgeted on his toned stomach as he stared up hazily, a soft curl of hair falling over his forehead.

I sat beside him and took his hand. His fingers wrapped around mine tightly. His eyes went out of focus then cleared, and a shuddering sigh wracked his body. I was scared. I'd never seen Nate this high on anything before. He wasn't the dependent type.

If that bastard Blu had done something to hurt Nate, I was going to kill him.

I stroked his hand softly. "What's going on? Did something happen on your date last night?"

Nate shook his head. "Last night?" A short, desperate laugh came out of his mouth. "No, nothing happened last night. That's the problem."

"What do you mean?" I leaned over and brushed the hair from his sweating forehead.

He let go of my hand and passed a trembling hand over his eyes. "Never mind. I'm not date material, that's all. No good to anyone."

My throat constricted at the pain in those words. "You're good to me, baby. Best friends, remember?"

Nate gave a hoarse chuckle. "Maybe that's the answer."

"Huh?" I was confused. "You're not making sense. Spill it."

He waved a hand. "You know, best friends. No strings, no ties." He patted the top of his towel and I swallowed. The towel was beginning to tent. "We could jack off together, get rid of some of this tension I have. Guys do that, don't they? Jack off in front of each other, because it's fun?"

My heart beat faster and I clenched my fists. After the shitty few days I'd had, my temper was close to the surface. Was he seriously suggesting we take out our cocks and jerk off? Didn't he realize what it might do to me? What it meant to me?

I guess not. I'd never told him.

"Nate, you're high," I said tightly. "You're talking crap. Anyway, I thought that's why you had dates." I spat the word out, the bad news of the day catching up with me. "It's a date's job to get you off, not a friend. So forget it."

"I had a date, Cody. A sexy, all-man version who wanted to have sex with me." Those words cut me to the core. "But when it came to the crunch, I couldn't do it. I wasn't ready." He sniffed. "So today was my pity party at how useless I am, and I wanted some weed to relax. Maybe I overdid it though. I feel a bit sick."

I couldn't deny the satisfaction knowing nothing had happened last night. And he did look a little green. I eyed the empty plant pot to my left, thinking it would be useful for a barf bag for Nate if he needed it.

"You're still getting over Jon. I can see that. And you're not useless, you idiot. Jesus, it was one damn date that didn't go well." I wondered if there'd be another one. "What did he say—your date?"

Nate closed his eyes, looking exhausted. "Blu was a complete gentleman. He said it was obvious I wasn't ready to move on and we could still be friends."

Oh. I hadn't expected that. "Well, that's good, isn't it? Making a new friend?"

He nodded. "But I wasn't getting over Jon. I'm over him already. It was someone else I kept thinking about." His face slackened and he lolled back in the deck chair, cheeks flushed, those long dark lashes falling over his cheeks. He was asleep.

Damn. But it beat seeing him upchuck so I was glad for that. My stomach wasn't good with that sort of thing and I'd probably have joined him.

I gazed at Nate's peaceful face with growing frustration. He wasn't getting over Jon? Then who the hell had he been thinking of when he denied Blu? I wanted to wake Nate up, shake him and ask him who he was getting over. I wouldn't though. There was still time to find that out when he wasn't stoned and I'd be able to trust what he said.

I knelt beside his still form. "You promised me donuts, you bastard," I muttered, running my fingers down his bristled cheeks. "Instead you left me with a twisty pretzel. That's so wrong. What the hell happened all those years ago, Clayman? I thought we had something special. You broke my heart when you told me you didn't want me, you know that?" I brushed a strand of hair from his forehead. "I still feel the same way about you as I did then. No one's ever come close to making me feel the way you do. Christ, I wish you hadn't walked away. Who knows what might have happened between us."

I couldn't resist planting a soft kiss on his cheek. "Instead I get to be your best friend. I'll take whatever you give me if it means I'm still in your life. Even if it's not everything I want."

I stood up with a sigh. It looked like he'd be out for a while and I couldn't leave him there wearing only a towel. I huffed out a breath and braced myself to cart Nate to his bedroom. I'd try to ignore the fact that carrying him in my arms like a baby made his cock bounce up and down as I walked.

I tried to ignore it.

But I was only human.

***

Two days later there was a knock on my door. I'd been back from work only for an hour. I glanced at my wall clock. Eight p.m. Living in a beach house not far from the ocean meant the person at my front door could have been anyone: a fellow surfer wanting to shoot the breeze about today's waves, or the next-door neighbor who made a habit of borrowing my homemade chilli sauce. Or it could have been Dev, who liked to drop in unannounced.

I opened the door and stared in surprise. Nate.

After the whole "getting high on weed" thing and putting him to bed a couple of days ago, he'd sent a subdued text the next morning thanking me for getting him to bed, and that had been it.

I'd told myself the usual excuse: I'd been too busy with the gallery and dealing with yet another diva of an artist to text Nate back.

He had come to my place before and knew his way around. Any taxi service he might have used stopped on the street right outside his front yard, and my place was only a stone's throw from the road. It was easy enough for him to find his way here, and each time he did I was so proud of him. I didn't want to appear patronizing because a grown man managed to walk ten steps down a backyard path. However, in my book, it was a big deal.

In only five months, Nate had come a long way.

"Wow, this is a surprise. I wasn't expecting you."

He fidgeted, his hand clenched around his cane. He looked tired. "Yeah, sorry. I tried calling but you didn't answer."

"Really? I didn't hear it."

He rolled one shoulder, looking uncomfortable. "Maybe you switched the volume down or something."

I snapped my fingers. "That's probably it. I was in a meeting this evening with a couple of clients. Come on inside." I ushered him into the house and tried not to ogle him. Nate always looked good in long denim shorts and a cut-off tee shirt, and I hoped I wasn't drooling at the picture he made of casual sexy guy.

"Sit down, make yourself comfortable. I'll get us some lemonade."

Nate sat down in the huge wicker chair, which was his favorite. "Homemade?" He laid his cane at the side of the chair.

I tut-tutted. "Of course. My very own Cody Fisher concoction." I poured us a glass each, passed it to Nate, who took it with a smile. He drank thirstily and my eyes were drawn to the sheen of sweat on his throat, the small drop of lemonade that ran down his mouth. He pushed out a pink tongue and licked it up.

My shorts grew tighter.

"So to what do I owe the pleasure?" I enquired as I sat in my chair and slurped my drink. "Not that I'm complaining of course." I picked up my cell phone sitting on the side table, peered down and sighed. Yep, it was on silent. I switched the ringer back on.

Nate's eyes stared to one side of the room, as if he couldn't face me, which was weird. His face flushed. I wondered why he seemed so uneasy.

"The other night, I was rather out of it. I'm sorry you had to put me to bed. I made you feel bad, I remember that."

"Nah. It was fine. I was surprised you'd overindulged to the extent of being comatose, but everyone deserves a moment of excess."

Nate murmured softly, "You've been avoiding me."

I didn't know what to say so I kept quiet.

Nate's lips twisted and he took a deep breath. "The date with Blu was great but when he wanted to"—his voice caught—"you know—"

"Nate," I interrupted, my throat constricting at thinking I might have to hear a story of Nate and Blu's failed sexploits. "You don't need to explain. In fact, I'd rather you didn't."

Nate huffed. "Why don't you want to hear about it? We've talked about our sex lives with other people before."

I stood, and went to stare out of the window to the beach beyond. "I know, but this time, I don't want to, okay?" My voice was sharper than it needed to be and I winced. No doubt Nate would pick up on it. There was a noise behind me and before I knew it, Nate was behind me, his hand on my waist.

"Cody? I'm dying here. I have no idea whether I'm about to fuck things up. Can you turn around and look at me?"

My heart was beating so fast, I thought it might take off and fly around the room in panic. I turned around and lost my breath. The catch in Nate's voice, the words he'd spoken— nothing prepared for me the look on his face. It was a look of both fear and determination, and more than that, it was a look I'd seen only once before.

"I heard you the other day," he said softly, his brown eyes staring at me with such intensity I lost my breath. "When you thought I was sleeping. I *was* out of it but not that out."

Jesus, he heard me? What the fuck am I supposed to do now?

"I had no idea you still felt that way. I've had some time to think and I need to tell you something."

I couldn't speak as his fingers trailed gently down my cheek. I closed my eyes, soaking up the feeling of those warm, tender hands cupping my jaw, running through my hair, tugging at my ponytail.

"God, I love your hair like this," he whispered.

The moment froze in time; two men with years of hot and needy between them.

When he leaned forward and touched his lips to mine, breath warm and sweet with lemonade, I fell into the moment, tumbling and rolling with emotions flooding me. I knew there'd be no going back this time.

Kissing Nate again was a dream come true.

I'd waited twelve years for this moment.

To be in Nate's arms again, his breath mingling with mine as our lips met and our hungry mouths sought each other out.

He tasted like everything I'd ever wanted. He was the breath in my body, the beat of my heart and the warmth of a summer's day.

This man was *mine*, but first, I had to make sure it was what he wanted. Remind him of what he was doing; make sure it wasn't a game.

I didn't want to be hurt again.

The first time had been painful enough.

I needed to be sure this time.

Chapter 9

Nate

The moment my lips pressed against Cody's I heard his breathy gasp and felt the way his body moved unconsciously against mine. Thank fuck, I'd made the right decision.

He wanted me as much as I wanted him. The words he'd spoken in that unguarded moment the other night had caused my heart to race and my pulse to quicken. A door had opened and I wanted so badly to walk through it, to tell him the truth about how I felt. The spark I'd banked from twelve years ago now burned brighter than before.

He tasted of sea and sunshine and home. His arms around me felt right, his mouth on mine a symphony of every tune I'd ever loved.

God, why the hell have we waited so long to do this? It feels so damn right.

He was *mine* and this time, I wasn't going to let him go for anyone. No threats, veiled or otherwise, were going to keep me from him.

His lips parted as I sought entrance and his heart beat against my chest, keeping rhythm with my own.

The kiss was tentative, almost awkward, but his mouth was warm and wet and heavenly, and when his tongue tangled with mine, I responded. The kiss grew fiercer as he took my mouth eagerly, greedily. I groaned and he pressed against me closer, his hardness poking me in the stomach.

There was no doubt he wanted me the same way I wanted him. The chemistry was still there and I wondered hazily how we'd ever avoided it. With this level of heat, we should have sparked up like fireworks then exploded like a supernova.

My guilt and fear, the things that had torn us apart so many years ago now, were a distant memory as Cody's body pressed against mine. Any reservations I'd had about us being together fled, leaving only my need and desire for the man currently exploring my mouth.

Hallelujah because this? This *is where I belong. Fuck the past.*

My cock ached, my body thrummed and I wanted to be wrapped up by everything that was Cody Fisher.

The only thing I regretted was not being able to see him. I had my memories of us now, and then, but to be able to see his face flushed with desire—for me... Yeah, I would always miss that.

I protested when Cody's lips left mine and I reached out only to find empty space.

The dream kiss faded and I was left bereft.

"What the hell is this, Nate? Rebound sex with your best friend?" Cody's unsteady voice laced with pain brought me back to reality. "I know you said you wanted to jack off together, but maybe you don't remember, I declined your kind offer?"

I raised a finger to my swollen lips and shook my head vehemently. "No, that's not it at all. You've got it all wrong."

Oh God, I've made a mess of this. I need to get him to listen to me.

"Have I? You couldn't make it with Blu, so you decided to come here and see if I'd changed my mind. So, you heard me the other night baring my soul. Big deal. No strings, no ties, you said, remember?" Cody's voice shook. "Well, I'm sorry, but I can't do that with you. Never with you."

The screen door squeaked open then slammed shut and I guessed he'd had gone out onto the deck.

Feeling helpless at being able to reassure Cody that what he was suggesting wasn't the case at all, I stood stock still, my stomach in knots.

I have to fix this. I have to.

I turned and retraced the steps to my chair to get my cane. Then I followed to where I'd heard him go. I'd spent a lot of time at his house and muscle memory was a great thing. I knew his home as intimately as I knew my own.

His erratic breathing told me where he was. I walked over and stood at his side. I reached out, happy when I found his arm even though it was stiff with tension.

"You got it wrong," I said quietly. "I had no intention of asking you to be my fuck buddy and I'm not making fun of how you feel. I'm sorry I asked you to jack off together when I was stoned. I didn't mean to dis you. It's why I'm here now."

Visualizing where I stood was easy to conjure; we were on the wooden deck, a few feet above the beach. It was dark, of course, as my world always was, but in the distance there'd be twinkling lights from the curved shoreline.

Behind me, Cody's rambling beach house would be awash with muted lights, splashes of vibrant jeweled color, and the canvas paintings from one his favorite artists, Clem Jobber, would be hung crookedly on the walls. Cody was great in the gallery but when it came to his own artwork displays, he couldn't hang a picture straight to save his life. It had been one of the things I'd done for him over the years.

His breathing had slowed and he was still silent. To our left, someone shouted, laughed and it went quiet again.

I took a deep breath.

Here goes nothing. I doubt I can fuck it up any worse.

"You want to know why I couldn't get into Blu?"

Beside me the air shifted and became fraught with what I could only think of was anticipation mixed with something else. *Hope.* I took solace from that.

He didn't answer but I heard the nervous drumming of his fingers against the rail.

"Okay, so you're not in the mood for guessing games," I joked, trying to build up the courage to say what I had to. "I couldn't do anything with Blu because he wasn't you."

The drumming stopped. I sensed the slow turn of Cody's head, his eyes on my face. His soft exhalation of breath encouraged me to tell him more.

"It was as if somehow I'd be betraying you, cheating on you." I swallowed. "I have no idea whether you feel the same and I might be making a fool of myself but, lately, hell, I've been thinking about you a lot, you know…" My voice trailed off.

"What you said the other night kinda got me thinking and I came to a decision. One I probably knew deep down, but never admitted until now. Becoming blind changes your perspective." I gave a wry chuckle. "In more ways than one. I guess what I'm trying to say is I feel far more for you than just friendship."

I remembered lying on my bed with my hand around my cock and Cody's face in my mind. "And I want all of you."

Cody shifted, and his arm brushed mine. "And what does that mean to you, Nate?" His breath was warm against my cheek then it was gone again.

Oh, he was going to make me work for this. I must be on the right track.

I thought I'd heard a trace of amusement in his tone, which was heartening and irritating.

I'm giving him my heart and he's finding it funny.

"You know exactly what I'm saying, you hippie bastard," I growled. A headache was forming. I let go of my cane, propping it against the back wall, and rubbed my temples.

Immediately there was a warm hand moving mine away, and replacing them.

"You got a headache?" he murmured. "Let me fix it. You know we hippies have this magic touch."

"Sorry. I didn't mean to—" My words were cut off when he kissed me. His hands slid from my temples to the back of my neck and pulled me toward him.

My question about his feelings answered, I surrendered with a gasp of both relief and awe. Everything else melted away and all I could do was hang on for the ride. Sensations I'd long thought buried climbed; tendrils of hope and desire suffusing my brain.

Cody was making soft noises of pleasure, his deep-throated hums resonating against my lips and finding their way into my soul.

When we finally came up for air my legs were strands of spaghetti on a body that ached for release.

"Oh my God," he gasped as he laid his forehead against mine and his strong hands moved down to my ass, gripping me with a possessive need. "That was awesome."

I managed to nod. "Yeah, that was epic. Reminds me of the old days."

"So shall we go inside, sit down, get a drink and talk about what the hell's happening here?" He took my elbow and steered me inside then pressed my cane into my hand as I sat down on his comfy, well-worn couch. "There you go. I'll get us a stiff drink. I think we both need one."

My head spun from needing him, wanting him, and marveled at how my body craved his presence.

A small, chilled glass was pressed into my hand, the glass wet with condensation. "Here you go." He sat next to me. "It's my best Aquavit. Brennivin."

Cody hadn't known his Scandinavian ancestors, but he enjoyed Aquavit and I'd had to develop a taste for it as well. We'd gotten drunk on it more than once, and I knew to take it easy because I couldn't drink it like he could.

I took a sip, enjoying the way the alcohol numbed my lips. The aroma of herbs and citrus flooded my nostrils, and I inhaled it in as if it were life-giving air.

"So" he murmured, "you're not looking for me to be your fuck buddy? Should I take that scorching kiss to mean more than you're horny?"

I smirked then reached over and found Cody's face and ran my fingers down his jawline. "I can show you better than I can tell you."

Cody needed no further urging. I was pushed back against the sofa, his lithe, strong body pressing against mine. There was something erotic about being manhandled like this and not being able to see. My heart raced, Cody's scent overwhelming, and now I knew what it was like to be blindfolded and under someone's control in a game of sex and want. I liked it.

I reached behind Cody's hair, pulling at his ponytail, and was gratified to hear a low, needy moan emanating from the lips currently plastered against mine.

Years ago, Cody hadn't had a ponytail to pull, but he seemed to be turned on now.

Good to know.

I returned his kiss with an equal measure of fervor and passion. It was dirty, and scorching hot. No other man had ever made me feel this way.

God, I need him. This man is mine.

His mouth was demanding, wet and needy. I was going to combust if this kept up. I was already in danger of coming in my pants. From the feel of the hard cock pressed against my belly, so was Cody.

I pulled away fearing Armageddon in my trousers. "Wait," I gasped. "Too much. I'm going to blow if we don't take a breath here."

Cody gave a sultry chuckle and lifted off me, his breathing deep and heavy. "You ready to talk then?"

Nodding, I winced as I tried to sit up. My cock got in the way. In the ensuing silence, I imagined he was doing the same thing I was—adjusting his out-of-control woody.

I cleared my throat. "I've been an idiot. Unwilling to take a chance on what had been buried deep for so long, and fighting it because I didn't want to upset our friendship. With Jon in the picture, I wouldn't allow myself to re-examine my feelings. Then he left. No more obstacles, and I can't hide it any longer. I wasn't sure you felt the same until I heard what you said the other night."

"You're kidding me, right?" Not the response I'd been hoping for. Where were the soft sighs of romantic acceptance, and perhaps another one of those incredible kisses? "Nate, I've been crazy about you since we were kids. Fifteen, in fact, when I realized you were a lot more than a best friend. And let's not even talk about what happened in the Keys."

"Yeah, I remember that, of course. When we split up, we went our separate ways and found other guys to be with. I thought you'd moved on like I did."

Not because I wanted to. Because I had to.

Cody made a strangled noise. He stood and I felt him passing back and forth. "What the hell? We didn't *split up*. We had this incredible, spontaneous, sex-filled weekend. I thought it was a dream come true to pardon the old cliché. I thought you felt the same." He heaved a frustrated sigh. "You went home, told your dad about us and bam, everything got quantum fucked up.

"Not only did you get kicked out of your home, something we weathered, but two days later you told me you didn't feel 'that way' about me anymore, that we were too young to be tied down to each other and that was it. I was left nursing a broken heart and living with the fact we were only friends again." Cody paused and I imagined him running his hands through his hair, pulling the ends with each pass. "Are you saying all these years you've been feeling this way and you've never told me?"

Now I was in deep waters. I so wanted to explain why I did what I did back then, but to bring the ugly into this fragile reawakening seemed too harsh. Painful truths could overwhelm and spoil the moment. I promised myself I'd tell Cody everything when I felt we were on more solid ground.

For now, I went with the more superficial and said, "I always knew I really cared for you but after we'd found our own guys, I pushed what happened out of my mind." *Mostly.* "You know I can sink things so deep they won't surface unless... Listen, the accident happened, which gave me a lot of time to think." My voice caught. "I realized I could have died. I could have been brain damaged, unable to make amends and I would've missed out on everything that meant anything to me.

"Jon and I had drifted apart. Then he left, and that didn't bother me the way it should have. Thinking about you, us, became all I could think about, even when—" I stopped, face flaming. "Well, when I, you know...ah, took care...."

"You jerked off thinking about me." Cody's voice was soft but there was an element of something else there I couldn't identify. Something sly and knowing that made me wonder.

I scowled and glared at him as best I could. "Yes, I did. Because you're...Cody. My best friend and the man that"—I flapped a hand in exasperation, looking for the right words—"the man that makes me feel special. You always have. Now more than ever, you don't see me as damaged or useless, but as someone who matters. Someone to be cherished. I finally realized the feelings I've had for you, I'd been denying them all these years."

Strong, calloused hands took mine as Cody knelt in front of me.

"You have *always* mattered to me." He took a deep breath. "I never fell out of love with you, you idiot. I didn't think we had a chance. You pushed me away, made me feel the friends thing was all I was going to get, so I played along. It was either that or lose you altogether. I wasn't going to have that happen."

I didn't process past the "never fell out of love with you" part. Even when we'd been horny teenagers, we'd never used the L word. Then it had been all about gratification and getting off.

I blinked. "You were *in love* with me? All this time?"

There was a tired huff of breath in front of me, warm, Cody air that tantalized my nostrils and caressed my face. "Crap. I didn't mean to say that. Can I unsay it?"

I gripped his hands tighter. "No. You know the rule. No take-backs. God, this is one of those times I *really* wish I could still see your face." My chest ached. "I want to see you again saying that to me." My throat closed up, and not for the first time I cursed my damned blindness.

"You *see* me." His breath brushed my mouth lightly. "You know me better than anyone." He sat next to me and pulled me into his arms, hands working through my hair, his touch gentle.

"Yes, I love you. I always have. Who else would put up with you like I do? All those diva moods, the crap jokes, the bad fashion sense." I heard the smile in his voice. "The genius—the brilliance that is Nate Powell. My Nate."

My stomach plummeted. I wasn't ready to say it back yet. It was too soon. My head was full of stuff I wanted to say and I wanted to do it right.

"I can't say it back yet," I whispered against his chest as his heart beat strongly in my ear. "I need a little time to adjust. I'm so damn sorry I've wasted so much time already, but I need a little more."

His hands continued their slow caress of hair and cheek. "I don't need to hear it, Nate," he murmured. "Just having you here like this is enough for me, for now. That is if you're sure about this new…thing we have."

I hated hearing the uncertainty in his voice, the unspoken question. *Are you sure this is what you want?*

Cody's voice was steely when he spoke next. "But I need to know. You need to tell me why you pushed me away all those years ago. Why you lied to me, if that's what it was."

My stomach clenched. Truth time. Nothing for it, the ugly was going to come out now.

"You know what happened. My father." I laughed bitterly. "I went home that weekend to my family, hoping they'd see past their bigotry to the fact I was happy. With you. I hoped they'd see that and not the rhetoric they'd lived. I was their only son, for God's sake. I thought I stood a chance at breaking through. But my dad tore everything apart like a lion savaging a zebra. He took something beautiful and bloodied it with his hate, and his holier-than-thou views. You know this bit though."

"I know that part, yes." Cody's fingers stroked the inside of my wrist. "I know how they treated you when you came out. It's why you came to live with us."

I nodded jerkily. "Well, apart from kicking me out, my father gave me an ultimatum. He wanted me to stop embarrassing him, and threatened to do some awful things to your family if I didn't do what he wanted, which was to leave you." I gave a harsh laugh. "He knew the best way to get at me was by hurting you or your family. So he threatened to shut down your father's business and turn his name to mud if I kept seeing you *that way.* He knew the chairman of the bank that loaned your dad the money for his business. My dad was going to have the loan called in. I knew that would have been a death knell to your dad's business."

Cody laid a hand on my arm "That could have been bad, but we would have dealt with it. Why didn't you tell me?" Not one trace of anger. God, he was amazing.

"He wasn't only going to destroy your dad. He was going spread nasty rumors that you'd been getting familiar with some of the younger boys on your surfing team."

Cody growled and swore filthily. In his youth he had coached some of the young team members. He'd been passionate about it, a mentor to the younger kids, and was well loved.

I splayed my hands helplessly. "I knew he'd do it. We were both going away to different colleges anyway and would hardly see each other, so I thought you'd be safe there, away from him. It seemed the best thing to do at the time. Cut you loose to placate my father, even if I had to lie to you. That way you and your family wouldn't get hurt. No way was I going to allow him to ruin your reputation like that. It would have followed you around all your life, no matter what we did to mitigate it. You know it would have." I blew out a breath. "So I broke up with you. It was the only way."

Cody moved away, the sudden loss scary.

"I can't believe what I'm hearing. You let your dad decide what was best for us, what was best for me? Why didn't you talk to us about it? We could have fought back, gotten my folks involved. So what if he threatened my dad's business and my reputation?" Cody sounded bewildered. "Nate, we could have gotten through that. We would have found a way around it somehow. You didn't have to deal with that all on your own."

His feeling of betrayal was palpable. I was right not to want to bring up the ugly. The fragile beginning of what we could be was disintegrating before we had a chance to try.

"You told me back then you didn't care for me. All these years you've been lying and breaking my heart in the process. I understand you have this need to protect me, I do. And I love you for it, but I also hate you for not telling me the truth."

His sandals made soft flopping sounds as he paced across the wooden floor. "I'm trying to figure out how to process all this." The pacing stopped, the sharpness of his tone making my heart sink to my boots. "I should be so fucking angry with you for shoving me away like that."

Something tinkled loudly and I guessed he'd walked into the wind chime hanging by the door.

I swallowed down the huge lump in the back of my throat. "I understand," I managed to get out, eyes burning with unshed tears. "I lied to you, wasted any time we might have had together. I can never get that back for us. I fucked up and I don't deserve you. In my defense, I was seventeen, scared of what my dad would do because you know he would have been as vindictive as hell. And we were going to be apart for four years anyway. I thought it was the right thing to do." I shrugged. "That's the only excuse I can offer."

He had every right to be pissed off. The deck door opened and I heard him walk outside. I wanted to follow but knew I needed to let him be. He needed time.

I sat on the old, worn sofa and put my head in my hands. Twelve years of being together yet apart was a lot to take in.

Shit, I'd waited too long. There was no coming back from this.

Minutes passed and I rested my head on the back of the sofa. Scents of sweat, coconut oil and men's aftershave teased my nostrils with memories of us watching movies, eating meals and sharing beers. Those days seemed so far away, and I closed my eyes and lost myself in those old times for a moment.

A waft of air, a nuance of Cody's unique scent, signaled he was nearby and then he was beside me. I opened my eyes and stared blankly at my hands resting on my legs.

His long fingers cupped my chin, forcing me to look up. "You know what? I should be really pissed off, but I'm not." Soft fingers caressed my cheek. "I look at you and the guilt you've been holding all these years. I look at how damn brave you've been not letting your blindness get you down and how hard you've worked to get to where you are now, and I wonder what kind of person I'd be if I got angry with you over something I can't change. Something that was done out of love to protect me and my family, however misguided it might have been."

My throat ached even as hope flared. He hadn't made me leave yet. I took that as a good sign.

"I was just a scared kid," I muttered. "My dad thought I'd get over it if you weren't in the picture. He didn't understand being gay is something you don't get over. It's who you are."

"Just like *you* are part of me." Cody's arms drew me in and pulled us up, his wiry strength enfolding me, making me whole. "I might need a bit of time to digest all this, but not having you in my life has never been an option."

We stood there, hearts beating in tandem, and I leaned my face against his chest and I thanked God for Cody Fisher.

"Why did he hate me and my family so much?" The pain in Cody's voice made my heart ache. "What did we ever do to him?"

I smiled sadly. "He never liked your parents' lifestyle, thought it was amoral and they were degenerates. It wasn't in line with his holier-than-thou beliefs. Their son hanging around with me, the son he wanted to follow in his footsteps and didn't, that was an insult. Somehow, in his mind it was all your fault. He even said you'd turned me gay because it was inconceivable that his wife would give birth to something like me."

"What a prick," Cody mumbled into my neck.

"Yeah, well, I'd never been the son he wanted. I wasn't into hunting and fishing, and he needed something outside his existence to blame for me not being who he wanted me to be. He couldn't cope with having a gay son. He was sure it would bring down his good name and making him a laughingstock. He hated to be embarrassed or shown up."

Oh boy how he hated it.

I reached up and cupped Cody's face. My family could go screw themselves. After all these years, I was starting a relationship with someone I'd loved since we were kids. "So can we agree that it's in the past? That what happened twelve years ago matters but doesn't define who we are now? We're together now with a chance to make it better. Can you live with that? Please?"

Cody's hands covered mine. "I still think there's something you're not telling me. But for now I'll let it go. When you're ready to tell me more, if there's anything else to tell… Maybe I'm making too much of this. Either way, I'm here. Deal?"

"Deal," I agreed with a huge sense of relief as I stroked the hard chest beneath my hand, reveling in the soft intake of Cody's breath as I found skin between the buttons of his loose shirt. "You were really good at hiding how you felt from me, too. I really thought you'd grown past it."

We stood quietly for a few minutes, Cody pulling me closer.

"So, to be clear. Are we, like, an item now? You know, in a relationship that doesn't involve the words 'best friends'?" Again with the insecurity in his voice. And I'd put it there.

I moved away and drew his face down to mine. "Yes, that's the plan. Now shut up and kiss me already. I need a little more convincing."

Cody's talented mouth rocked my world. His beautiful, eager mouth stole my breath and my sanity. He gave everything when he kissed me and I took it deep into my heart.

The feel of his body against mine got my senses swimming; the scent of him imprinted on my skin; his hands cupping my face as he kissed me were warm, strong and possessive. The world outside shut down until all I heard were the sounds of our breaths and the buzzing delight in my head. When my fingers found the skin of his belly, his moan of pleasure shot into my mouth and filled up my hungry, needy body.

I belong here, in his arms. This is what I've been missing.

When we drew apart, Cody said, "Hell, Nate." His voice dreamlike. "If that's what kissing you is like, imagine the sex we're going to have. We're gonna need a stronger bed. Not right now, because first, I want to get used to this idea of you and me as a couple. But later…" He shivered. "Later, I intend on fulfilling every fantasy I've ever had about you. It's going to be awesome."

I laughed, a little disappointed there'd be no sex yet, but I understood why.

Then Cody drew me in for another thirsty, gut-wrenching, cock-hardening kiss and I was lost.

Chapter 10

Cody

Being in a relationship with Nate was weird. Seriously weird.

It was like slipping into old, comfortable and familiar clothes that made you feel warm and fuzzy, mixed with something sexy and tantalizingly different. I hadn't wanted to cheapen anything we had by falling into sex straightaway, no matter how frustrated I was. I wanted to make sure we were both committed. Sex could blur our new relationship, and I'd been burned before after our sweaty indulgences. But Christ it was tough, and I knew I couldn't hold out much longer.

Nate's kisses and sly touches had made me rock-hard in one second flat, and I'd been seriously struggling not to pin him to the floor and do dirty, nasty, wonderful things to every inch of his luscious body.

And the bastard knew the effect he had on me.

So I stood now, days later, watching him work in his light-filled studio. I had a boner the size of the Coit Tower and was as rigid as steel from the constant self-denial.

Things had been a little awkward. The transition from what we'd been to who we'd become hadn't been easy for either of us. Sure, we still joked around, teased each other, and in that respect, it wasn't so different.

It was the rest of it that made me take a deep breath. It was sitting together on the sofa, not knowing whether to snuggle up or not. The fact Nate chose to hold my hand when we were out in public, wherever we were. The times I'd brushed some stray crumb from his beautiful lips and not have to drop my hand right away. When he held onto my arm as we walked together, and brushed his hands against my skin in erotic gestures of possession.

Nate liked to tease. Yesterday morning he'd held out a piece of mango and told me to eat it, let his fingers rim my mouth in the most pornographic way possible, which had floored me and I'd had to force myself not to forget the go-slow program.

Yep, my man was a deluxe bitch. He was ready for the physical relationship whereas I… I wanted to find the right moment to make it special for us both.

Engrossed, watching Nate put the final touches to a set of three beautiful conch shells he'd created with such intricate detail, I was blown away. He shouldn't have doubted whether his art was still exceptional. These pieces were destined for an exhibition at Artisana next week and I couldn't wait to sell them to a deserving buyer. A buyer with plenty of money because Nate deserved the best price he could get for his work.

He sensed me watching him, and turned to face me, his face alight with satisfaction and his brown eyes sparkling.

God, he was gorgeous. Seeing him like this, back at work, doing what he loved—I said a silent prayer of thanks to the universe. I couldn't imagine my life being any better.

"Hey, babe. Good day at the office?" He grinned and turned back to his sculptures, face rapt.

I moved over and brushed his cheek. "Yeah, not bad. We sold that Manuela Riposte sculpture you loved, the one of the guy on horseback? A good customer of mine in Brazil bought it for his private collection." It had been a busy but profitable Saturday.

I moved away, not wanting to distract him from his work.

"Uh-huh." Nate lovingly pressed creases and ridges into the last shell. "That was a fantastic piece. Glad it went to a good home."

Nate had this thing about the artwork, wanting me to grill prospective buyers about any piece I sold. Where did they live? Where would the piece be kept? Would it be showcased or locked in a vault? Did the buyer appreciate the artwork or was this just an investment?

Laughing at his checklist of questions, I'd told him I didn't get the CIA to check out my buyers but I did my homework. Of course, at the end of the day, cash was cash and with my prices being at the upper end of the market, it was generally accepted the buyers truly wanted what they purchased.

One day when I'd told him a story about an incredible piece of art I'd sold, he'd almost cried from distress. It was a ballerina pirouetting, hands above her head, beautifully crafted and intricate. I'd sold it to some elderly man in the U.K. who'd put the piece in his kitchen, next to a spice rack and what looked like a basket of wilting vegetables. The customer had sent me a proud photo. Nate had been horrified. It hadn't mattered the guy was as rich as Croesus and an art patron. All that had mattered was that this work was the result of someone's blood, sweat and tears and the guy had put it next to vegetables. In a kitchen.

"You're such an art snob, you know that?"

He chuckled. "I guess I am." He surprised me by lifting his face to me. "Don't I get a proper hello kiss?"

"God, you are so contrary sometimes," I grumbled. "When you're working, you tell me not to interrupt and now you're asking for a kiss."

He rolled his eyes. "It's what you love most about me. Shut up and kiss me, damn it."

I did and for a few moments, life got even rosier. Kissing Nate was always like the first time.

Eventually, we pulled apart. He cupped my face. "Your mom was due to get her test results today."

I nodded. I'd told him about it days ago and he'd commiserated, kept me strong. The results of the test had been the highlight of my day—apart from coming home to Nate. "Yep. All good. No sign of the big C."

My mom had broken down on the phone when relaying the good news and I'd cried with her. In the background, I'd heard my dad trying to comfort her in his choked-up voice.

Nate's smile split his face. "That's awesome news. I was worried about her. I'll give her a call later."

He motioned over to the other side of the studio. "Go take a look over there. I have a surprise for you."

I looked over to the potter's wheel to see a lump of clay, a huge bowl of water and various tools all laid out neatly beside it. I squinted, looking past the covered piece of work next to the wheel. The piece Nate was working on that he'd never let me see. He'd been all mysterious about it, saying it was a secret and I'd find out soon enough. I'd never wanted to lift a piece of cloth so badly in my life. I'd been a good boy though—so far.

"You going to work on the wheel today?" I ambled over to the worktop and regarded the implements.

He laughed. "Nope. *You* are."

I looked at him in dismay. "What? You know I'm useless at this stuff."

He huffed. "Cody, dude, you have a Bachelors in Fine Arts. You've done practical work like that before, don't tell me you haven't."

I narrowed my eyes, looking at the wheel with suspicion. "Yeah, but I never said I was that good, like you. I got by."

He stood up and stretched, his clay-spattered tee shirt riding above his flat stomach and showing an expanse of firm, toned skin. I was mesmerized by the thin, dark treasure trail leading down into his gray sweatpants. It looked as if he was going commando. The outline of his resting, half hardened cock lay against his right thigh.

God, the man was trying to kill me slowly.

I cleared my throat and didn't miss the smirk on his face. The little bastard was messing with me.

"Come on," Nate wheedled as he moved across the floor. I marveled that he seemed to do it so effortlessly. "Come sit down, and let me reacquaint you with throwing techniques."

I muttered under my breath but sat down on the stool. Nate stood behind me, warmth radiating off his body.

"So, we're going to make a bowl. Something you can have your Rice Krispies in or that weird salad stuff you like so much." He made a gagging sound. Nate wasn't big on salads or healthy eating.

"That's kale, you idiot, and it's good for you. You should eat more of it yourself."

He sniggered. "Greens are for rabbits. You know me. I like my meat."

My groin flamed at those sly words, but I chose to ignore them given the current seating arrangement.

He made sure I was situated properly, everything at hand and within reach. Then he stood beside me and gestured.

"Come on, you can't have forgotten that much about throwing a pot. Pedal to your right, clay in front of you. You've done this before. It's nothing new. I kneaded your clay and warmed it up for you earlier. That's what boyfriends do."

His words held a dirty promise and I ignored them.

I wet the clay, ran my hands over it then pressed the pedal. The wheel spun slowly. I watched it go around and around, almost hypnotized. My fingers trailed over the wet, dark material and found the rhythm of clay and fingers,

Nate's amused voice jolted me out of my reverie. "Okay, stop for a minute. Make sure the clay is in the middle of the wheel, it's important to center it, then hold the clay firm, thumbs up, fingers around it." His voice went husky. "Pretend you're holding my cock, and imagine you're slowly sliding your hands up toward the tip. Create a cone with your hands."

I pressed the pedal and the wheel turned once again. I held the visual of holding Nate's cock in my hands and transferred it to the clay. My groin ached at his teasing words. "You do know your cock isn't this thick? I hate to burst your bubble—"

He nipped my ear with his teeth. "Shut it. Concentrate. Make sure you keep wetting your hands and fingers. It needs to be kept moist."

I crinkled my nose. "I hate that word," I complained as I watched the lump of clay take on form. "It sounds so icky. Moist. Blech."

Nate laughed. He leaned into my back, his hands running down my arms. There was the unmistakeable press of something hard against my spine. I didn't know how the hell I was supposed to focus on making a damn bowl when the evidence of Nate's arousal was insistent at my back.

The scent of him, mixed with the smell of the wet clay, and the slight acrid burn of the wheel as it spun were intoxicating.

"Now, here we go." Nate leaned in and covered my hands with his. I gasped as his hard-on burned through my clothes to my skin with its heat. His breath whispered against my ear, driving me wild.

He adjusted my hands, so that one cupped one side of the clay while the other was placed over the top, fingers over my other hand. "Using the heel of this hand," he tapped on the one over the top, "start to press down firmly in the middle of the clay, creating a depression. Keep it steady, and use your fingers to press your hand against the clay, keeping it in place. Use the water, make sure it's kept wet. Things are always better when they're wet."

I swallowed but obeyed, my cock now in an unbearable state of ready-to-launch mode.

"You, my friend, are a plagiarist." I wasn't sure if that was the right word to use for someone who copied film scenes, not literature, but it was all I had. I was proud I was even able to speak. I watched as the clay began to shrink downward, creating more of an uneven bowl-like shape.

"What do you mean?" Nate's fingers rubbed against mine teasingly.

"Oh come on. *Ghost*? The movie with Patrick Swayze and Demi Moore? You mean to tell me you aren't re-creating that scene—my favorite scene of the whole film as you well know—for my benefit? And from the feel of it, your gratification?"

Nate's tongue licked my ear as he chuckled, and that sexy sound drove me crazier. "I knew you'd get it. I've been waiting ages to do this with you. It's such a turn on."

He nibbled at my ear and pulled my ponytail at the same time. A surge of pleasure went straight to my cock and I gasped. I'd had enough of his teasing.

I took my foot off the pedal, and the wheel slowed. I didn't care what happened to the clay at this point. It could dry up and become a misshapen blob for all I cared.

This was war.

"Step back, Nate, I'm getting up." I didn't want to surprise him moving too quickly, and send him flying. As I stood, I moved in one fluid movement and grasped his biceps. I manoeuvred him back against the nearest wall and pressed against him, grabbing his wrists and holding him still.

Nate's eyes were half closed, his face flushed, and there was the faintest trace of a smirk on his delicious lips. He looked sexy as hell.

I pressed my lips against his ear. "I've been trying to be a gentleman and make sure we were both ready for this but you've tipped me over the edge." I reached one hand down and into his sweatpants, grabbing his cock. He was already slick, hot and smooth in my hand.

Nate's eyes opened, desire swirling in their dark depths and his full, pink lips parted as he breathed out warm, coffee-scented air. His free hand rested on my hip.

"Now this is what's going to happen," I growled. "I'm going to relieve you of the hard-on that's been pressing into my back and driving me wild, then you're going to get on your knees for me and relieve mine."

Nate smiled, a huge beautiful smile that made my heart ache. He pushed himself into my hand, and his lips brushed mine like the soft caress of a whisper.

"Please," was all he said, and the need in his tone undid me.

I claimed his mouth with a ferocity that surprised me. I wasn't usually this forceful but Nate seemed to bring it out. Our tongues slicked together in a kiss borne of need, and anticipation that had been years in the making.

Fisting his smooth, rigid cock, I stroked him, loving the sounds that he made, the small gasps and pants that invigorated me to work him harder. The smell of semen and musk in the air was an aphrodisiac.

"God, Cody," Nate whimpered when our lips parted, "Waited so long for this. Please, harder. Finish it. I need to come."

"I've got you," I whispered against his lips. "I've always had you, Nate."

Those words were the catalyst for Nate to come, his orgasm wracking his body with shudders and a stuttering of his hips. He let out a soft moan and liquid heat spilled over my hand and between my fingers. I uttered a groan at feeling that evidence of his arousal—what I'd done to him—coat me in its sticky slickness.

I released his wrist and took my hand out of his pants. Watching his face in the aftermath of his sexual bliss, I raised my hand and slowly began to lick off the sticky essence.

"Right now I'm cleaning your come off my hand with my tongue," I said.

His pupils dilated. "That is so hot," Nate whispered. "God, I wish I could see you."

I kissed him fiercely, letting him taste himself, and stuck two fingers into his mouth.

"Suck it clean," I instructed and he did, his tongue greedily licking away the last vestiges of his release.

When he'd finished, I hugged him close, letting him feel the hardness of what he was about to take care of.

"That was amazing," he murmured into my neck. "I'd almost forgotten how good we are together."

I kissed his sweaty forehead and grinned. "Yep. And now it's your turn to show me." I squinted at him as he raised his face, those unseeing eyes fixated on my face. I shivered at the intensity of that stare.

Without saying more, Nate dropped to his knees, pressing his face against my groin. I couldn't help the moan that grew in the still air as Nate rubbed his bristled cheek against my cock.

"I remember this," he said, his fingers trailing down my length. "I remember it being inside me, filling me up. I remember the taste of it, the feel of you in my mouth…"

Frantic with need, all I wanted to do was wrestle Nate to the ground and take him right there in the studio. I knew that if I did that though, it would be a short-lived pleasure.

Burying myself inside Nate again would be the trigger to explode the minute his heat was around my cock. I wanted more than that this first time. Taking the edge off, notching up the heat again and slowly making out until I could slide inside him and feel him naked and warm against me was a far better plan.

"Nate, are you planning on doing something anytime soon?" My voice sounded strained and husky. "Because I swear, you rub me one more time like that I'm going to come in my pants."

As it was, I was sure the minute Nate got his mouth on me I'd blow my load. This wasn't going to be a drawn-out experience judging from the build-up in my groin.

Nate chuckled. He stopped what he was doing and unzipped my jeans, pushing them down to my thighs. "Impatient bastard," he murmured as his hot mouth surrounded my cock and I nearly screamed in delight with the sensation.

Nate had a masterful mouth. When we'd been in the Keys, his blowjobs had made me feel like king of the world, and his tantalizingly teasing tongue and lips had driven me over the top.

Nothing had changed. And yet everything had changed.

I closed my eyes, stopping an unmanly squeak as Nate did a flicking thing with his tongue. I braced myself against the wall as my cock was licked, sucked, rolled around like a marble in his talented mouth.

My boyfriend's talents were awesome. And I was right. It didn't take long. My balls ached, retracting against my body, and my skin tingled as that prize and long-awaited orgasm let loose.

I rode my climax like the most incredible, perfect wave as it took me to the peak, then I descended in a moment of heart-stopping exhilaration. I shouted, one long, stuttering sound that made *my* ears ache.

Nate lovingly held my still warm and sticky flesh in his mouth, relishing every drop of spunk if the expression of beatification on his face was anything to go by.

Once I'd stopped shaking and my heart rate slowed, he proceeded to drive me crazy by cleaning me up with his mouth. I watched, and it was the most erotic act I'd ever seen.

By the time he was finished, I was already growing hard again.

Nate stood, tucked me back into my pants and hitched up his own. His dark hair was mussed, his lips swollen and wet still; he looked debauched and beautiful and downright edible.

I reached out and pulled him close, pushing my tongue in his mouth. He opened up beautifully for me, and we stood there for a while making out like the teenagers we'd once been when this had all started.

It was as if the years dropped away and we were seventeen again.

Needing to breathe, we stopped kissing but held each other close.

"I guess that clay on the wheel is dry by now?" Nate's husky voice held amusement.

I looked over at the clay I'd been working on and grimaced. "Yep, a bit. It'll make a great paperweight though. If you like misshapen, bowl-shaped doo-dahs."

We both snickered then fell silent.

"What time is it?" Nate asked.

I looked down at my watch. "It's eight-thirty. Time to get something to eat, and I feel like a beer. Then maybe we can sit down and talk about the first thing that comes up?"

Nate rolled his eyes at the silly old joke. "Right. Food. Your stomach. Of course."

He moved away, navigating his studio like a pro in the dim light of the fading day, which, unfortunately, he couldn't see—the sky was a bright pink. He found his cane where he always left it, behind the door, and cocked his head like a bird.

"Ready? Let's go feed you. I have linguini, sauce and some mussels. We can make a seafood pasta."

He moved toward the door and I glanced over to the corner where the thing beneath the covers lay and tried once more to find out what it was. It was a rite of passage on leaving the studio and no doubt he'd be expecting it.

"Nate, please tell me—"

"Nope." The smile on his face lit the room up, and although I grumbled at being left out of the secret, the grin warmed my heart.

"Fine, you secretive bastard. I'll have you know I will find out."

"You'll find out when I choose to show you. And no peeking and breaking and entering when I'm sleeping either."

I followed Nate out of the room. "I wouldn't dream of it." I *hoped* I sounded convincing but I couldn't deny the whole clandestine break-in scenario had occurred to me a few times.

Nate snorted as he closed and locked the door. "I know you. You probably had Scooby-Doo scope the place out so you can both come down here later and sneak in."

"Hey, enough with the Shaggy references." I pushed his shoulder hard, causing him to overbalance and stumble. Panicked, I caught hold of him and pulled him back against my front. He smelled like home, his spicy aftershave so familiar, his scent of warm man, clay and sweat an aphrodisiac. The needy thing in my pants grew and pressed against Nate's ass.

His hand snaked around the back of my head and he pulled me in for another kiss. Quick this time and fleeting. "I'm guessing that's not going away by itself? We'll be taking care of that later?"

I bit his earlobe sharply, palming his groin, loving the hiss of pain that escaped his throat. From the feel of his front, he liked it too.

"Oh yeah. Tonight I'm burying myself in that tight, perfect ass and we're getting as close to nature as two naked, sweaty, horny men can get."

I stuck my tongue in his ear.

Nate squirmed and spoke huskily, "God, stop it. We need to eat first and cooking with a hard-on, *and* the thought of you in me later is damn distracting." He moved away and continued up the path, muttering to himself. His cane clicked softly against the stone.

I grinned. So far, everything was better than perfect.

Chapter 11

Nate

Being in a relationship with Cody was both intoxicating and unnerving.

Christ, he could be a dominant and bossy bastard when he wanted. People underestimated him, seeing only the laissez-faire attitude, the surfer-dude look and a constant, winsome smile.

I knew better.

Beneath that façade of the golden boy next door was a man with nerves of steel evidenced by the chances he took when out in the waves. Cody was a tough businessman, having built a local gallery into a worldwide and buzzing enterprise.

And in the bedroom, all those years ago, he'd taken charge and blown my mind along with my cock.

Hell, I loved it when he took charge. I wasn't into anything strenuous or painful, but being told what to do, being dominated, was a fucking turn-on.

When we were seventeen and had spent hot, sweat- and spunk-filled days in the balmy confines of a beach house on the Keys, Cody and I had explored each other's bodies and experimented. That's when I learned I enjoyed being controlled.

I'd discovered I was happy to switch between bottom and top, as had Cody. However, he'd seemed to have taken special pleasure in trying to drive me through the bed, and I'd been happy to let him.

I was looking forward to tonight, to reconnecting with Cody emotionally and physically. And while our romp in the studio had been amazing, I wanted more.

Dinner was tasty but fraught with sexual tension. It radiated off us, palpable and sizzling hot.

We finished eating, and I drained my beer. I'd only had one because I wanted nothing to impair my performance. I imagined Cody felt the same as he too had only one drink.

As I'd done most of the cooking, I was directed to the armchair while Cody cleaned up. I checked my messages, noting with pleasure that Suzanne was coming over Monday morning. Our sessions had tapered off and she was more of a friend now, coming by to check on me rather than being a life coach for the blind.

I was listening to one rather surprising message when warm hands covered my eyes and a voice whispered in my ear.

"I think it's shower time. You want to go first or should we get clean together?"

I turned off my phone and shook my head. For some inexplicable reason, I didn't want our first time to be in the shower. I wanted romance, a bed and soft sheets.

"No, I'll go first, you can jump in after me." That way I could at least prepare my bedroom a little. Controlling my environment had become important since the accident.

Cody kissed my ear then moved away. "Cool. Okay, you go get nice and scrubbed up for me, and I'll putter around in here. I'll meet you in the bedroom."

My groin warmed at that thought and anticipation rocketed through my body. I nodded and got up, taking my cane and moving toward the hallway. "By the way, my friend Blu left me a voicemail. You might want to sit down for this one."

Cody is going to find this as amusing as hell.

"Huh?" Cody's interest piqued immediately. "That sounds intriguing." The couch sagged as he plunked himself down. "Spill."

I nodded, trying to keep the smirk off my face. "Well, it seems *my* friend met *your* friend at the Empty Closet and they kinda hit it off if you know what I mean."

"Which friend are you— Ohhhh." He cackled loudly. "That's awesome. Those two fit. Blu and Dev sitting in a tree, K-I-S-S-I-N-G," he sang.

I shook my head as I moved into the hall. "You're such a kid, you know that, right?"

He was beside me in an instant, warm breath fanning my cheek as he groped me.

"A kid? Really? I don't think this," he palmed me hard, "feels like a kid."

"Ah, no," I gasped. "I'm going to go shower now."

I moved away before my boyfriend—how weird did that still sound—could torment me any further. I washed quickly, ignoring the boner prodding insistently against my stomach.

Huh. Probably no point in putting on any clothes. He's gonna take them off anyway.

And didn't that thought both thrill and scare the shit out of me. I stroked my cock, almost salivating at the thought of what was coming.

I pulled back the bedcovers, making sure there were condoms and lube under the pillow—we didn't want to use the damn condoms but we were waiting for our tests results—then I sat down on the edge of the bed. My legs shook and my heart beat as fast as a hummingbird's.

Shit, I hope this works out. I haven't been this nervous since using my cane for the first time on my own.

I took a deep breath. My bedroom smelled of sandalwood, coffee, aftershave and fresh linen. The alarm clock ticked on the side of the bed. The dream catcher over the window blew gently in the breeze of the open window, a familiar knocking sound as it tapped against the glass.

Outside, trees rustled and there was the soft call of some night bird.

At the sound of water running in the shower, I got into bed, draping the cover over my bottom half and wondered whether Cody would be wearing anything when he came to bed. Not for the first time I cursed my lack of eyesight. I would have given anything to see Cody again, see the curves and muscles of his body, and the cock I'd seen so many years ago and now would never see again.

I sensed his presence before I heard him, smelled the familiar clean scent of him. I gripped the sheets, swallowing the surge of panic.

"Hey," he murmured as he slid in beside me. I could feel the radiating heat of his body. "You okay? You look a little worried."

I shrugged. "Nervous."

Cody shifted and without warning, his heated, still-damp body pressed against mine. His hair smelled of my shampoo, and my soap.

He was a warm and tasty treat on a cool, early-October night and I was so damn hungry for him it took my breath away.

"Don't be nervous, Nate," he whispered against my neck as his lips found my throat and he nibbled my oversensitive skin, his lips whispering promises all the way down. "It's you and me, you know? Just in a different way this time." The smile in his voice warmed me. I held my breath when he moved over me, arms alongside my body, and gasped when his hardness pressed against mine.

He rutted against me gently. "It's like old times," Cody said wondrously. "Like coming home. God, Nate, you feel so damn good. I've missed you so much."

I pulled him down, trying to find his mouth in a frenzy of need. His lips were warm and sweet, his tongue tangling with mine and thrusting deeper, fiercer with each press of his open lips against mine.

Our cocks were slick and smooth as they rubbed together and I knew I wouldn't last if he kept that up. I wanted to come with him inside me. He had been the only man to ever manage to make me come from simply filling me up.

I wrenched my mouth away from the desperate kiss. "I need air," I gasped. "Take this a bit slower or it will be over before you know it."

His sexy chuckle sent a jolt of electricity down my body.

"Yeah? I can do slow." Cody's fingers brushed my cheek. "We have all night. Just lie there and let me do my thing."

What followed was reminiscent of years gone by, and what I expected death by sensuality would feel like.

Cody could have taught classes in the art of seduction and erotic foreplay.

The teenager I'd once known had grown to be a man who knew well how to play his captive audience—me—and torment them within any definition of mind-blowing, orgasmic torture.

The fact I couldn't see enhanced his every sexy, teasing and intimate act.

I was his buffet.

I groaned as his teeth and lips pulled on my nipples, sucking and licking them until they were hard. "Jesus, who taught you to do that?"

His quiet laugh reverberated against my stomach as he moved down. "Glad you like it." He wriggled his tongue in my belly button and his hand brushed my aching cock. The moan I made was worthy of a porn star.

My hips were his next target, and in my heightened state of arousal, each brush against my skin drove me closer to falling off a cliff. He trailed wickedly teasing fingers along my body as his breath ghosted over my heated skin. He'd lick then blow on the wet patch, driving me wild with the sensation.

I reached a hand down to touch my cock and he stopped me. "Leave it." His fingers flicked the tip, and I whimpered. "That's mine to make you come when I'm inside you."

"But I'm so past horny it's not funny," I pleaded as his lips bit the skin at my hips and I sucked in a breath. "You're killing me here."

Soft hair brushed over my cock, and in my mind I saw Cody's blond hair draping over my body, tantalizing me. That thought was soon forgotten when my almost bursting hard-on was engulfed in heat and wetness and my hips bucked upward to meet his mouth.

"Oh God," I managed to get out. "You do that much more and I'll be over. Kaput. You bastard."

He laughed against my cock, tongue lapping at me like I was a popsicle. I reached down and pulled that laughing mouth off me. "I think I've had all I can take of this damn edging. Fuck me, please."

Cody's hand took mine and he wrapped it around his cock. "Feel that?" he said unsteadily. The hard length of him, slick with his desire, was a lot bigger than I remembered, especially when I considered where it was going. "You do that to me, Nate. You've always done that to me. And now I get to push my cock inside you, feel you around me. Do you know how long I've waited for this moment? Tell me again. You sure this is what you want?"

"Yes, it's what I want." I waved at my groin, writhing against the sheets, the scent of sex and musk and sweat assailing my nostrils. "Doesn't this show you that?" My legs moved restlessly against his. "For God's sake, the stuff is under the pillow. Get a condom on that gorgeous cock of yours and fuck me."

He fumbled for the supplies then there was a brief pause as he no doubt got himself ready. The smell of vanilla scented the air and I cheered silently.

Finally, he has the lube, ladies and gentlemen.

The room grew still and I frowned. "Cody, you okay? Are the condoms the right size? I bought large, but I have smaller ones somewhere if you need them."

His voice was strained when he answered. "Don't be stupid, the condoms fit fine. Really? Medium? That's what you think I am?" He leaned in and I sensed the anxiety wafting off him. "Nate, this is like, a really big moment. I've built this up in my head so much and for so long… I know it's kitschy, but it's a dream come true. I want to make it good for you."

"Baby, everything you do is good for me. And believe me, I feel the same way. It's going to be incredible." My sexual frustration had built up to beyond intolerable. "Now could you get on with it? Please? My ass is getting agitated. It wants your cock."

Cody snorted as the cool, slippery glide of fingers breached my ass, and I gave a strangled yelp.

Calloused fingers pushed deep into my core. Warm and strong, he touched every pleasure center I had and drove me up the wall. The scent of male sweat and sex pervaded the air, while desperate pants and moans formed a soundtrack to this decadent seduction. Cody's murmurs of pleasure, coupled with his breathy sighs were a heady mix as his mouth sought mine greedily.

My brain switched off from normal mode and entered the realm of *hurry up and get busy* as I pushed myself onto Cody's fingers like a man possessed. His breathing grew deeper and I was about to swear and tell him to get his cock inside me when it happened. His body covered mine as he slid home, pushing inside me, and I grasped his hips, willing him deeper.

Usually, I was fairly silent during sex, but this grown-up Cody brought out the beast in me. I'd never sworn, groaned or moaned so much in my life as he filled me with steady thrusts, the sound of skin on skin exhilarating. I rocked beneath him as he murmured unintelligible words against my mouth and throat, his hips a pistoning machine that seemed to want to drive itself right into the depths of my body.

"So good, Nate. Knew this would be epic. God, I love you. Always love you."

His whispered words created pictures in my head of how we must look together, and I moaned at the erotic tableau it conjured.

"Baby, I knew it would be good because it's you. It's always been you."

That appeared to spur him on, and he sought out my mouth, his teeth clicking ferociously against my lips and drawing blood. He kissed me and muttered into my mouth, "Sorry, sorry, didn't mean to hurt you."

I grabbed him closer. "Kiss me harder," I begged, wanting that domination, that almost-cruel pleasure/pain. His body shuddered as he acquiesced.

I was near to exploding, and from the feel of him, so was Cody. His thrusts were becoming more erratic, his moans echoing in the room.

"Close," I whispered. "So close. Only you can make me come like this, only you."

He cried out and gave one final push into my body as he came, his hips melding into mine. Feeling him lose control, hearing his desperate gasps and the wanton way he whispered my name as he buried his face in my neck, was my undoing. I cried his name as I climaxed, my cock jettisoning sticky, messy fluid over the both of us.

Heart hammering, blood pounding in my ears, truly, I had never come so hard, never felt so spent. I gripped Cody's hips as if they were a life vest and I was a drowning man. I had no doubt he'd have bruises, and the thought that he would wear my mark made my orgasm even more intense.

Cody collapsed on top of me, and his lips found mine for a kiss so tender I wanted to cry.

"That," he gasped in between heaving breaths, "was better than I even dreamed. To hell with being seventeen. I like us at this age."

I chuckled, my body satiated and so relaxed it felt as if all my bones had liquefied. I had a habit of going straight to sleep after sex, and after *great* sex, I was surprised I was still awake.

"Mmm, that was pretty awesome." I closed my eyes, feeling sleep settle in. Valiantly, I tried to recover. I didn't want to miss out on the afterglow of an event that had been twelve years in the making. "Sorry about the mess."

The bed sprung as Cody got up. "I'll grab something to clean us. Then we can snuggle."

"Uh-huh." I closed my eyes for a second. When I opened them drowsily, something damp and warm was wiping along my body and my now flaccid prick.

"I'm awake," I slurred and he chuckled warmly.

"Go to sleep, Nate. I've cleaned you up. I remember this bit, the 'I'm done in after sex.' I thought you might have grown out of it by now."

I snuggled deeper into the duvet and smiled. "Nope. Get into bed. You said something about snuggling."

Cody's warmth enveloped me and I pulled his arm around my waist as I pushed back against his groin, tucking myself in.

"Love you," I murmured and he stilled. Then his lips kissed the back of my head.

"Love you too. Sleep tight, baby."

This—*this* was what I had wanted. Cody's warm, willing body in my bed, his soft, loving kisses on my hair when he thought I was sleeping, and the feeling of truly belonging to someone special. Someone who wanted me just as I was.

I slid into sleep with a stupid grin on my face.

***

It felt completely natural to have Cody stay over the rest of the weekend. Neither of us had questioned it. He borrowed some of my clothes, used my shower, and made himself at home in the kitchen.

We'd always been comfortable at each other's places, but now knowing I could walk around naked, and although I didn't have the pleasure of seeing him doing the same, it was all so much more intimate and cozy.

Sunday started with lazy, mutual jack-off sex, kissing until my lips were numb. Then Cody jumped out of bed and proclaimed he was going to make us breakfast. Food fueled another make-out session, followed by binge watching *Daredevil*. The Netflix Audio Description function was a fine thing, and I was a fan.

When he left late Sunday evening to return home, I felt lost. In our short time together, I'd gotten used to us being a couple in my home and I wondered whether it was too soon to broach the "move in with me" question. I knew Cody loved his place near the ocean, and I was happy in my blind-proofed home with its useful gadgets and now customized areas, which enabled me to feel safe and comfortable.

Perhaps it wasn't the right time yet. We'd only started out in this new version of our relationship and to put that sort of pressure on the both of us was probably not the best idea.

But God, when I heard that front door shut and the familiar sound of his car with its distinctive growly exhaust pulling out of my driveway, I wished he was still here with me.

Chapter 12

Nate

This Monday morning would be a little different from my usual routine. Today was about getting up, taking the spunk-spattered sheets off the bed, putting new sheets on, and doing an extra load of washing.

Male pride washed over me as I thought, *Huh, look at me with the remnants of my debauched weekend of hot sex with my delectable boyfriend.*

That word, as it applied to Cody, still sounded strange. I had taken to saying it out loud simply to hear how it sounded.

Once I'd done all the household chores, made breakfast, and tidied up, I made my way to my studio. I was almost finished with my current project and halfway through another. I was itching to finish them both.

I'd been working for a couple of hours when the doorbell rang. I walked over to the intercom mounted in the wall and clicked it on.

"Hello?"

A cheery voice echoed down the line. "It's Suzanne. Can I come in?"

"Of course. I'm down in the studio."

I buzzed her in. This was a new setup I'd had installed that made life easier and safer. I controlled who I let into my house without having to make my way up and down the backyard path. The installation guy had told me it was top of the line and had the capability to have people enter their fingerprints so they could open the door themselves. I hadn't been keen on that idea, especially since I was now hoping to have regular sex sessions and didn't want anyone just strolling in and finding us *in flagrante delicto.*

Cody had cackled with laughter when I mentioned it. "Come on, Nate, be an exhibitionist for a change. Let our friends find us doing the dirty. Who cares?"

I cared. What he and I had was special, and while he may have been willing to put on a show, I certainly wasn't. Call me old-fashioned.

Sometimes his relaxed attitude to all things sexual made me blush.

I busied myself putting some final touches to *Nate's Folly*, as I called it, and got distracted to the point I didn't hear Suzanne come up behind me and place a firm hand on my shoulder.

"Nate, I called and called, and you were so absorbed you didn't hear me. You were so caught up in that piece."

She leaned in and I smelled the fragrance of her hair and the scent of her perfume.

"That is incredible." She moved closer.

I wasn't ready to share this with anyone yet. *Nate's Folly* was special. It was a culmination of every longing I'd ever had, every regret, and every good thing that had ever happened in my life.

I reached over and fumbled for the cloth, draping it quickly over my unfinished creation. "It's a work in progress, and until it's done, you can't see it." I kept my tone light. "It's bad luck."

"I understand that." There was something knowing in her tone and I hoped she hadn't seen enough to know what the bust was turning into. What it had always been meant to be.

And there's someone who needs to see it first. Along with the other piece I'm making especially for him.

It was intended to be a second Christmas present for Cody.

"You should never have doubted yourself, Nate. Your talent still shines in everything you do."

Her praise touched me, warming my heart.

"Thanks. I appreciate it."

Suzanne moved around the studio, her shoes squeaking on the floor as soft murmurs of approval salted her words. She seemed curious about everything I was working on and I had no doubt she picked up pieces and checked them out. Usually, I didn't like people touching my work, but knowing Suzanne I was certain she treated the pieces with such reverence, I knew they'd be fine.

"Are those new shoes?" I reached out and rearranged some things on my workbench. Scented air wafted past my face as Suze moved past me.

"Ah, yeah. Comfy. Hey, this shell arrangement is beautiful. Is it for Cody's gallery?"

I nodded as I cleaned my hands and my tools. *Conchious Effort* was a piece I was really proud of. It was the first work I'd done with confidence.

"Yeah. He's putting them in an exhibition at Artisana next week. It's his regular October pre-Halloween event. He says he'd already had enquiries but being the businessman he is, he's going to try and push the price up for me. You know, play the patrons against each other and make the most money for the starving artist." My voice was wry but the statement wasn't as glib as it sounded.

While I had money, I didn't live above my means, and the accident and the subsequent alterations to the house and the gadgets had taken a significant chunk of my savings and inheritance.

Cody insisted I needed to become more mainstream and get out with the public more to showcase my art. I was intrigued by the idea but worried about being typecast as that "gay, blind sculptor" as opposed to being seen for my work. I knew how labels worked.

He'd scoffed; saying whatever the public wanted to believe didn't denigrate my talent. That man had more faith in me than I had.

"He's right. Your work is stunning and unique and deserves the best attention it can get." Her voice shifted into something sly. "So, tell me. Did you have a good weekend?"

There was a definite emphasis on the word "good."

I nodded, trying to keep the smile from my face at the thought of how good it had been. "Yes. It was memorable." I stopped, trying to decide how much to tell her about Cody and I being an item now. We'd kept it quiet from everyone but I'd guessed she knew something was up. If I could see, I was sure it would have been written all over her face, since I heard it reflected in her voice.

"Uh-huh." Her warm hands clasped mine. "Anything you want to tell me? If you were a woman, I'd tell you that you look radiant." She chuckled as I made a disparaging sound. "You look so damn happy. Is everything good?"

My heart beat a little faster at the knowledge that yes, everything was good. More than good.

"You're a little harpy, you know that? You're fishing."

She giggled and the air changed around me as she swept around the studio, the fabric of her dress making soft, swishy sounds.

"I might be. Or you could put me out of my misery and tell me what's put that goofy look on your face. Would it be a certain man called Cody Fisher?"

I couldn't help the grin that split my face and she squealed and stopped her swishing.

"Oh my God, it is. Have you two stopped being idiots and decided that the only way forward is together? Like in, together, together?"

I nodded, no doubt beaming. "Yeah, it seems we're in a relationship now. He stayed over this weekend, and we, you know"—my face heated up and I flapped a hand—"talked."

"Ohhh," she drawled. "You talked, huh? How much 'talking' did you do? Was it a deep, in-depth conversation, with lots of up close and personal?"

I laughed. "Not telling you anything about our conversation. Suffice it to say we managed to figure out what we wanted."

Suzanne moved in for a hug and I lost my breath as she nearly broke a rib. "I'm so pleased the two of you came to your senses and saw exactly what you mean to each other. You deserve each other, Nate."

We did. I was going to make sure of it.

We walked up into the house, and I demonstrated more of my Braille reading techniques. I was slowly mastering the simple alphabet and words. I couldn't read as much or as fast as I wanted, but I was getting by. I tended to buy audiobooks.

She left a couple of hours later, giving me a big kiss. "I'll have you and Cody over for dinner one night at my place. I'll call you. You've got a birthday coming up on the twenty-eighth, haven't you? We need to do something to celebrate."

She gave me another fierce hug. "You two belong together. I'm so glad you finally see each other for what you are. I think you've always been soulmates."

Apparently. And despite, or maybe because of, the accident, everything bad that had happened turned good.

I had Cody back in my life the way it always had been meant to be.

***

The week that followed was as athletic, adrenaline-inducing and torturing (in the best way) as the weekend had been. It seemed that Cody and I were making up for twelve years of being apart as lovers.

I wasn't complaining.

One of the best things about the week had been sharing our latest medical results and both having been given the all clear. With nothing between us, the sex was even more intense, if that was at all possible.

An hour ago, I'd walked into his beach house and been manhandled at the door. Cody had thrust his tongue halfway down my throat as he walked me backward to the sofa. It took mere seconds before I was lying flat, my trousers around my ankles while Cody straddled my body. Somehow, he'd gotten naked while I still had my shirt on.

My heated skin was all about the naked man on top of me whose hands were running down my flanks while his ass ghosted against my cock. My arms were pinioned to my sides by his strong legs, curtailing my mobility. The heady scent of his cock, frustratingly not close enough to touch with my lips, caused my mouth to water with the anticipation of getting it near enough to swallow down.

"Come on," I wheedled. "No fair. For God's sake, bring that cock here so I can taste you."

He shuffled closer, and I opened my mouth. Instead of the velvety smooth skin of his erection, I found something sweet and wet being pushed into my mouth. Strawberries. I knew I'd smelled fruit. I closed my mouth around the juiciness of one large piece, chewing down on it, moaning a few seconds later when his mouth found mine.

The remains of the strawberry mixed with the taste of Cody was intoxicating. He placed another piece between my teeth, except this time it was his to swallow. I couldn't say how many times we devoured the sweet fruit, or each other. The sensation that stayed with me was Cody's sweating, lithe body, slick and smooth, hands rough when they touched me in places I ached to have him fill even more.

My brain short-circuited, and when he finally whispered to me that he was ready, I could only mumble in dazed obedience. When he lifted himself up, his hands on my shoulders, and lowered himself onto my hardened and aching cock, I wondered dimly whether this was what heaven would one day be for me.

To have the man I loved riding my cock with such passion and fervor, his pants and sighs a symphony to my senses. My own moans and entreaties tantamount to the clash of heavenly cymbals that made a love serenade, an orchestral movement in the sunshine; two men joined in that most intimate of acts, the soft whispers and touches against heated flesh that made the world dazzling and stupendous.

Being inside Cody was a climactic event that made me shudder. I wanted nothing more from this life. Not even my sight. And when I exploded inside him with a surge of lust and desire, knowing my come was flooding his most secret places, I made him mine in a way no one could ever question. I knew I'd found my heaven on earth.

I smelled and felt Cody's orgasm as he jetted over me, coating me with his come and mashing his mouth against mine in a heady cocktail of strawberries and hope.

"Happy birthday, baby," he whispered and I smiled.

Lying together afterward, murmuring endearments and touching each other as if scared we'd miss something, my heart swelled with the rightness of it all.

"We'd better get ready," I murmured in post coital bliss. "The guys will be waiting for us and we don't want to be late." In a way, I was sorry we'd made plans for dinner.

Cody caressed my chest softly. "Yeah, I know. Just give me a minute to savor this moment. Then we'll shower and dress up."

Dinner tonight was with Suzanne, Blu and Dev. It was a birthday celebration and, yeah, once the afterglow subsided, I was looking forward to being with everyone. I was also curious about Blu and Dev. I knew they'd hooked up, but according to Suzanne, it had become more than that.

The restaurant was one of my favorites, and I had been there before the accident. Adagios served up delicious Italian fare. In previous visits, I'd enjoyed the décor: red and white old Italian kitchen look, and the smooth Italian music, most notably Sinatra, that filtered from corner speakers. It was just enough to be background music. I hated places where you walked in and the music choice blared out, making conversation difficult.

From the sounds and smell of it, nothing had changed. I was thankful for that. It was good that some things were just as I remembered them.

Cody nudged me as we walked into the restaurant, my hand in the crook of his arm. "Will you look at those two?" he whispered to me after we'd announced ourselves and were shown to our table. "Blu and Dev are all over each other. I never thought I'd see Dev look at a guy that way. All doe-eyed and dorky." He stifled a laugh, which came out like a snort. "He's even worn his best shirt. The blue one that he always said brings out the color of his eyes."

I chuckled. "Suzanne tells me you look at me the same way. Has she been lying to the blind man all these months?"

"I don't look at you like *that*," Cody said, sounding flustered. "She's laying it on a bit thick."

I squeezed his arm. "And who was it agonized over whether to wear the green shirt or the red one? I seem to recall a certain someone bemoaning the fact he couldn't decide which one to wear with his new jeans."

My man wasn't a fashionista by any stretch of the imagination, but tonight he'd wanted to do me proud. I'd been touched, told him he looked good in anything he wore, which led to a kiss, which led to a deeper one, which led to...well, you get the idea. Luckily we hadn't been too late to my own birthday celebration.

"Turn it all around on me, why don'tcha?" Cody said indignantly.

I grinned.

There was a cheer as we neared the table.

"'Bout time," Dev shouted, and whistled, a shrill sound that made my ears hurt. "What have you two been doing? I always thought the birthday boy should be here before his guests. You're lucky we saved you both a seat."

Suzanne joined in, her voice teasing. "You do both look a little flustered. My imagination is working overtime."

I laughed at the good-natured banter. "Sorry, guys. We got a bit delayed."

"Yeah, it takes time to look this good, you Philistine," Cody retorted. "I mean, look at my guy." A chair was pulled out and he gently pressed down on my shoulder to sit. "He's the sexiest man here. We should have stayed home and partied together, if you know what I mean, not come here to be with you."

I sat and laid my cane flat on the floor, beneath the table. It was a never-ending struggle to find somewhere to place it where no one would trip over it, and it wouldn't keep falling down or get kicked to hell and gone so I couldn't find it.

"You look good, Nate. Really great." Blu's soft voice was on my left and I turned my head to him. "Being a couple suits you both."

"I've heard similar stories about you and Dev," I teased, relaxing into my chair. I laid my hands on the table, checking what was in front of me.

It was the usual arrangement of placemat, cutlery and a crisp napkin.

On my right, another chair scraped the floor. My boyfriend sat next to me and placed a hand on mine. "You're all looking well. Suzanne, may I say that red dress looks stunning on you."

Suzanne gave a pleased laugh. "Thank you, Cody."

"So, before the waiter gets here, can we have a role call?" Cody had initiated this method of all the people at the table calling out their name so I got an idea who was at the table and where they were.

Names were called from my left to right, and I nodded, visually filing away their location. One good thing, my memory had improved since being blind, no doubt out of sheer necessity. "Thanks for coming tonight. I appreciate you all being here."

A waiter came over and our drink orders were placed.

"So what did Cody give you for your birthday?" Dev asked slyly. "Let me see. Did it involve something up close and personal? Did it end well? Could you eat it? Want to tell us about it?"

My face heated. It had indeed been something personal but I damned well wasn't telling anyone around this table about it.

"No, Nate isn't going to tell you all our dirty secrets, so stop fishing." Cody chuckled. "Blu, control your man. Dev has never been the subtlest of people."

"Yeah, well, someone has to keep him on the straight and narrow." The fondness in Blu's voice was hard to mistake. "Dev tends to shoot his mouth off, or says the most cringe-worthy things at the wrong time. Last week, down at the beach, he told this joke to a bunch of people before I could stop him. He didn't realize there were some kids behind us who immediately started asking their parents some serious questions. Dev didn't make it any better when he joined in."

"Ooh, tell us the joke," Suzanne exclaimed.

I heard the grin in Dev's voice. "Okay. How did the Burger King get the Dairy Queen pregnant?"

There was silence at the table.

"I have no clue," Cody finally said. "Go on, tell us."

"He forgot to wrap his Whopper." Dev delivered the punch line and cackled.

Suzanne burst into giggles, I chuckled, and Cody guffawed once or twice.

"There you have it," Blu added wryly. "After that, the kids kept asking their folks how a burger can get an ice cream pregnant, and some asked what *was* pregnant anyway? Dev didn't help by trying to explain that one should always practice safe sex, so a Whopper was in fact a representation of a condom, which grossed the kids out no end and led to even more questions."

Laughter burst out around the table.

When everyone had laughed their fill, Blu carried on. "Eventually the parents moved away with the kids, but not before a few dirty glances were thrown our way."

Dev argued. "You make me sound like a pervert. I *so* did not know those kids were there. Maybe you should find yourself someone a little more circumspect," he huffed.

"Baby, you're perfect just the way you are. Big mouth and all," Blu said softly.

Dev's tone perked up. "You like my big mouth for other things."

That led to a ribald discussion about the pros and cons of big mouths and I listened with gratitude that I had such good friends. Not only was my social circle the best, the affection between Blu and Dev was unmistakeable.

I wondered idly what might have happened had Blu and I gone further that night, and whether we might have gotten together. In hindsight, everything had worked out just the way it was supposed to.

Cody was my future now. Actually, he always had been.

***

A week later, something happened that triggered a series of events that I could have never imagined. If I'd known then what would happen, I would have never made that first phone call.

On a bright November morning I was enjoying the warm sunshine streaming in through the bay window in the family room. I sat on the sofa honing my constantly improving Braille abilities when a news flash on the radio made me sit up and take notice.

"And now to the latest news. In Christchurch, New Zealand, a magnitude 6.2 earthquake rocked the country. It is not known yet exactly how many casualties there are, but the current number stands as sixty dead, and many more injured or missing. Some of the worst hit areas are still being searched and it is hoped more survivors may be found beneath the rubble of this thriving city. We cross over to our Brenda Ondine, who is in the disaster area, for more details. Brenda, are you with us?"

Fuck, fuck, fuck. My family lives there.

I didn't wait to hear what Brenda had to say. Dread trailed sneaky tendrils through my brain and chest. My heart had clenched at the radio announcer's first two sentences and I'd already been scrambling for my phone with trembling fingers.

While I knew my vindictive and manipulative father would never forgive me for being me, not to mention what I'd done in his boardroom all those years ago, or the decisions I'd made; and despite not speaking more than a few words to me in twelve years, never mind my entire family's complete and utter lack of concern that I might have died in an accident, I needed to find out if they were okay.

I dialed my parents' home number—Uncle Tim had given it to me—with clumsy fingers.

The phone rang. And rang. And rang. I waited for what seemed interminable minutes for someone to answer. Finally, in desperation, I re-dialed.

This time, the phone was answered after the fourth ring. "Hello, this is Duncan Powell." My father's authoritarian and brusque tone traveled down the line, bringing back painful memories.

My gut churned and I gripped my cell tightly. "Hello, Dad."

"Nathan? Why are you calling here?" My father's voice rose an octave, but there was no mistaking the querulous tone with a healthy dose of disgust.

I cleared my throat. I was thirty years old and still my father had the power to reduce me to that young man he'd rejected so many years ago. "There was an earthquake. I wanted to make sure my family was all right. Are you all okay?"

He harrumphed on the other end. "We're all fine, not that you really care. Is that all? I have things to do."

I closed my eyes. Christ, even now the old bastard could make me feel like a piece of shit stuck on the bottom of his shoe.

"Hell, Dad, way to treat someone who's only calling to see if you're safe."

"Nathan, you know we have nothing to say to each other. Have you stopped that disgusting habit of being with men?"

Fuck, I wish things could be different. I wish my family could accept me for who I am. Surely that's not asking too much?

I took a deep breath. "No, I haven't. Have you stopped being with women?"

"Don't be bloody stupid, Nathan, and don't get cocky with me. That isn't the same thing and you know it." The anger in my father's voice reached out and choked me.

"I didn't choose to be this way, it's how I was born. Why can't you all accept that?" I knew the truth wouldn't carry any weight with him. But still, I had to try.

"Don't you say that. Your mother didn't give birth to some faggot. She gave birth to a boy who should have gone on to be like his father and not some simpering queer using art as a crutch to make a living."

Blackness filled my head and I struggled to breathe. "That faggot and simpering queer has just won another award for his art, this time in San Francisco."

I'd been informed I would be awarded the Objet D'Art for a statute I'd made a year ago called *Solitude*. Cody and I were scheduled to attend the ceremony next week.

My father snorted. "San Francisco, the Queer City? Just goes to prove what I've been saying. It means nothing. Anyway, I thought you were blind. How can you do anything worthwhile when you can't even see?"

The scorn in his voice was palpable and I began to shake. "Being blind doesn't mean I can't do anything. I've proven that." I became aware of someone behind me and knew it was Cody. He pressed a hand against my cheek, letting me know he was there.

"Make it quick, baby," he whispered, his lips ghosting over my cheek. "Don't let him hurt you anymore. He's done it enough."

I nodded, my throat tightening. "Is Mom there? Can I speak to her?"

My father's harsh laugh reminded me of all those times he'd insulted me after I'd come out. "She doesn't want to know you either, Nathan. You've shown you're a failure as a son and a brother. The accident you had proved that God works in mysterious and heavenly ways to punish sinners."

I couldn't speak.

My father ranted on. "Did you know you have a nephew now? He's three years old, and our first grandchild. At least Trudy can make her family proud, which is more than you can say. Now, are you finished? I really have to go."

I exploded. The rage and hurt having built up for years finally made its exit. "You bastard. You couldn't even call when I had the accident and at least I was man enough to call you to see if you were okay after the earthquake. What kind of father are you? You're nothing but a homophobic son of a bitch who bullies everyone around you and imposes your will on everyone. *You're* the reason Mom won't speak to me. And as for Trudy, you poisoned her with your version of what you call the truth. I—"

"Nate, love, forget him. He's not worth it." Cody murmured in my ear as his hands tried to wrest the phone from me. I gripped it and shook my head, determined to say all the toxic things that had been fermenting inside for me for too long.

"You destroyed the family, not me. You and Mom decided to cut me off because I was gay, even though I was the same person I'd always been."

"I cut you off for a lot of reasons. That was one of them." My father's tone was vicious. "Was that Cody Fisher I heard, the other little trouble-making faggot? You should have gotten rid of him when I told you to. Instead you chose him and homosexuality over your family. Don't give me that whole pitiful 'you disowned me' shit. You disowned yourself staying friends with that little bastard and his disgusting hippie parents. Not to mention your actions when you accosted me in my own boardroom and lost me a valuable contract and made a fool of me." His breathing was labored. "I should have destroyed his father like I wanted to. It would have given me great pleasure."

I hoped desperately Cody hadn't heard that last part. I also wondered for the millionth time why my father hadn't done what he'd promised to do all those years ago. But now was not the time for that question—not with Cody listening.

I pressed the phone closer to my ear and pushed Cody's hands away. He moved from me with an exasperated and dirty expletive no doubt aimed at my stubbornness.

But I had something that needed saying.

"Cody was my best friend, someone who always had my back with no judgment or conditions. His family treated me like a son, as you should have done. And you know what, Dad? Now Cody is my boyfriend and my lover and we have a relationship. We even have sex like normal people," I spat viciously. "Maybe I'll send you a photo postcard—"

"You make me sick. How dare you say these things to me?" my father growled.

The line went dead. I stared at the phone, hardly aware of Cody moving it from my now limp fingers. He guided me over to the couch, sat me down and curled up beside me, pulling me into his chest and stroking my back and my hair with his warm, calloused fingers.

He said nothing, and I was grateful for that. My mind was numb, my body aching and I wanted to forget the whole conversation had ever happened.

There was a good reason my father and I were on separate continents. I doubted either of us would survive the fallout if we ever met again.

Chapter 13

Cody

"Crap and shit," I grumbled as I sorted through the paperwork on my desk. "Have I ever told you how much I hate this part of my job?"

Rachel looked over at me, a glint in her eyes. "Oh, only about a zillion times. Come on, Cody. Nate's going to be thrilled *Conchious Effort* sold for such a good price."

I stared down at the photos on my desk, the pictures of Nate's three intricately designed conch shells. He'd come up with the name one evening after sitting out on the deck at my place while the sun's warm rays caressed our naked bodies.

I'd been loath to let the piece go because it appealed to the beach boy in me, but I knew I had to. At the auction, we'd achieved a price of twenty thousand dollars from some buyer in New Zealand. It was going to make Nate's bank balance much healthier. The buyer had been determined to outbid everyone else for the artwork, and it had appeared money was no object. The reserve price had been ten thousand. I imagined they'd fallen in love with the piece, and I wasn't surprised. It was outstanding work.

The buyer was also getting the work of an award-winning sculptor. Nate and I had attended the Objet d'Art Festival a few days ago and I'd been so damn proud of him when he'd gone to collect his award on the stage.

The evening had been a star-studded Who's Who of the art industry, and seeing Nate on stage in his tux, confident and sexy, had led to a debauched night of extreme sex. Nate had finally found out what car sex was all about and I thought smugly there would so be more of it based on his enthusiasm.

My ass still tingled when I thought about it, and I still had a bruise on my hip from where the console had dug into me.

"Mr. Hedgewick seemed to go ga-ga over the piece," I remarked as I finalized the paperwork. The sculpture was already on its way to the buyer, and would take some weeks to get there. "No doubt I'll get the third degree from Nate when I tell him. 'Did you make sure he's a bona fide buyer and he appreciates them? Did you find out where they'll be sleeping, oh and find out the temperature and humidity of the room they'll be in before you send them?'" I scowled. "He's such a perfectionist, the little shit."

"But you love him," Rachel remarked as she finished her part of the deal, scanning the Certificate of Authenticity.

I couldn't help the smile. "Yeah, I do."

Things were great between us and I couldn't wait to get home. I had something serious to discuss with him. We'd *officially* been together for a month, and I was willing to take the final step to give up my beach house and move in with him. It was a no-brainer really. His place was geared up for him, he was comfortable there, and the commute to my Los Angeles gallery would be shorter.

Sure, I'd hate to have to rent out my own home—there was no way I was selling it—but. Dev was chomping at the bit to take it over since his current place was being sold. And while I'd miss living by the beach, it was a small sacrifice to make to live with Nate.

I know he'd been thinking about it too but had been afraid to broach the subject. I wasn't. Now seemed to be the perfect time.

Among the thousands of reason I wanted to live with him, one that crossed my mind again and again was I'd be there in case he ever had the crazy need to call that bastard deadbeat father.

It had taken Nate a few days after his meltdown to get over his father's vitriolic comments. I swore I'd never let that happen again. Nate hadn't told me the whole of that conversation, but I'd heard enough to make me want to fly to Christchurch and bury my foot up Duncan Powell's backside. I wanted to make him wish he'd never been born and he'd be lucky to be the size of a hobbit once I'd finished beating him down.

Thoughts of doing that and reducing the man to a blob of quivering jelly must have made me smile because Rachel slapped my arm.

"Hey, boss, are you okay? You looked like a baby that shit its diaper. All happy and warm."

"Really, that's the metaphor you want to use? It's disgusting." I wrinkled my nose, sure I could smell that diaper as I leaned back and wrapped my hands around the back of my head. "And we're done. I'm going home now to my man, and I'm going to participate in a little monkey sex then take him to dinner."

"You realize most of us do the whole dinner then sex thing?" Rachel remarked drily. "Trust you to get it ass backwards."

I smirked. Did Rachel just make a good gay joke? "Nate can't resist me. I bet you twenty dollars he jumps my bones the minute I get home. Is it my problem I'm irresistible?"

My second in command rolled her eyes. "You tell yourself that." She stood and stretched and I couldn't help notice the new tattoo on her stomach as her shirt rode up.

"Love the angel tat. Special occasion?"

Her face flushed and I blinked. My Rachel was blushing? She never did that.

"Yeah, I met this guy who's a tattoo artist and he did it for me for free."

She seemed evasive and I squinted at her.

"Is he a new beau?"

Rachel had a propensity for the bad boy of tattoo parlors, inked within an inch of spare skin. I didn't see the attraction. Nate, however, had always wanted a tattoo. I could say with confidence that he didn't have one anywhere. I knew every inch of his body intimately.

Rachel shrugged. "We've been out once. His name is Jackson and he has a place down on Sunset."

I narrowed my eyes. "Do you think he'll give me a special price? Nate said he wanted a tattoo and I might surprise him with a visit to the strip to get it."

Rachel's eyes brightened. "Oooh, where does he want it and what does he want? Jackson does body piercings too. Maybe a Prince Albert or something for you?"

I shuddered. "Don't be stupid. No needle is getting anywhere near my dick. It's far too precious and Nate would die without it."

"So what is Nate thinking of doing? A dragon? A tiger? Perhaps your name tattooed across his ass?" She snickered.

It was my turn to roll my eyes. "No, none of the above. Although my name on his ass does have a certain appeal." I lost myself in that thought for a while then came back to my senses and away from a fantasy of licking my tongue across my name on Nate's delicious rear end.

"He designed one himself. It's an image of the three conch shells he made, but more surreal. Apparently conch shells symbolize truthful speech and strength. It won't be a big tattoo. He wants it across his left shoulder blade."

I was turned on by the thought of Nate and a tattoo. I might not want one myself because I was a hissy-fit baby when it came to pain and I hated needles, but on Nate? The idea was making me grow a chubby. I shifted in my seat.

"Anyway, let me know if this Jackson guy can do me a solid and give me a discount. I might get it for Nate for Christmas."

Rachel came over and pecked me on the cheek. "You're such a romantic, Cody Fisher. I think that's lovely. Now get off and get home to your man. I'll finish up here and lock up."

I was only too pleased to get on my way. And getting home to a randy boyfriend was even better.

True to form, when Nate got hold of me, I was kissed, fondled and manhandled into submission. As we both lay gasping on the bed, I stared at him hazily, my brain blown by my most recent orgasm.

"Hell, did you scoff down a whole load of oysters or something? You were on fire tonight."

Nate chuckled lazily and trailed fingers down my belly. Tendrils of heat emanated from them and I regarded my cock with a certain satisfaction as it stirred once again.

"We've both been busy this week, and this," he waved a hand, "has been lacking. I thought we needed some *us* time."

I hummed in pleasure as his hands cupped my balls and moved up to stroke my nipples. "Well, let me tell you, it was worth the wait."

Nate's fingers slowed down and I opened one eye to see his eyelids shutting, dark lashes falling against his cheeks.

I grinned. In typical Nate fashion after sex, he'd succumbed to the lure of sleep. I always marveled at the way he seemed to switch off and simply drift away into the land of Nod.

"We're supposed to go for dinner," I murmured against his shoulder as I kissed his freckled skin. "How can we do that if you fall asleep?"

"Just a few minutes," he mumbled, and I sighed.

"Okay. I'm going to catch a quick shower because somebody attacked me like a ravenous beast before I'd even had a chance to say hello."

His soft chuckle accompanied his smirk as he crunched the pillow under his head.

I got out of bed and went into the bathroom.

An hour and a half later, we were both seated in a small, intimate restaurant down the road, enjoying our first course of lobster with asparagus and lemon butter sauce. The wine was flowing and I'd relaxed enough to broach the moving in subject with him.

"So…" I wiped my mouth with the white napkin, leaving smears of yellow sauce across it. "I have a couple of things to talk to you about. I'm hoping one is excellent news and the other good news."

Nate's brow drew together and he stopped what he was doing, which was licking his fingers. I'd been watching the decadent display for a while and I was glad he'd stopped treating his fingers like some sort of fellatio practice object.

"Give me the excellent news," he said, fumbling around on the table for a clean napkin. Silently, I handed him a clean one.

The butterflies in my stomach fluttered madly as I wiped my sweaty palms against my trousers. "I was thinking about our living arrangements."

Nate stopped wiping his mouth and he laid the napkin down on the table.

"Oh? What about them?"

There was no way to do this other than be the bull in the china shop and throw caution to the wind. Yeah, I knew there were a couple of boring clichés in that sentence. I never professed to be particularly creative in my use of the English language.

"Well, you know I'm paying a mortgage, and we're commuting to see each other. It seems stupid, given that we spend all our time together." Nate's brow furrowed and I hurried on. "Of course, I want to spend more time with you, rather than spend it in the car, so I thought perhaps, it might be time to give some thought to combining our residences? You know, live in one place rather than two?"

Nate blinked. I took that as a good sign.

"Also, I did the math and it looks like we can both save some money if we moved into one place—yours because it's all set up for you already. All our expenses will be split between us. That's only fair. Maybe we could get some more gadgets for your place to make life easier for you, because they can be expensive. And Dev says he'll take my place over, because he loves it, and he can screw Blu's brains out there on the deck. It's a fantasy he has, and who am I to put the brakes on a man's fantasy? So what do you think?"

I stopped my sales pitch, out of breath.

Nate blinked again and his mouth twisted in a smirk. "Cody, are you asking to move in with me at my place, and allow our friends to have carnal relations on the deck at your house?"

It was my turn to blink. "Well, yeah. That was the gist I hoped to get across."

Nate pursed his lips. "Hmm. Tempting. Have Cody Fisher at my home all the time. Have his annoying sneakers kicked off anywhere so I fall over them…"

"That was once," I said hotly. "And you made me pay for it, if I remember."

Oh yeah. He'd edged me within a hair's breadth of imploding and messing up the walls before letting me come. I'd take any punishment he wanted to inflict on me if it meant I got to have him that way. I'd even considered leaving my shoes out on purpose for him to fall over, but no. Even I had limits.

"Have the fridge filled with all that icky healthy stuff"—Nate's lips pursed in distaste—"and suffer the toilet seat being down when I need to take a piss."

"That was also the one time," I said weakly. "I said I was sorry."

My heart was plummeting. Did this laundry list mean Nate didn't want me living with him? I'd come a long way in being the boyfriend of a blind man. I'd learned a lot and it wasn't fair he was bringing up all my earlier transgressions.

"Have the man I love with me all the time, sleeping in our bed, making breakfast for each other and sitting listening to movies while we cuddle on the sofa?" Nate's voice was tender, and he reached over and found my hand. "I can't think of anything I'd want more."

My chest lightened and I stared at him. "Really, you're good with this? Me moving in with you?"

Nate tugged my hands, indicating he wanted me to move closer. I did, and he framed my cheeks and drew me in for a long, lingering kiss that melted my heart and hardened other bits.

"I am, baby," he whispered. "So good with it."

I beamed then waved the waiter over to order some champagne. *This needs celebrating. But first I have a burning question.*

"Seeing as how we're moving in together, does it mean I get to know the meaning behind your password at long last? I mean, I know you use it for nearly everything, including the buy-on-demand television programs."

Nate chuckled. "I'm surprised you never figured it out. I'd have thought it was obvious." His hand sought mine again, and I placed it on top of his. "It's either Clayman—my nickname obviously"—he hesitated—"and the number seventeen. Our age the first time we made love together."

I lost my breath as he continued. "The other one is the same, seventeen and your birthday. The ninth of February."

I sat there, still unable to speak.

"You've always been with me, Cody," Nate said softly as he caressed my hand. "Every time I used that password, I was remembering that weekend together. And you."

"Oh wow," I sputtered. "That's quite the romantic gesture." I swore my toes were curling in pleasure.

Nate chuckled as the waiter came over with the bottle of champagne. I poured, and passed a glass to Nate.

"Okay, now you know my secret, give me the good news." Nate flashed me a sexy grin.

I was still on a high and I mimicked a trumpet fanfare. "I sold *Conchious Effort* today for an incredibly good price." I stopped for dramatic effect.

Nate punched me on the arm.

"Ow, you bastard. What was that for?" I rubbed my bicep as I winced.

"For keeping me in suspense." Nate went back to eating and I watched as he picked up another chunk of seafood and popped it in his mouth.

It always amazed me how he managed to make it look as if he wasn't blind, as if he knew where everything was. It was the habit he'd gotten into of prepping his food with surgical precision so he could eat it without fearing he'd make a fool of himself. Everything was carefully cut up, sorted and placed on his plate so he could get to it without any fuss.

I looked down at my rather messy plate with everything randomly scattered across it and not for the first time thought how I took my sight for granted.

Nate talked around his food. "So, while you know I'm not really into the money side of things, tell me what it went for, and who it went to."

I finished my mouthful and put down my fork. "We used the new online auction system Rachel set up and I was pleased with the result. It sold for twenty thousand dollars."

Nate choked and spat something out. A piece of asparagus went flying across the table to land on my plate.

I regarded it with a grimace. "Yeah, thanks, sweetheart. I'm not a baby bird and I don't need pre-masticated food. Thanks anyway."

I picked the offending morsel off and wrapped it in a napkin.

Nate flapped a hand as he tried to get his coughing under control. He picked up his wineglass and took a slurp. I stood, worried he'd choke, and smacked his back. Finally, after his coughing fit subsided, I sat back down.

"Twenty thousand dollars?" Nate's voice was squeaky and he took another sip of wine.

"Yup. This guy wanted it bad. No doubt he saw the program that tells people how much this work meant to you, how it was your first real work since you were blinded. He paid us a few days ago and it's been shipped already. It'll take a while to get there, but he seems happy."

I regarded him slyly as his face got less pink and returned to his normal color. "Of course, there are those other pieces you're working on that I'm dying to see. The secret projects. No doubt those will be coming my way and I can sell them too?" I tried to sound innocent but Nate knew how much I wanted to see the pieces he'd been sweating over for weeks, probably months.

He snorted. "Nice try. And those pieces won't ever be for sale. Back to *Conchious Effort*. Do you know who the buyer is?"

And there it was. I was about to get the third degree. Best head it off at the pass.

"The buyer's name is Anthony Hedgewick. He's some big-shot entrepreneur in Christchurch, New Zealand—there's a coincidence, seeing as how your family lives there—and he's looking forward to getting his sculpture, Rachel said. He told her the pieces would be put where they rightfully belonged, and that he'd take really good care of it."

I noticed Nate's stillness. His hands lay flat on the table and he hardly drew a breath. His face was shadowed, his brown eyes dark. I wasn't sure what the expression on his face was. I couldn't read it and hadn't seen it before.

"Nate, you okay?" I reached over and covered his hand with mine. His hands were ice cold. "Babe, what the hell? Are you still struggling with your breathing?"

Nate shook his head jerkily. "No, it's—" He sat back in his chair and closed his eyes briefly. "My dad's middle name is Anthony, and my mother's maiden name was Hedgewick. It seems a bit out of the blue, I guess, that he lives in Christchurch as well. It couldn't possibly be my dad that bought that piece, could it?"

I nearly spat out the wine I'd sipped. "Hell, no. Why would he do that after the conversation you had with him last time?"

Nate shrugged, his face uncertain. "I don't know." Hope dawned over his face and my heart fell.

Please don't believe it, Nate, I thought desperately. *Your father can't possibly be this buyer. Surely you can't be this naïve after everything that you've gone through?*

Part of me loved the fact Nate never gave up on his family despite everything they'd put him through. The other part despaired at knowing he could and would get hurt again.

"Can you—" Nate fumbled with his napkin, and those beautiful eyes stared right through me. "Can you find out the address you sent it to? Maybe we can make sure."

I stared at him, feeling helpless. "Baby, I can check the shipping address on my phone app, but are you sure this is what you want? Maybe you should let sleeping dogs lie."

I broke off, seeing the need on Nate's face. I had such a bad feeling about this.

"Please, Cody. I want to know. I *need* to know." His fingers grasped mine. "Maybe speaking to my dad last week sparked something off. Perhaps he had a change of heart."

Ah—no. Duncan Powell had always been a bastard and I didn't see him changing anytime soon. However, this was Nate's decision to make.

I sighed. "Fine. Let me pop out and find a mobile signal because it's shit in here. Then I can pull up the invoice and check the address for you." I stood. "Be back in a sec."

I left my man sitting at the table buoying himself up with hope that I was sure I was about to shatter.

A few minutes later I'd screen shot the invoice and the shipping note. I went back into the restaurant and sat down. Nate's fingers drummed a nervous tattoo on the table. He looked up expectantly.

"Did you find it?" he leaned forward, face alight with hope.

God, please don't hurt him with this. He's been through enough.

I murmured assent. "I don't know your folks' address, so I'm not sure if it's theirs."

I reeled off an address in the affluent suburb of Canterbury in Christchurch and watched Nate's reaction. It wasn't hard to see the dawning pleasure filling his face and my mouth opened in shock.

"It's your folks' place? No shitting me?"

Nate nodded, eyes sparkling and mouth curving into a wide grin. "That's where I've been sending cards the last twelve years." His shoulders straightened and he almost bounced in his chair.

"This must mean something, right? If my dad paid that much money to buy my work, it's a good sign, surely. Do you think he's finally relented? Maybe that conversation we had brought things home that I'm not going to change who I am to suit him?"

I still didn't like the whole vibe. Something was off. Nate's father wasn't the sort to relent to anything. I thought Nate was being naïve but I had to agree on one thing. Who the hell would spend twenty thousand dollars like that if they didn't want the piece? What could their end game be?

The feeling of dread in my belly intensified and for a split second, I contemplated whether, by some miracle, I could abort the shipment and give Nate's father his money back. That thought left me as soon as it arrived. Nate would never forgive me if I interfered. Besides, it was probably too late now to do anything.

I pulled my chair closer to my now beaming boyfriend and tried to play devil's advocate without completely bursting his happy bubble. "Baby, it seems he definitely bought the piece. I don't know what else to say. But..." My voice trailed off and Nate stiffened beside me.

"But what? Why would a man spend that kind of money if he didn't care?" His tone had turned brittle.

I swallowed, choosing my words carefully. "I agree it's something to consider. But if he wanted to make amends, why not give his real name? Why give an alias? He had to know I'd mention the sale to you, and you might ask questions and put two and two together. And this is your dad. He's not the forgiving kind."

Nate's lips thinned. "He doesn't know how I get about my art— how could he? I haven't seen him in so long. And perhaps he used a fake name for tax purposes or something." His tone hardened. "He didn't know I'd care about where my pieces ended up, so chances are he might reach out later and tell me he's got it. Maybe this is his way of extending an olive branch. Miracles happen." He drummed his fingers against the tabletop, eyes staring down at the noise.

I still wasn't convinced any miracle had occurred.

"Yeah, maybe. I guess we'll find out." My stomach clenched. "Nate, please tell me you aren't going to call him and say anything yet. Let the piece get there, it'll take a few weeks. Then we can talk about what happens. I'm still not convinced everything is as it seems, I don't want you getting hurt."

Nate's eyes remained fixed on the table. Then he shrugged, nodded and looked up. "Sure, let's wait until it gets to the destination and is signed for. Then, I'm warning you, Cody, I'm going to speak to my dad again. Find out what's going on."

Nate's tone brooked no argument and I rolled my eyes, glad to have staved off what I thought might be a cataclysmic and emotional event. Leopards like Duncan Powell did not change their spots, no matter what Nate believed.

"Sure, that's fine. I hope it all works out, honey, I truly do. If there's a chance for you to reconnect with your family, that would be awesome." I nudged his shoulder with mine. "It would also mean a trip to New Zealand at some time. I've always wanted to see those houses the hobbits live in. Do you think we can visit them?"

Nate and I got into a heated and silly debate as he lectured me that hobbit houses weren't real and I insisted they were because I'd seen them in the *Lord of the Rings* movies.

When we left the restaurant a couple of hours later, with an endearingly tipsy Nate clinging onto me and trying to feel me up all the way home, I was glad I'd taken his mind off who bought *Conchious Effort.*

I was sure when we got home I could do an even better job of distracting him.

Chapter 14

Nate

It was stupid, but the Christmas season was one of those times I felt the downside of being blind. I'd always been a big Christmas person. The colors, the sparkles, the shops decked out in their decorative cheer, the shop windows with their seasonal themes and glitzy baubles—it was like being a child again, in happier times.

Decorating the tree, putting it in the big front window and seeing it sparkle as I drove home or walked back from a stroll, had been one of the seasonal highlights.

And now that we were a week into December and Cody was moving into my house in time for Christmas Day, I was gutted that I would be denied seeing *our* home alive with Christmas cheer as we decorated and put up the tree later this week.

I'd miss seeing Cody's reactions to our first Christmas together as lovers.

I was also about to do something I'd promised Cody I wouldn't do unless he was with me. I was about to call my father and find out exactly what had happened with *Conchious Effort.* I was surprised I'd made it this far without giving in to the burning question I'd had ever since I'd found out the real buyer.

As I sat listening to the ringing of a phone somewhere in a house in New Zealand, I thought that I'd at least followed *some* of my lover's orders and given it all some time to process. So strictly speaking, I was only contravening one part of what we'd agreed.

I didn't feel much better though. Inside my stubborn brain, a small voice told me this wasn't a good idea.

The phone stopped ringing and I heard my mother's voice for the first time in forever.

"Monica Powell here."

I was struck by an old memory of the smooth timbre of her voice, the slight Southern twang that still resonated from her upbringing in South Carolina.

"Mom? It's Nathan."

I waited as she gave a long, indrawn breath. "Nathan? What on earth are you calling here for? I thought your father made it quite clear last time you were not to get in touch anymore. He was really quite upset by your conversation last time."

My eyes stung and I swallowed back a lump in my throat. "Well, it's December. Season of goodwill and all that. I thought I'd call, see how you are. Plus, I have something to ask Dad. Or you even, if you know anything about a sculpture he bought back in November."

The chill on the other side of the phone was unmistakeable. "Oh, *that*." Her dismissal and evident scorn should have been the trigger to put the phone down gently and walk away. Instead I chose the option of self-torture.

"Wait. I'll put your father on. I'm sure he'd love to tell you what he did with it." The phone clattered down and I closed my eyes, humiliation flooded my body at her complete lack of care for anything *me*.

The phone trembled in my hands and I reached out to put it down. Get back the impersonal dial tone and go back to my own life and, this time, forget I had family at all. Cody and his family were all the family I needed.

My father's voice though made me raise the phone back to my ear.

"Nathan?" His tone was smooth. "I believe you're enquiring after something I purchased from that gallery your queer boyfriend runs?"

For a moment I thought to put the phone down once and for all, but that stupid voice in my head said, *"You know you can't do that. You* have *to know what happened."*

My father continued, his tone gleeful. "Well, Trudy's husband, Dirk, saw the gallery program online. He works in the art world too. He showed it to me."

I still couldn't find words. It didn't seem to matter because my father had plenty.

"After the disgusting conversation we had on the phone last month, I wanted to make my point. Get my own back a little. I read the blurb which said how much this piece meant to you, how you'd overcome your blindness and still had the talent you'd apparently had before you had the accident, and how this piece was special to you. I thought I'd like to see what was so special about a bunch of shells cobbled together from mud."

Sickness roiled in my gut at the mocking voice echoing in my head. Like a deer in headlights, I simply stood and waited for the impact that would kill me.

"And when I got it here, we looked at it and wondered what all the fuss had been about. Then I took it outside and put it in the garbage. I think it's been taken away now. You see, I told the gallery I'd look after it and make sure it was placed where it belonged. I used a different name to buy it so your boyfriend wouldn't realize it was me straight away. He would no doubt have made things difficult for me to purchase the piece if he knew. I was going to send the gallery an email later in the week telling them where the thing ended up. I had a feeling the news would get to you somehow. Pillow talk, perhaps." He spat the words out with derision.

Finally, I found my voice. "You motherfucking bastard." The ache in my throat intensified.

Don't fucking cry. Don't give him the satisfaction.

A work of art I'd put my heart and soul into had been discarded like a piece of trash. Just like my family had discarded me all those years ago.

"Why would you be so cruel? Haven't you done enough?" My voice gave out. I had nothing left to say anymore.

"Really, Nate? You ask me that? Remember, after I thought we had it all settled, you stormed into my boardroom when I was busy in an important meeting with investors? Do you remember slapping me across the face and pissing in the plant pot, right there in full view of everyone?" He hissed in disgust. "I was mortified. You embarrassed me. Did you forget the fact that little stunt of hysteria of yours cost me an important business deal, one I really wanted?"

My lips were numb. "I remember." It hadn't been one of my finest moments; in fact, it had been one of my stupidest.

After that magical weekend in the Keys, one so full of promise, being forced to tell Cody I could no longer be his lover—I'd been devastated. The look on his face had bruised my heart and it had eaten away at me. So, idiocy had set in, and two days later, after a marathon drinking session, I'd been full of piss and vinegar and had interrupted my father's business meeting to tell him some home truths about his demands and his homophobia. In hindsight, my actions could have further damaged Cody and his family, despite the fact I'd met my father's original demands.

I guess my father was making up for lost time from that event so many years ago.

"Yes, well, the bottom line was they said if I couldn't control my own son, how in hell's name could I manage a project in Rio that big. Then they left." His tone was vicious. "After you disgraced me like that, I was so tempted to go those extra steps anyway and ruin the Fishers and your boy-toy as I'd promised."

"So why didn't you?" I whispered. "I waited for you to do it for months." The burning question I'd wanted the answer to for years slipped from my lips.

My father's voice was toxic waste when he replied. "One of those investors knew Samuel Fisher and his family. She would have suspected who was behind any measure to cause trouble for him because you'd just aired all our dirty laundry in front of her. Your mother talked me out of it. She said you weren't worth it and said it wouldn't look good for the business if I did what I should have done. You should thank her for that because I was so tempted to damn the consequences."

"Sure." I laughed bitterly. "Make sure you tell her thank you for me. You were both only saving your own skins. If you could have gotten away with it, you would have done it."

My father didn't dispute that. "I couldn't salvage the deal, no matter what I said in mitigation. They didn't want to know me. Then you called and stirred it all up again with your disgusting admission of your life. And when Dirk told me about that piece of mud, I thought, I could afford it. Best twenty thousand I've spent in a long while." My father's voice was triumphant. "Is that all, Nathan? *Don't* call here again. No one will speak to you. And remember— you're dead to us. All of us. Try to stay that way, will you?"

He hung up.

I slid down the wall to the floor. The tears came; hot drops that spilled down my cheeks and burned my skin. Each tear contained all the pent-up emotions I'd held inside me for so long, along with the last remnants of hope I'd ever had that my family cared about me.

I'd always wondered why my father hadn't made good on his threats. Now I knew.

I didn't even remember going to the studio. I only remembered standing inside and thinking of the happy hours I'd had here creating something that now resided in a garbage dump. Much like any residual emotional attachment I might have had for my family.

I'd been a fool. Cody had been right to question my eternal optimism. I'd held out hope for too long, and once again it had destroyed me. This time, for good.

There would be no moving on from this. I would never contact them again.

In the empty quiet of my studio I screamed my defiance until I was hoarse. Sobbing hysterically, I stumbled around, completely losing my bearings. I couldn't find my cane, and was clueless as to where I was spatially. I reached out, seeking some landmark to ground myself, and heard something smash to the floor. It shouldn't have been possible to feel any worse, but I did. I searched around frantically, hoping what I thought was lying smashed to smithereens on the floor wasn't so.

"Please," I begged, "please don't let it be you."

My seeking fingers found the familiar layout of my current workspace, the tools I'd left there, the old rag cloth I'd used and the packet of mints I'd left on the worktop. The one thing that wasn't there was *Nate's Folly*. The familiar bust of my lover's head, the piece I'd created from love, regret and desire, wasn't there anymore.

Bile spewed forth as I retched, burning my throat. I slumped to my knees on the floor, ignoring the sharp pricks of pain as shards of clay broke through my jeans and pierced my skin.

Nate's Folly lay in pieces on the floor and nothing could have prepared me for the devastating loss I felt deep in my gut and heart. I leaned over it, trying to sweep the pieces up with my fingers. Fingers that hurt from being cut by the sharp fragments.

"I can fix this," I muttered desperately. "I can fix it."

It was all a lie. I knew there would be no fixing this.

"Nate? Baby, what the hell is going on, you're bleeding."

Strong hands pulled me to my feet and I fought them, wanting to salvage what lay in pieces before me.

"Leave me, Cody, I have to fix this. My dad isn't going to win this time." I scrabbled at the hands holding me up, even as my legs threatened to give way.

"Nate, it's broken, honey. I don't think it can be fixed." Cody's soothing voice washed over me, but I heard the touch of fear lacing his tone. "Please, let me check you over. You're bleeding."

I shook my head frantically. Light bursts flashed before my eyes, annoying little flashes that I knew meant nothing, that I was stressed. It had happened before.

"Nate, did you call your dad already? Is that what this is all about?" The anguish in his tone was hard to miss. "What the hell did he say to get you in this mess?"

He escorted me across the room, and I clung to his hip. Then there was the sound of water running. My hands were pushed under the cool liquid and I hissed in pain.

"I destroyed it, like I nearly destroyed you the first time. I am so tired of this shit. He fucked us up, like he always does."

Cody's fingers gently massaged mine and they were wrapped in something soft and dry. "Nate, you're not making any sense. What did you destroy?"

"Us, you," I shrieked, and laughed. "My dad once again got his vicious claws in everything I held dear and took it away. He destroyed *Conchious Effort*. He bought it with the sole purpose of chucking it away and letting me know he'd done it. Just to get his revenge on me for what I did all those years ago, and for what I said when I called him last month. He's a fucking monster. A bastard."

Cody took me to the old, worn sofa and sat us down.

"Christ, Nate, I'm so sorry. That's a disgustingly vile thing to do. I'm so sorry, baby," he whispered as he stroked my hair and I wept against his chest.

My hiccupping sobs finally stopped and I curled my fingers in his shirt and wished the world would stop. My man smelled like comfort and home, and I needed him so badly I could hardly breathe.

"What else happened all those years ago? Something else went on that you haven't told me yet." His tone was even, but underneath something lurked that sounded like fear.

I was exhausted. I didn't care about keeping secrets anymore. I needed to tell him the whole truth. Even if it meant I lost him too, because, hey, that would be the cherry on top of this disaster.

I moved away from his comforting warmth, swung my feet up onto the sofa, shoving them onto his lap, and hunkered down into the familiar corner of the sofa. I pulled the worn cushion over my chest and hugged it like a child. There were loose strands in the cover and I picked at them, my fingers and heart aching in tandem.

"Those nights at the Keys meant everything to me," I murmured. "You meant everything to me. I was worried we were going to different colleges and we'd be over three hundred miles apart, but I thought we could do it. Being with you that weekend was bliss. Sheer bliss."

His hands stroked my ankle gently. "Tell me everything."

"You know about my dad's threats. What you don't know is the stupid thing I did afterward that could have made everything worse."

I removed my hand from his and wrung it like an old lady. "After a couple of days of wallowing for having to break up with you, I'd had gone on a bit of a bender, which made me monumentally stupid. I went to his office and confronted him about what he'd made me do." I hugged the cushion closer. This was the part I'd never told Cody or anyone else.

"Go on. I'm listening."

I nodded. "I hijacked his business meeting. He was busy with a load of investors he was hoping to get on board with some big project. In front of everyone, I'd told him he was a bastard, and what he'd wanted to do to your family was disgusting. I laid out all his threats right there for everyone to hear. He slapped me, told me I was lying and that I was nothing but a deviant and a pervert."

I swiped at my swollen eyes as the tears fell again. "I lost it. I walked over and slapped him back, took out my dick and pissed in the plant pot. Everyone in the room stood up and left. He lost an important deal that day because of me."

Cody's hands tightened on my leg. "I knew there was more behind this story."

I nodded. "I waited for months for the bomb to fall. For him to do what he said he would do after I'd humiliated him and cost him a shit-ton of money. I was sure he was going to ruin you. Every day I waited for the sky to fall in on us." I took a shuddering breath. "I was so damn ashamed of what I'd done, what I could have started. I could have ruined you, your dad's business, your whole family."

Cody's breathing was rapid and his fingers clutched my leg so tightly it was like a tourniquet. I reached down and unclenched them a little.

"Today I found out the only reason he didn't go through with it was because one of the investors in the boardroom knew your dad. If my father had done anything to your dad or his business, she'd probably have guessed it was my father and that would have become public knowledge, no doubt. My dad had a reputation to uphold so he had to back down." I took a few deep breaths. I was so fucking tired. "At the time, I didn't know that, so I spent months waiting for him to circulate the rumors, or ruin your father's business. Then we went to college and I thought we were safe, but I figured it was best I not get involved with you romantically in case my father was biding his time. There was no point in adding fuel to the flames."

This story had been buried deep for so long that telling it was cathartic, but so draining. "When they moved abroad two years after the boardroom blow-up, it was the first time I relaxed a little. It seemed the threat and my dad were gone.

"When we finished college and came back here, it seemed better to stay friends. You had a boyfriend when you came back, and so did I. I pushed everything I felt deep inside and told myself it was truly over. That was the easiest way to cope." I stroked Cody's hand. "Eventually I believed it myself. Having you as a friend meant everything to me and that's how we ended up. Until now."

"Christ," he said, his voice shuddery. "This is like a damn shitty soap opera." His voice tensed. "Was this why when you came to live with us you were so off? I mean, we were still friends, but I thought the fact we'd had sex had really weirded you out or something." He moved his hand away.

I nodded. "Yeah, I was waiting for something bad to happen. Living every day with the fear you and your family would be hurt. I felt guilty and was glad when we went to college—I didn't have to face you and your family. I was so ashamed." I raised my hands, palms out. "We were lucky it didn't. No thanks to me."

Cody put his hand back on my leg and squeezed tightly. "I don't care about what you did, facing up to your dad. Part of me admires you for it, even though it was a stupid thing to do. You did it for all the right reasons and I love you for it. It could have gone so much worse if that woman you mentioned hadn't known my family, but that's all water under the bridge. The worst didn't happen. If it had, at least we would have faced it together, and weathered the storm instead of you throwing yourself on a damn sword out of some kind of mistaken altruism." He sighed heavily. "You asshole. Losing you was horrible."

We were both quiet and he reached out and took my trembling hands in his warm one. "Anyway, it is what it is and no point in regretting the past now." He kissed my cut fingers tenderly. "What was that piece you broke, the one you're so upset about?"

My throat clenched at the reminder of my loss. "I called it *Nate's Folly*. It was a bust of you, from memory. I was going to give it to you for Christmas." I cleared my throat. "He got me to destroy you all over again, like the first time."

Cody's arms reached out and pulled me into a hug. "Oh God, I'm so sorry. I know how much heart and soul you put into your art. But you still have the real thing right here." He took my hand and placed it on his chest. His warm heart beating rapidly. "That should count for something."

I pulled away. "Do I still have you?" I felt unsure. "After all this gut spilling, and knowing I've lied to you all these years, you still want to move in, and be with me?"

He hugged me tighter. "Stupid question. Water under the bridge. We can't go back and undo the past. And nothing could change what I feel for you. I love you madly, Nate. Always have, always will."

His lips found mine and I sank into them with a sigh of relief and bone-deep need. Cody's fingers ran through my hair and I moaned, his touch grounding me.

When we pulled apart, he brushed my cheek with tender fingers. "Come on, let's get you up to the house. I want to double-check those cuts on your hands, and I think we both need a drink. You up for that?"

I nodded. "I could use a drink. And a shower." I wrinkled my nose. "I'm a wreck. I must look terrible."

He nudged his nose with mine. "But you're *my* wreck. And you could never look terrible. A little straggly, maybe, and your eyes are red. And you look like you've been sliced and diced a bit, but you still look great to me."

I gave him a smile. "Thanks. Just what a guy needs to hear." I hesitated. "Could you help me clean up before we leave? I don't want to leave you in bits on the floor."

Cody's hands brushed hair from my face. "Sure. Let me get the broom."

He disappeared and I heard him rummaging around. He was back in seconds then the broom moved across the floor. "Actually," Cody drew out the word, his tone reflective. "This isn't as bad as you thought. Yeah, part of my face is missing but a lot is still intact, mostly the skull part. It looks cool. Surreal." He huffed. "I still can't believe you can get a lump of inanimate clay to look like this. You have serious talent, baby, but you know that."

He pressed what was left of the bust into my hands, cradling them tenderly. "Feel it, see what it looks like. Maybe you should keep this piece, think about it differently." He hesitated. "Maybe the part of me that's missing in this piece now is you. This is me, unfinished, before we got together."

I hadn't wanted to cry again, but those words, uttered so simply and yet cutting to the core of what that piece had been about, made me weep. Cody wiped more tears from my face and tut-tutted.

God, I'm an emotional wreck. I need to man up.

"Did anyone ever tell you you're a really sensitive soul?" my man teased as he left the sofa to clean the shards off the floor. I cradled *Nate's Folly* close to my chest, hoping that perhaps all was not lost.

Perhaps, with the right motivation, anything could be salvaged with a bit of TLC and a whole lot of love.

*** *

The next three days we spent in sheer, hedonistic bliss as we shut the outside world out and simply enjoyed each other.

We'd made love in virtually every room in the house, anointing every surface. The shower stall had never seen as much action. Texts from friends and family were ignored after we'd told them we were fine but were switching off for a while.

One thing I'd insisted during our "hibernation" had been for Cody to refund my father's money. Cody had argued that it was my right to keep the bastard's cash but I'd refused. I wanted nothing to do with his fucking blood money. When I'd offered to settle a future commission since Artisana had lost money through the refund, Cody had simply glared daggers at me. Wisely I'd let it go.

After our self-indulgent, sex-fueled few days, Cody left to visit his family. The last week had been overwhelming, and to be honest, we both thought we needed a little space apart before Cody moved in.

Ordinarily I accompanied Cody on the trip to Topanga Canyon to see his family—they were my family too after all—but this time, I thought he needed alone time with them. I'd insisted he take time out, go surfing and spend time with his folks. He'd hemmed and hawed but finally agreed to see them without me.

We'd kissed each other good-bye, hot, wet, sloppy kisses with so much need in them—then he'd gotten into his car and driven away.

I missed him already.

***

I wasn't surprised when the doorbell rang the next morning. I'd switched my mobile on the previous day to find a load of concerned texts and voice mail messages. I opened the door, and found a party of three on the doorstep.

Suzanne, Dev and Blu had come to visit, no doubt to bolster up my spirits and get nosy about what was going on after we'd gone into silent mode.

"If this is an intervention, you're too late," I said, dead-panning as I let them in. "I've already kicked him out. He's gone back to his folks."

There was dead silence.

"You threw Cody out?" Suzanne gasped, voice incredulous. "Oh God, Nate, why?"

I shrugged, fighting back the grin on my face. "The dude snores and farts enough to cause a tornado. And he leaves the toothpaste cap off. Who the hell can live with that?"

I couldn't help chuckling as she punched my arm. "Asshole," she exclaimed. "I thought you guys had broken up or something."

She moved away, muttering the word "asshole" again under her breath.

I found myself drawn into a hug, and recognized Blu's familiar scent.

"Hey, buddy, we hadn't heard from you in a few days. We were worried when neither of you stayed in touch."

I hugged my friend back. "We had some stuff to work through. He's gone to see his folks but he'll be back in a couple of days."

Dev was a little more reticent. He shook my hand. "Hey, Nate, good to see you. You're looking good."

I got everyone settled out on the deck with drinks before I sat.

Time to face the myriad questions I knew were coming my way.

I should have guessed Suzanne would be the first.

"So spill it," she demanded. "Cody said you'd been upset over something your family had done and needed some space. Who do I have to kill?"

I laughed. "No killing needed. I'm getting over it."

Blu touched my arm, getting my attention. "This the family that disavowed you when you came out?"

I nodded.

Blu sighed. "Shit, that's always rough. I work with the LGBT shelters, with the homeless runaways, and that sort of thing will break your heart." I remembered a conversation we'd had one night. I knew his little sister had been blind and at four years old, she'd gone paddling in the lake one evening on her own, slipped and drowned. Blu had never forgiven himself for that; he was the one who should have been looking after her. He'd only been ten at the time.

"Babe, your heart gets broken regularly. You get too involved." Dev's tone was filled with affection. He had a voice like warm toffee and I tried not to imagine it saying dirty things to Cody when they'd been in bed, or in a car, or a bathroom.

Saying dirty things to Cody was my job now. I still had quite a few in my repertoire I wanted to try out.

Blu sounded wistful when he replied. "Yeah, I know. People tell you all the time not to let these guys into your heart, but when you see them huddled down with no light in their eyes because everyone they thought would love them has rejected them—it's tough. They need someone to care. I guess sometimes I do it too much, if that's possible. You wouldn't have me any other way, though, right?"

There was the soft sound of one mouth taking another in an unmistakeable kiss and I shook my head.

"Guys, I might not be able to see but my hearing is really good. You making out in front of me has me wishing Cody was here, so knock it off."

Suzanne tapped my knee. "Excuse me, lady here liking the floor show. These two are way cute together."

I pretended to gag. "Straight lady in the room, could you please refrain from describing two men as 'cute'? I hear it all the time and it's like, urggh."

"But they *are* cute!" Suzanne defended herself and I bit back the smile. I loved baiting her. "Is it something guys don't like hearing, some cardinal sin or something? 'Cause if it is I'll try not to say it anymore."

By now all three men were chuckling loudly at her flustered state and the sudden "lights on" moment that I was teasing her surfaced.

"God, Nate, you can be such a bitch," she huffed. "I thought I'd said something to offend. I'm still learning all this stuff with what to say and not to say."

I affected a camp voice. "Sweetheart, I'm gay and I think they're cute." My voice went back to normal. "Suze, honest, I don't think anyone minds. We may prefer to be described as manly, sexual gods with dicks the size of a submarine, but cute will do in a pinch."

The rest of the afternoon was spent in idle chatter and we all had a few more drinks. I went to bed later that night buzzed.

I might have been a little more buzzed than I thought when I listened to my texts the next morning. I vaguely remembered speaking some slurred words into my phone as I lay in bed.

Me: *Missing you so damn much. Lying here naked thinking of you.* I checked—it had been sent to Cody, so that was good. I hadn't sent a random sext to someone I shouldn't have.

Cody: *Missing you too. Naked you say? What are you doing?*

Me: *What would you like me to do?* Ooh I had been coquettish. Nice.

Cody: *I want you to wrap a hand around that gorgeous cock and stroke it, while you think of me kissing you.*

My cock liked this conversation. It was rapidly inflating and from the dim recall, it was going to get better.

Me: *I'll do it if you do it too. Think of my mouth on you. Love to taste you, touch you there, where you like it.*

Cody loved having his balls played with.

Cody: *God, the things you say. Why don't we take this to an actual call? Want to hear your voice gasping my name.*

Me*: I've already gasped it, like, ten times already. Going to come with it on my lips.*

Cody: *Babe, I'm going to call you. I want to hear your voice when you come. Answer your phone!* ♥

That last one sounded rather desperate. I smirked at that.

There were no more texts but now that I'd heard the texts, I remembered Cody's sexy bedroom voice in my ears as I finished jacking off with him. The dried semen on my bedsheets were proof something had come and gone.

I was already hard and horny so I thought before taking the sheets off I might as well give them something else to remember me by.

Whoever said romance was dead hadn't met my Cody.

Chapter 15

Cody

I stood and stared around at my new home and drew a satisfied sigh. My shoulders ached from picking up and carrying boxes, and my legs were tired from all the tramping back and forth between my place and Nate's. I supposed I should get used to calling it "our place." I grinned. That phrase had a good ring to it.

I still had to pinch myself to truly understand where I was now, both physically and emotionally. The fact Nate and I were a couple and moving in together—giant WOW factor.

"Move over, you lazy bastard." I found myself shoved out of the way. "Hell, I'm blind and I'm doing more than you are."

Nate's amused voice made my grin bigger. "Yeah? I'll have you know, I managed that box of books that's bigger than the Taj Mahal all by myself, as well as all that stuff you call art."

I chuckled at his gasp of mock horror.

"Babe, how dare you?" His smile warmed me more than sunshine would ever do. "You wound me deeply. You truly do."

He set down the box he'd been carrying and wiped the sweat off his face with his tee shirt. The sight of his sexy, lean body, muscles glinting with perspiration, made me think dirty things not conducive to the current moving in activities.

From the smirk on his face, he knew it too. His beautiful eyes stared at me, and though I knew they couldn't see me, I knew he *saw* me. He always had.

"You okay?" He reached out a hand and found my face, running his fingers over my lips. "There's no frowny pout, so I guess you must be."

He tried to keep his tone light but I knew better. I reached out and drew him in, inhaling the scent of sweat and coffee, and what was uniquely Nate.

"I'm good. Stop worrying this isn't what I want. It's been on your mind all week, I know."

Nate shrugged as he buried his face into my shoulder. "You love your beach house," he replied, voice muffled by my skin. "I want to make sure you're still cool with moving in with me." His tongue trailed licks of fire up my sweat slicked shoulder and I tried to keep the conversation on track.

"I love you more. And besides, you know what Dev's face looked like when he saw my place empty? He looked like a man who'd been given the keys to Cock City."

Cock City was an imaginary place we'd always joked about when we were teenagers, a luxurious golden palace full of naked guys with cocks. Of all shapes and sizes. Yep, it was that simple.

"Dev didn't know what to do with himself. He darted about like a demented bumblebee, figuring out what to put where. My place will be in good hands. I couldn't ask for a better tenant."

Nate's sightless eyes narrowed as he looked up. "I'd forgotten about Cock City." A deep low rumble of laughter started in his chest. "God, the fantasies we used to have about that place."

"And now we have our own place to act them out," I said slyly, brushing a damp strand of hair from his cheek. My hands framed his gorgeous face and his eyes closed as if anticipating the kiss. I didn't leave him hanging.

The slow glide of tongue against tongue, the breathless sighs from both of us, the eagerness in lips claiming lips—it was an experience I'd never tire of.

"Hey, you two. Stop getting off while everyone else does the work." Suzanne's exasperated tone brooked no argument. She walked into the family room, huffing and puffing, red-faced, as she clasped yet another box to her chest.

Dev followed close behind her, and out on the road, I saw Blu struggling with my surfboard. I'd been damned if I was leaving it behind for Dev to get his paws on. I'd never see it again. And I'd be surfing since getting to the nearest breaks was no big deal; Manhattan Beach was only fifteen minutes away.

Everything was going into the family room, leaving the rest of the house clear for Nate, so he didn't have a minefield in front of him. He'd been warned the room was off limits. I didn't want our first day in our home together tainted by him falling over.

"You're jealous I have this hunk in my arms, and you don't," Nate teased as he moved away and promptly stumbled over the box he'd set down. I grabbed for him, keeping him upright before he face-planted.

Nate swore. "Shit, I forgot I put that there." He bent down and rubbed his shin. "Get used to everything being in its place, because that's the way things have to roll around here unless you want me in the hospital."

The insecurity in his voice stung. I needed to nip this in the bud—fast.

I motioned to everyone to put down what they were currently carrying. Blu had walked in and he leaned my board against the wall, crossed his arms and waited. Dev stood beside him, one eyebrow raised.

Nate stood, seemingly confused by the sudden lack of activity. "What's going on?" His forehead wrinkled as he frowned.

I jumped on top of one of the boxes, one I knew would hold my weight—I think it held those damn books—and raised my arms dramatically.

"Ladies, gentlemen and dorks," I yelled, looking at Dev and smirking. Dev rolled his eyes and grinned. "I, Cody Fisher, wish to proclaim that this man"—I reached down and grasped Nate's shoulder as he looked up in astonishment—"this man is *my* man, my one and only.

When you realize you want to start the rest of your life with somebody, you want to start the rest of your life as soon as possible."

Dev was laughing, Suzanne and Blu simply looked confused. Nate's face was slowly turning pink but the look of love on his face was hard to miss. He knew where I was going with this. Together we'd seen all these films I was quoting from.

I swallowed through the sudden lump in my throat and forged on. "We're gonna have to work at this and it's not going to be easy, it's going to be very hard. We're gonna have to work at this, every day, but I wanna do that because I want you. I want you, Nate

Powell, and I want to live here with you, and nowhere else. So if that means I never get to leave anything out of place ever again, then that's what I'll do. I'm a boy standing in front of a boy asking him to love him. Because I love you and I'll do whatever it takes to make a life with you, forever."

I'd paraphrased that second to last line, but it had needed doing. The last line was all me.

Blu's eyes were glazed, Dev started to clap and Suzanne was about to blubber.

"Did you quote, like, three different movie lines in that little speech?" Nate said, his hands gripping my hips and pulling me off my box. I stepped down and placed my forehead against his.

"Yep. You can tell me where they're from later," I teased. "If you can't remember, you'll have to pay a forfeit." I made what I thought was a villainous chuckle.

"Way to embarrass me," Nate muttered, his cheeks pink. But I could see the delight. He gave me a soft kiss on my cheek, leaned down and picked up his box, and walked toward our bedroom. I was tempted to follow him but…there were people around. I sighed heavily.

Tonight our bedroom was going to rock.

Dev walked past with my board. "Way to go, man," he said, and we high-fived.

Blu simply shook his head in pity, but he was laughing inside, I could tell.

He murmured as he went past with his box, "You're definitely going to get lucky tonight with that speech."

I smiled smugly. Why yes, I think I was.

"Oh God, that was beautiful, Cody." I found myself squashed against a distinctly girly bosom. "You're such a dork, but an adorable one."

Suzanne took the opportunity to wipe her eyes against my tee shirt then turned and carried the stuff she'd brought into the kitchen. "I think that's the last of it, guys. There's only a few bits of clothing left, but I'm sure Cody and Nate can manage those."

I stood basking in the knowledge that I'd hopefully put my man's mind at ease. With a sudden frisson of anticipation, I realized Nate was still in the bedroom. Perhaps I should see what he was up to.

I was disappointed when I walked in and Nate was still fully clothed. I'd half expected he'd gotten naked and was waiting for me with a come-hither look. I thought my creative speech deserved that at least.

Instead, he was standing in the middle of the room, a box on the bed, half open. He looked up as I entered and moved swiftly to stand in front of it.

"You need a hand with anything, lover?" I asked. I tried to edge past him to see what he was hiding.

Nate laughed and pushed me onto the bed. "Nope. Sit down, though. I've got a present for you."

"But Christmas is still three days away." I didn't mind. Presents were for every day of the year.

Nate shrugged. "After your speech, I really wanted to give this to you. I think, as it's the first night together in *our* place, it's fitting."

He reached into the box and shifted around a load of purple and pink tissue paper. From the depths of the box he pulled something out that took my breath away.

I knew Nate had been working on something since the accident with *Nate's Folly*. That piece had been cleaned up and we'd planned on putting it in the dining room, on the sideboard. It would forever be a reminder to us both of how something that was thought to be broken had simply endured and grown stronger.

Our love was like that.

But this piece was even more extraordinary. Tears welled as he held up one of the most beautiful pieces he'd ever made. It was two men sitting naked, limbs entwined, foreheads pressed together, arms draped over one another's shoulders. The detail was incredible, each muscle defined, even down to the genitals and the curve of the men's buttocks. Over them, a wave washed, in intricate detail, protecting them, shrouding them. What was even more amazing, it was instantly recognizable as us. Our faces were forever enshrined in smooth, cool clay.

I stared at Nate in wonder. "How did you do this? It's…" Words failed me. "I can't believe the work you must have put into this. It's absolutely stunning."

He handed it to me and I held it with reverence.

Nate's face flushed with pleasure. "I did most of it here in my studio, and what I needed help with—Michael came over and gave me some guidance. Once I'd gotten the image in my head and could create the detail, it was fairly easy."

He motioned to the windowsill, the bay window that was currently empty. "I thought we could put it in our bedroom, right there. To remind us how far we've come together." He took a deep breath. "I called it *Wavelength*. Because we've always been on the same one. And you love the waves."

I placed *Wavelength* back in the lined box and drew Nate to me. I was finding it difficult to speak through the tightness in my chest. My heart swelled with love for the man in front of me.

"Baby, I will never forget how far we've come. How much we've overcome, especially you. You're my hero, Nate. My forever guy. Nothing will ever change that."

Nate's eyes lit up and I knew I'd never see a more beautiful sight. He sighed softly as his mouth sought out mine.

I lost myself in his warmth, his scent, the feeling of his skin against mine. I didn't need anything else in my life. This was it.

When Nate drew away, I was left breathless, speechless with his passion and desire for me.

He tugged my ponytail gently. "You are the best thing in my life, Cody Fisher. You've always been the one person I could count on. The only person who's ever seen me the way I needed to be seen. I'm not good with words, so I hope that your present tells you how much I love you."

"You know I love you, Nate. Nothing will ever change that."

We kissed again and when we came up for air, I noticed how quiet the house had gone. Maybe everyone was outside enjoying the sunshine. I had my own sunshine inside and I didn't want to leave it.

"But I'll still be getting another present on Christmas Day?" I murmured against his fragranced throat, as I smiled.

Nate mock groaned. "Yes, you'll still have more presents to open. God, you are such a kid."

I kissed the top of his head. "All I need is you. Honest. And perhaps that new surfboard I've had my eye on. Ooh, and that subscription to the GQ Sports Edition I've never quite got around to." I paused, hearing Nate's soft chuckle. "And I've always wanted a puppy. A spaniel, maybe—"

My ramblings were cut off when my man took my mouth, and the world stopped. I simply took the time to enjoy Nate's closeness, the hardening of his groin against my own and the fervent hands that pawed under my shirt, trying to reach skin.

I fell under his spell, the one he wove so effortlessly around me, and made me dream of the future.

No doubt, we both thought about falling onto the bed, but we knew if we did there'd be no going back. And we did have guests.

Sometime later, I wasn't sure how much, we both stumbled, half-dressed, swollen-lipped, with uncomfortable groins, into the hallway. The house was quiet.

We stepped into the family room, and I looked around. There was no one there. I saw a piece of paper propped against the lamp that glowed dimly on the sideboard. I picked it up, recognizing Dev's scrawl. I read it out loud.

While you guys were getting your rocks off, we finished bringing in the stuff. Go us.:) You'll find cold chicken and salad in the fridge. If you guys can stop making out long enough to eat, enjoy. If not, enjoy.:) You two deserve this chance together. Don't fuck it up.

I was sure that last bit was directed to me. I scowled.

"Why does he think I'm going to fuck things up? That man is such a doubter."

Nate's arms encircled my waist from behind as he put his chin on my shoulder. "He might mean me. Or both of us. Either way, we won't be messing anything up. This is our home now. We both belong here."

I sighed dreamily and leaned back against his chest. "It feels right, you know? Being here, with you, like this. It's meant to be."

Warm hands found their way under my shirt. I drew in a breath as they caressed my stomach.

"What time is it?" Nate asked.

I squinted at my wall clock lying on the couch. I'd have to put that up somewhere. "It's nearly eight p.m. Time to eat, and then I think it's bedtime."

My stomach growled as I said the words and we both laughed.

"Food first," Nate said huskily. "I'll go with that plan." He let me go and walked toward the kitchen. "I think we need to eat fast though." He threw me a wicked, sensual grin over his shoulder and opened the fridge.

I watched as he reached inside, finding the food and bringing it out. Opening the fridge door caused light to shine out into the darkness of the room and was like the beacon I'd been waiting for my whole life.

And Nate was my lighthouse, my port in the storm.

My chest constricted. "Hey, Nate?"

He turned, eyes searching for me.

I took a breath. "I love you. With everything I have. Just wanted you to know that."

His smile was another beacon in the dim light. "I know how you feel because I feel the same."

He cocked an eyebrow. "Now come and eat so we can go to bed and I can show you how much."

I hurried over.

Only a fool would refuse an invitation like that.

The End

AUTHOR'S NOTE

This book was a tough one to write. Not only did I need to write from a blind man's perspective, and remember that I had to use his other senses to describe how Nate acted, I also had to remember American spelling. That was no mean feat. This book is also set in the U.S., in Los Angeles, so again, writing about a place I've never been to, my research had to be spot on. That's why I was so glad I had both Nicholas and Michelle Klayman, my editor, to guide me when I messed up. Thanks, guys. I hope I did it justice, and any errors made are completely my own.

I'm also thankful for the myriad of resource material out there on being blind, and for the various aides and groups available to people to make their lives easier. Reading the blog of someone trying to adapt to their new situation was both humbling and eye-opening. Listening in the forums to people talk about their own, very real circumstances, as they tried to tell me what their lives were like, was inspiring.

ABOUT THE AUTHOR

Susan Mac Nicol is a self-confessed bookaholic, an avid watcher of videos of sexy pole-dancing men, a self-confessed geek and nerd, and in love with her Smartphone. This little treasure is called 'the boyfriend' by her longsuffering husband, who says if it vibrated there'd be no need for him. Susan hasn't had the heart to tell him there's an app for that.

A lover of walks in the forest, theatre productions, dabbling her toes in the cold North Sea and the vibrant city of London where you can experience all four seasons in a day, she is a hater of pantomime (please don't tar and feather her), duplicitous people, bigotry and self-righteous idiots. She likes to think of herself as a 'half full' kind of gal, although sometimes that philosophy is sorely tested.

In an ideal world, Susan Mac Nicol would be Queen of England and banish all the bad people to the Never Never Lands of Wherever-Who Cares. As that's not going to happen, she contents herself with writing her HEA stories and pretending that, just for a little while, good things happen to good people.

CONNECT WITH SUSAN

Interested in reading more of my books featuring men who make you swoon, steamy scenes and an engrossing relationship story? If you sign up for my newsletter at **www.susanmacnicol.net**, I'll send you a complimentary copy of one of my standalone titles, or perhaps the first book in my Men of London series, *Love You Senseless.* I don't do too many newsletters, so it's a low volume list. You have no obligation to buy anything, and you can of course unsubscribe at any time.

Did you enjoy this book? Drop us a line and say so! We love to hear from readers, and so do our authors. To connect, visit www.boroughspublishinggroup.com online, send comments directly to info@boroughspublishinggroup.com, or friend us on Facebook and Twitter. And be sure to check back regularly for contests and new releases in your favorite subgenres of romance!

Are you an aspiring writer? Check out www.boroughspublishinggroup.com/submit and see if we can help you make your dreams come true.

Made in the USA
Las Vegas, NV
18 June 2022

50425317R00118